TORPEDO BOAT

G000134466

Also by Duncan Harding

Duncan Harding

Torpedo Boat

Futura Publications Limited
A Futura Book

A Futura Book

First published in Great Britain in 1976
by Futura Publications Limited

Copyright © Futura Publications Ltd 1976

This book is sold subject to the condition
that it shall not, by way of trade or
otherwise, be lent, re-sold, hired out or
otherwise circulated without the publisher's
prior consent in any form of binding or
cover other than that in which it is
published and without a similar condition
including this condition being imposed on the
subsequent purchaser.

ISBN 0 8600 7376 9
Printed in Great Britain by
Hazell Watson & Viney Ltd
Aylesbury, Bucks

Futura Publications Limited
110 Warner Road
Camberwell, London SE5

'The only policy . . . is to mark down the personalities of the Bolshevik Government as the objects upon whom justice will be executed, however long it takes.'
'Do you mean – *assassinate them*, Churchill?'

Exchange between the Minister of War,
Winston Churchill and Prime Minister
Lloyd George, Cabinet meeting, Sept 1918.

BOOK ONE

THE WAY IN

'You see, that main channel is the one spot in the whole of Russia where the Bolshies wouldn't expect anyone in his right mind to try to penetrate the place.'

Lt. Bird to Sub-Lt. de Vere French. 1919.

ONE

A MEETING WITH C

'The word has gone out – kiss the Hun and kill the Bolshy'

1

Behind the two men waiting at the top of the cliff, somewhere a village clock struck midnight with hollow finality. There was no other sound save the sad lap-lap of the North Sea at the bottom of the cliff on which they stood.

'You know, sir, that the mission is impossible,' said the young Lieutenant-Commander with worried eyes and the wing-collar of the pre-1914 Royal Navy.

'Why?' his strange visitor from London asked softly, leaning back into the shadow thrown by the shed, as if he'd spent all his life hiding in shadows.

'Because I don't believe in suicide, sir,' the other man replied stoutly. 'The skimmer is a tremendous weapon and undoubtedly will change the nature of coastal operations. That's why we're doing our trials at this time of night – we don't even want our Allies to get onto it. But what you're expecting, sir – if you'll forgive me – is sheer suicide.'

The big, bluff civilian with the wooden leg was in no way offended. 'This chap Bird is the best man you've got in the skimmer squadron, isn't he, Commander?' he said softly.

'Yessir.'

'And he's a regular officer too, isn't he?'

'Yessir. But I don't quite—'

Noisily the civilian scratched a match across the rusted metal of the corrugated-iron boat shed, interrupting the Navy man. It burst into a spluttering pool of light, as the civilian lit his pipe. In the sudden flare, the Lieutenant-Commander caught a glimpse of cool, deep blue eyes set in a hard middle-aged face, before the flame went out again. 'So,' he said, puffing at his pipe, 'regular officers of his type must be prepared to commit suicide. Always has been thus, always will be.' He smiled, but his eyes did not light up. 'Lieutenant Horatio Bird will have to risk it, like the rest of us.'

If the worried Lieutenant-Commander had any further objections to the crazy scheme put to him only two hours before, he had no chance to express them. For at that moment, the heavy silence was broken by a banshee howl of racing engines. In an instant it split the night apart. The civilian clapped his hands to his ears. Down below, a long, leaping shape shot into view, two great white wings of water at its stern as the secret craft hissed across the sea's surface, heading for its anchorage in the little, remote Yorkshire bay.

'The skimmer, sir,' the Lieutenant-Commander roared, as the wild howl of the craft's engine died away, 'Lieutenant Bird has arrived!'

*

The CMB [1] squadron's operations' room, lit by a powerful, unshaded light, was cheerless. The furniture consisted of well-worn charts of Northern European waters, a fly-blown, highly coloured portrait of the bearded monarch and his spectacularly bosomed queen, a deal table covered by a Navy blanket, and a dozen, ancient horsehair chairs littered with dog-eared magazines. But the civilian had no eyes for the furniture. His gaze was concentrated on the door, as the heavy sea-boots crunched up the gravel outside.

Abruptly it was flung open. A tall, light-haired young man stood there, spray dripping off his black waterproof, blinking rapidly in the sudden fierce light. 'We got a tremendous performance out of her, sir,' he cried with youthful enthusiasm. 'The Thorneycroft behaved like a—' he broke off suddenly, as he spotted the stranger sitting next to his squadron commander.

The civilian noticed the newcomer's strong jaw, determined mouth and alert eyes, noting also the faded ribbon of the D.S.C. on his tunic below the open oilskin. 'The fellow was worryingly young,' he told himself. 'But he'd already proved himself at Jutland in Sixteen. If he'd done it once, he could do it again.'

1. Coastal Motor Boat, the official name for the 'skimmer'.

'Lieutenant Bird – *Horatio* Bird?' he queried quickly before the Lieutenant-Commander could make any attempt to introduce him by his real name.

'Yessir,' the young officer replied smartly, wiping the spray from his wind-reddened face. He smiled suddenly. 'But I like to keep the Horatio undercover, sir. My pals usually call me—'

'Dickie.'

'How did you guess, sir?'

The civilian smiled, but still those cold eyes of his did not light up. 'Oh, I know *all* about you, Lieutenant Bird. But no matter.' He turned to the Lieutenant-Commander, who was watching the exchange anxiously. 'I have your permission, Commander?' It was not a request; it was an order and the Navy man knew it. He shrugged a little helplessly. 'Of course.'

Swiftly the civilian turned his attention back to Bird. 'Take your coat off, Bird, and sit down,' he barked, 'I want to ask you something.'

A little mystified by this autocratic stranger, who had appeared out of nowhere in the night, but presuming that he might have something to do with the top secret skimmer project, the keen-eyed Lieutenant did as he was told, and waited attentively.

'Now Bird, you had an excellent record for such a young man in the last bit of bother. D.S.O. as a sub just out of Dartmouth, at the Battle of Jutland. Commended by their Lordships for your work in the Channel during '17, and a volunteer from the cruisers for the Coastal Motor Boat Service in '18 in order "to get a little more action," ' he concluded.

Bird laughed softly, trying to size the strange civilian up. He wasn't anything to do with the engineering branch, that was certain. 'It didn't do me much good, sir, I'm afraid. I've been stuck out here in wildest Yorkshire ever since I volunteered. All the action I've seen since '18 is from the seagulls' dive-bombing attacks on us as we come back into the cove. I don't think they like us much. I suppose it's the racket we kick up.'

The civilian did not respond and the young officer added hastily, 'But don't misunderstand me.' He flashed a look at his CO, who for reasons known only to himself, was avoiding his eyes. 'The skimmer is a beaut, sir. Fastest and most reliable motor boat in the world, in my opinion. On tonight's run, I got forty knots out of mine!'

The civilian absorbed his enthusiastic opinion with a curt 'Good.' He hesitated a moment, before phrasing the question he had come all the way from London to this secret Yorkshire base to pose.

'What do you think of active service, Bird?' he asked finally.

'I don't quite understand, sir.'

'Well, although the war is over and most of you chaps seem to have had a bellyfull, are you still prepared to go on active service again?' His piercing eyes bored into the young officer's rugged face, well aware how important it was for the success of the mission, to gain Bird's support. 'Active service of a kind more dangerous than most of you went through in the last show.'

Lieutenant Dickie Bird hesitated only a fraction of a second. The experimental skimmers were tremendous fun for anyone like himself who loved high speed craft. But otherwise he was bored with Yorkshire and the routine nature of peacetime service in the U.K. Besides he was a regular officer and ambitious. Already he'd learnt in the four years since he'd left Dartmouth in 1915 that the way to make rapid promotion was to be involved in some form of violent action: you either jumped a rank, as they said in the wardroom, or made a pretty corpse.

'Of course, sir,' he snapped. 'I'm a regular officer – that's what I'm paid to do, *fight*. Besides,' he grinned suddenly, 'those damned seagulls are getting closer every day.'

The strange civilian's face lit up and this time his smile was genuine. 'Good, very good, indeed,' he said, the note of relief, obvious in his voice. 'But perhaps now, I'd better tell you who I am.' He leaned over the table, his voice suddenly very low. 'In London, they call me C.'

If he expected some kind of spontaneous reaction from Bird, he was disappointed. All the young man's face revealed was his mystification. 'C, sir?' he queried.

The stranger nodded. 'Yes C – the head of what you chaps on the outside call *the Secret Service*!'

'I wonder if you could get us something to drink, Commander?'
C broke the silence which had greeted his announcement. 'Anything wet and warm would do. A cup of cocoa perhaps?'

'Of course, sir, I'll pop over to the cookhouse,' the Lieutenant-Commander answered. 'I'm sure the duty cook will be able to rustle you something up.' Hastily he rose to his feet. The request for a drink had been the signal agreed on two hours before, once Bird had decided to accept the mission, as the Secret Service chief had been sure he would. For his part, he was glad to be finished with the matter convinced it was sheer suicide. Grabbing his cap and flashing Bird a last look of unease and sadness, he went out into the night.

C waited till he had gone. 'Now listen, Lieutenant Bird,' he continued severely. 'Everything I am going to tell you now is highly secret. I won't ask you to sign the Act. But if you so much as breathe a word of what I'm to tell you to anybody, you're for the high jump. You understand?'

'Yes sir, I understand. But—'

—'There are no buts. I'll have you out of the Royal before your feet can touch the deck, Bird. Now then, I don't need to remind you about what is happening in Russia since those diabolical Bolshies took over under Lenin?'

Bird nodded, but said nothing.

'Thank God our people are beginning to wake up to the danger the Bolshies present. Since Churchill took over the War Office a couple of months back, the word has gone out, "Kiss the Hun and kill the Bolshy". And it's not a bad piece of advice, believe me, young man.'

Bird was completely apolitical. Ever since he had been a very small boy, his sole interest in life had been the Navy. All the same, from his casual readings of the papers, he knew that Red agitators were whipping up trouble among the workers, now losing their jobs by the thousand as the munition factories closed down; also among the Tommies on the Continent, angry at still being in the Army, six months after the end of the war. As a result, many thought that the Bolshevik Revolution in Russia might well spread to Britain, if it were not stopped in time.

'Unfortunately,' C continued, 'Churchill hasn't got the full support of all his colleagues in the cabinet. They don't see the need to wipe the Reds off the face of the map because there isn't enough relevant information coming out of Russia at the moment, for him to convince them, in particular, the Welsh Wizard—'

'You mean the Prime Minister, Lloyd George, sir?'

'Yes, without information about that devil Lenin's real purpose, he can't convince them of the danger to this country.' He looked hard at the young officer. 'And that's where you come in, Bird.'

'How sir?' Bird asked slowly, wondering suddenly what he had let himself in for.

By way of an answer, C limped over to the opposite wall and selecting a cord, pulled hard. A large-scale chart of Northern Europe came into view suddenly. 'The Baltic,' C rapped a hard knuckle against the chart. 'Finland here,' he rapped the chart again. 'Finally cleared of both Bolshies and the Hun, and now waiting for Anglo-American recognition of its new independence. Pro-British on the whole, with General Gough's Military Mission here at Helsingfors [1], trying to co-ordinate all anti-Red action in the area. *Quite clear?*' he barked suddenly, as if he were back on the quarter-deck of the dreadnought he had once commanded, before he had entered the secret service.

'Yessir,' Bird answered, now completely mystified, as to where he came in on all this.

Again C indicated the chart. 'Estonia, now also free of the Hun. With General Yudenich's White Russian Army located about here, poised to strike against Petrograd, whenever the Welsh Wizard decides to supply him with enough money and arms for his rag-tag army.' He hit the map hard, as if to annihilate an area. '*Petrograd*, the cradle and centre of the Bolshevik plot. It's there that those devils are planning to destroy us and the British Empire too – if we don't destroy them first.'

1. Today Helsinki, capital of Finland.

He paused momentarily to let his words sink in. Then his voice resumed its normal soft tone, as he spoke again. 'Now since Russia got out of the war, we have had our main intelligence group there, watching their movements for obvious reasons. We call it the R-Network. I can't tell you more, in case you ever—'

He did not finish the sentence, but Bird could guess what it was – 'in case, you ever *fall into their hands.*'

'Unfortunately, we've had a problem with the R-Network for the last two months or more. Ever since Yudenich posed his threat to Petrograd, the Bolshies have taken very stringent measures to seal off their frontiers with Estonia and Finland, especially the latter. Their damned secret police, the Cheka,[1]

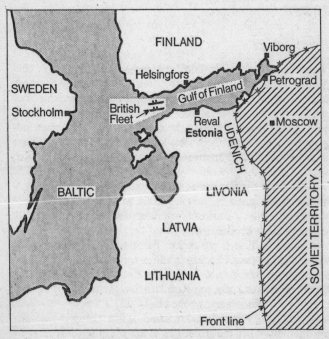

The Situation in the Baltic, Feb. 1919

1. Russian secret police.

15

are all over the border areas, and have really fouled up the works.'

'You mean the R-Network has been crossing the frontiers with the information you required?'

'Correct, Bird. And now that is impossible. So ever since Christmas, we've been racking our brains to find some other means of getting information in and out of Petrograd. That is why I came down here as soon as I heard that your skimmers had reached the final development stage. That's why I asked your C.O. for the name of his best skipper – you.' He paused for a second and scanned Bird's stern young face for the answer he was searching for. '*Lieutenant Bird, I want you to volunteer to go into Russia for us . . .*'

3

'Now then, Dickie, what's all the dashed mystery about, eh?' Sub-Lieutenant de Vere French raised his voice above the crash of the North Sea breakers three hundred feet below them. 'For the last forty-eight hours since you came back from the trials, you've been running around the camp like the proverbial blue-rear-ended fly. Frightfully busy – not even time for a pink gin in the wardroom of an evening. Come on old boy, spit it out, won't you, *P.D.Q.*!'

Lieutenant Bird smiled at de Vere's three favourite initials – 'pretty damn quick.' Then he shook his head, 'I am afraid there isn't a P.D.Q. answer to your question this time.'

'Rank Hath Its Privileges, I see,' de Vere said in his somewhat affected drawl, which like the longish hair, the elegant white handkerchief hanging from his tunic pocket, the expensive kid leather gloves, belied the toughness of his skinny frame. 'I always knew you Regulars thought we Wavy Navy [1] chaps had six fingers and webbed feet.'

The older officer smiled. He found de Vere irrepressible. An ex-Etonian of private means, he'd left a cushy staff billet to

1. Navy term for the Royal Naval Voluntary Reserve originating in the 'wavy' stripes the officers wore.

join the skimmers in the hope of seeing some action before he was demobbed to go up to Oxford. 'Listen,' he said firmly, suddenly making up his mind and lowering his voice. 'I've got something to tell you.'

'I'm all ears, old chap.'

'Oh shut up! This is important, de Vere. Two nights ago, I was offered the chance of active service.'

'*What?*' De Vere exploded, his pale, horsey face flushing with excitement. 'What did you just say, Dickie?' Bird, his face grim, realised what he was letting the younger man in for, if he accepted. 'Active sevice,' he repeated the words deliberately. 'And de Vere, I am empowered to ask you if you'd like to join me on my mission.'

For what seemed an age, de Vere stood there, his mouth open, while the wind howled furiously between the little huts. Finally he spoke. 'You're not codding me, are you, Dickie? Honest!'

'Of course I'm not kidding you, de Vere. Come here and look down there.'

He pointed down at the gang of ratings in dungarees, caps at the backs of their heads, working on the two sleek grey skimmers – the fastest motor-boats in the world drawn up on the gleaming wet shingle below. 'And why do you think the C.O. ordered those two forty-footers hauled up on the beach like that yesterday morning, eh?' he asked.[1]

'Search me, Dickie. Routine overhaul, I expect.'

'Routine! We only had them out on the blocks six days ago. You remember, don't you? Or have you forgotten already?' He gave a mock sigh. 'They didn't do too much for the old grey matter at Eton did they?'

De Vere launched a punch at his grinning face. Bird avoided it easily. Down below 'Ginger' Coates, his smart, red-haired Cockney mechanic, the inevitable Woodbine stuck behind his ear, looked up and grinned at the two officers playing around on the top of the cliff like two silly schoolboys.

Bird froze him with a look. Pulling down his tunic and look-

1. The skimmers, invented by three young Harwich-based destroyer officers came in two lengths – 40 and 55 foot; hence they were known among their crews as 'forty-footers' and 'fifty-five footers.'

ing down with an expression as severe as his father, the Admiral might have worn. He hissed. 'All right, de Vere, you silly ape. Take that stupid grin off your face and show some respect for your superior officer! Well, what's it going to be? Are you on?'

'Am I on?' de Vere yelled excitedly, unable to contain his youthful enthusiasm. 'You can bet your sweet life I'm on – P.D.Q.!'

*

'But Dickie,' de Vere said, when they were alone in the ops room with the door locked carefully from the inside, 'the only thing is – I don't think I'd make an awfully good spy.'

Bird smiled faintly at the younger man. 'Funny. That's exactly what I said when he told me what the mission would entail. But don't worry, they don't want us to be spies. With that horsey face of yours, they'd spot you as an Englishman within the hour in Petrograd!'

De Vere muttered an obscenity.

'Tut-tut, de Vere! I'm afraid you're picking up all the wrong things in the Royal. What will your mater say when you go back home?'

'Mater smokes cigars – black ones - and cusses like a trooper, for your information, Dickie.'

Bird smiled, but briefly. 'This is the situation, de Vere.' He tapped the big map of the Northern Baltic behind him. 'This is the Gulf of Finland, dominated, as even you chaps of the Wavy Navy know, by the port of Petrograd. I have learned a devil of a lot about it in these last forty-eight hours. Now when Czar Peter, the Great, built the city named after him over two centuries ago,' he lectured, 'he selected an unrivalled strategic position for it. One doesn't need to be a Haig to spot straight-off that the only approach to Petrograd is by sea and through this strait here, guarded by the Island of Kronstadt. Clear?'

'Clear as mud,' de Vere said irreverently. 'But do go on. You've got me interested.'

'Hope you'll still be interested when I'm finished,' Bird grunted. 'Well, to make the place's defences even more foolproof,

Peter the Great covered the main entrance channel and the mouth of the River Neva by a series of small forts to the south – here, here and here! And on the northern bank – here – he completed the place's cover by erecting a group of other forts. Naturally they're a bit antiquated by the standards of 1919. But with modern artillery, they're still pretty effective. Now, if that weren't enough, during the war – according to the C chap – the Russians laid down an extensive minefield between the Island of Kronstadt and the southern shore – here, just in case the Hun fleet tried to raid the place. Still with me, de Vere?'

The Sub-Lieutenant nodded, his face fascinated, as if he could already visualize what was to come.

'Well, again according to our friend with no name, the Reds have retained the minefield, knowing it is their best weapon to keep out our own Baltic Fleet, under Admiral Cowan. So, as far as the Russians are concerned, Petrograd is effectively sealed off by its forts and minefield.' Suddenly he shot his forefinger at de Vere. 'But is it?'

'Is it what?' de Vere asked, startled.

Instead of answering, Bird fired another question at the younger man. 'What is the draft of your skimmer, de Vere?'

'Well, one can't be completely accurate. But give and take a couple of inches, two foot, nine inches, say.'

Bird smiled. 'And do you know the depth of the minefield which bars the main channel into Petrograd? It's located at four feet. That would give any skimmer trying to cross it a leeway of one foot, three inches.' He looked at de Vere almost triumphantly. 'Do you get it?'

The other man gasped, suddenly grasping the full enormity of what Bird was saying, 'You mean they want us to go into Petrograd with the skimmers?'

'Yes. That main channel is the one spot in the whole of Russia where the Bolshies wouldn't expect anyone in his right mind to try to penetrate the place.'

'I agree, Dickie,' de Vere said hastily. 'I agree. But what would they want us to do, once – and *if* – we could get across that minefield?'

'That would be the easy part, according to C. We'd have to find some lonely spot on the coast of the estuary and bring out the R-Network courier I told you about – and see him on his way to Gough's Headquarters in Finland at Helsingfors. From there he'd report to C in London. You see,' he hurried on, 'we'd set up a base here on the Finnish coast, east of Viborg. I've been doing a lot of research in these last forty-eight hours and apparently there are a lot of small abandoned yachting harbours between Terrioki and Raiajoki. These days there's not much pleasure-sailing going on in the Gulf of Finland since the Revolution, as you might guess.' He poked his finger at the big chart. 'Here at Seehafen might be as good a spot as any.' He paused momentarily. 'Well, de Vere, what do you think of my plan?'

De Vere sucked his somewhat protruding teeth for a moment. 'Not bad, not bad,' he said finally. 'So we're going to act as a sort of courier service for these spy chappies in Petrograd?'

Bird nodded.

'But how are we going to get in touch with them for a start, if your C fellow has already lost contact with them for the last two months?'

Bird was ready for that one. 'According to C, one of the R-Network's couriers was cut off in Finland when the *Cheka* cracked down on the frontiers last December. That courier will go back with the first skimmer to get through the minefield and the defences into Petrograd—'

'*If*,' de Vere said sourly. '*If* it gets through.'

But Bird did not hear the interruption. 'He'll re-establish the contact with the R-Network and set the ball rolling. Then we'll run a regular service in and out of the harbour,' he added, with more confidence than he felt.

'And when and where will we meet this hero?'

Bird shrugged. 'Search me, de Vere. C didn't tell me that. I expect he'll contact us when we get to Finland.'

De Vere nodded. 'Ay, there's the rub, old bean,' he said slowly and thoughtfully.

'What do you mean?'

'Well, if our people have got spies in their camp and the balloon's expected to go up at any moment in the Gulf of Finland, it stands to reason that the Russkies will have their own people out in the area keeping their eyes open, checking what's going on, eh?'

'*So?*' Bird snapped.

'So,' de Vere smiled lazily, as if it were the most obvious thing in the world, 'how are you going to get the skimmers into the Gulf of Finland without those nasty Bolshies spotting them? Tell me that, *P.D.Q.* . .'

4

Time was running out rapidly.

At their one and only meeting, Lieutenant Bird had promised the mysterious head of the British Secret Service that his two skimmers would be ready to sail from Hull to Finland within seven days.

It had been a rash and highly optimistic guess at the amount of time he would need, to lick his little force of two mechanics and one officer into shape, and get the skimmers ready for action. There were a hundred and one things to be done, and looking back Bird could never recall having been so tired as he was that week. Even at the Battle of Jutland he'd managed to grab a few hours' sleep during the lull in the action. There were fake seamen's passes to be found, civilian clothing of foreign origin, foreign currency, and that universal currency of 1919 – the British sovereign. One thousand new golden coins from the Bank of England.

Meanwhile de Vere ran fresh sea trials on the two skimmers they were taking, and fitted them out for their mission. Their mine-laying gear was dismantled and replaced with two torpedo tubes, per boat. As an afterthought, Lewis guns were fitted – a decision he was later to come to bless, but that was later. De Vere also decided to take along compressed air cylinders, a necessity he judged, in starting the skimmers' 500 HP Thorneycroft engines in the icy weather of Northern Russia. Bit by bit, piece by piece, the hundred and one things they would need to make a success of their bold mission were put aboard. Lieutenant Bird, in his dismal hut, with the North Sea gale rattling the salt-stained windows, pondered the damnable question of how to get the skimmers to the Gulf of Finland without their being noticed.

For a while he toyed with the idea of using a naval transport, supplying troops at Reval in Estonia, the only port in British hands on the southern Baltic coast. From thence he could run the boats across the Gulf by night to Seehafen, which he had picked now as their base. But Reval, according to all accounts, was full of Red spies, and a bad choice. He turned his attention next to Finland, spending hours poring over his maps. Helsingfors, the capital, was out of the question. It, too, was full of spies. Besides the forests were supposed to be filled with Finnish Reds and Field Marshal von Mannerheim, the new Finnish strongman, did not want to risk any further confrontation with them by allowing British naval craft to land at the capital. Then Bird struck lucky.

Gazing out moodily over the green, swaying mass of the North Sea, he spotted the slow, coal-burning progress of a Swedish timber ship returning home from Hull; its deck covered in large crates which the Hull dockers had not been able to stow in its holds.

On impulse he seized his binoculars and focused them on the old tub, running his eyes along her rusting, dirty, white length until he came to her name and port of origin. 'Stockholm.' With a thoughtful frown, he remained gazing at the ship until she finally disappeared, then walked slowly back to his maps, a plan beginning to form in his mind.

The two skimmers could easily be hidden in crates and placed on the deck of a ship of that kind, passing through the narrows of the Kattegat without arousing any suspicion. And even if they did, the enquirer would find they were heading for Stockholm; a long way away from their future base of operations, only a matter of miles away from the Russian border.

But what then? He studied the map carefully, following the direct route across the Gulf of Bothnia until he came to the Finnish port of Abo[1], north of Helsingfors. According to the map there was a railway line running south-east from Abo,

1. Known today as Turku.

which branched off to Helsingfors on one line, while the other penetrated the relatively uninhabited interior, swinging through Labti and going on to Vyborg not far from Seehafen. Wouldn't it be possible, therefore, to transport the skimmers in their original neutral crates across Finland by rail to their destination?

The more he thought about it, the more he liked the scheme. In the end he decided to telephone the unlisted number in Whitehall, which C had given him for just such an eventuality. The voice which answered did not belong to the one-legged Head of the Secret Service. The nameless man at the other end was obviously in the picture though, for he listened to Bird's scheme in silence before hanging up with a laconic, 'Thank you, Bird. You'll be hearing from us.'

Two hours later the ancient local 'postie' from the nearby village of Flamborough, came pedalling into the naval base as if the devil himself were after him. Crimson-faced under his helmet and puffing mightily with the effort of his one mile ride, he staggered from his Hercules and demanded from the grinning sentry to be taken to see a 'Lieutenant Dickie Bird' at once. There was an 'urgent from Lunden and 'taint every day we get one of them out 'ere in t'Riding.'

The sailor brought him to Bird's hut, still clutching the 'urgent' possessively in his gnarled hand.

Excitedly and oblivious to the sentry's broad grin at the postie's use of his nickname, Lieutenant Bird tore open the buff envelope and read the message it contained: 'AGREED. WILL BE TAKEN CARE OF.'

There was no signature . . .

*

A few days before they were due to depart from Hull's Alexandra Dock on the Swedish timber ship the *SS Edward Esbjerger*, Bird paraded the little group behind locked doors, in the clothes he had bought for them personally in a sailors' slop-shop just off Hull's George Street.

De Vere was perfect. He wore a battered, scuffed leather seaman's cap of Continental origin, a striped shirt under a shabby three-quarter length coat which the Germans call a

Joppe, and baggy, patched pants tucked into a shocking pair of knee boots that even the poorest Lascar would have turned his nose up at.

'Great Scott,' Bird exclaimed in delight. 'You look like an Apache in that gear!'

'Apache, mein lieber Mann! Ich bin kein franzosischer Gauner – ich bin ein ehrlicher deutscher Seemann,' de Vere cried indignantly. 'I'm a German seaman!'

'I didn't realize you spoke German, de Vere,' Bird said in surprise.

The Sub-Lieutenant winked. 'The result of a decent Etonian education, my boy; not like that cramming shop you went to. Plus a summer stay with my aunt in Baden-Baden before the last spot of bother.'

The two ratings were a disappointment, however. 'Ginger' Coates and Leading Seamen Bull, a well-named gigantic, red-faced Yorkshireman who would crew de Vere's skimmer, had pressed and cleaned the 'slops' so that both of them looked exactly what they were – two British sailors in civilian clothes.

Bird groaned when they presented themselves to him. 'Stand at ease, the two of you,' he ordered. 'You stand out like a couple of sore thumbs.'

'I thought we'd done our best, sir,' Bull said in that slow way of his. 'They was pretty shocking when we got 'em, sir.'

'That's just it, you damn great oaf – you've done too well!'

Ginger Coates, the sharp little cockney grinned up at his pal's sorry face. 'See, you silly great Yorkshire pudding? You've gorn and put yer big plates-of-meat in it agen.'

'Shut up, Coates,' Bird snapped without rancour. 'All right the two of you, I want you to go away and sleep in those clothes until we ship out of here. And don't shave again until I tell you to! And that's an order!'

Now it was the ginger-haired cockney's turn to be surprised. 'Cor stone the crows!' he exclaimed. 'Did I hear you a-right, sir? *No shaving in the Royal!*'

'You heard me, Coates. Now cut along, the two of you.'

Coates pushed Bull outside, muttering something about the 'real old Fred Karno's' he'd let himself in for now.

*

On the last day of February 1919, they set sail from Hull on the Swedish coal-burner. As the ship nosed its way down the grey littered channel of the Humber, Bird buried his face deep into the collar of his threadbare civilian overcoat and stared at the Yorkshire coastline.

Now in the winter gloom, with the lights beginning to twinkle all along the shore, even the ugly mud-banks seemed somehow beautiful and welcoming. For a moment, he felt a vague trace of fear at what he had let himself in for; he dismissed the thought and remembered C's telegram to him that morning, unsigned as usual, but still symbolizing the ex-sailor's trust in him. 'GOD SPEED – AND REMEMBER, ENGLAND EXPECTS!'

He knew, whatever his own personal fears were, he must not let him or the country down. His handsome young face set in determination, he walked to the forward deck where the two big crates, containing the skimmers, were lashed. Here the men were waiting for him.

'Gentlemen,' he began, 'I would like to explain your mission to you now.'

De Vere looked at him strangely. It was not customary to address men from the lower deck as 'gentlemen,' but he said nothing. He was too eager to hear the real purpose of their mission.

'Well, I can tell you for a start that you're not going to the Med, as the two of you might have thought.'

'You're right there, sir,' Ginger Coates said, his thin cheeky face already blue with cold. 'It's proper brass monkey weather.'

Bird grinned. 'And it's going to get much colder where we are going, Ginger.'

'Are we bound for Archangel, sir?' Bull asked, knowing that there was a small British expeditionary force up in the ice-bound Russian port. 'Or Murmansk?'

'Not quite, Bull. You see this isn't going to be an official show like up there. We've been selected for a special mission – a show of our own.'

'I don't think I want to stay and see the picture,' Ginger said, with mock fear. 'Can I go home now?'

Lieutenant Bird raised his voice to drown the mournful tolling of the bell on the Bull Lightship, the last in the Humber Estuary. 'I'm afraid you can't, Ginger. You see, we've been picked to transport Secret Service couriers in and out of Petrograd harbour.'

'Cor stone the bleeding crows!' Ginger breathed, his trembling stopped abruptly by the surprising news. 'What 'as Mrs Coates' little boy got 'imself into now? Muvver, sell the pig and buy me out!'

But it was Bull, big, heavy and imperturbable as ever, who took the announcement in his stride. 'That cook of theirs said,' he declared in his flat East Riding accent, as if it were a matter of great importance, 'that he'll be serving supper as soon as we get out of the Estuary – and there's steak and potatoes tonight.'

To the big Yorkshire farmboy's surprise, his impressive announcement was greeted by a burst of laughter, banishing the sudden nervous tension. Bull led the way to the passenger accommodation, his red, honest face bewildered by their inexplicable reactions and the others followed, laughing hysterically.

Behind them the coast of England died away in the winter gloom. For some of them, it would be the last they would ever see of their native country ...

TWO

THE FINNISH CONNECTION

'It is your mission to take in the courier to link up with the R-Network, yes? . . . Well, I am that courier!'

1

Daylight came late in the Gulf of Bothnia. It was almost ten before the pale yellow ball of the winter sun rolled over the green swaying horizon and lay there, as if too exhausted to rise any further. Then the snow came back again in swift, vicious flurries so that the little Finnish coaster, nosing its way through the drifting ice into Ako Harbour, seemed to glide through the water like some ancient grey ghost.

But for once Lieutenant Bird, his head buried in his collar, his eyes narrowed to slits against the driving snow, did not mind the terrible weather. Turning to de Vere, freezing next to him on the dirty rusty deck, he said: 'Good cover, eh? I mean the snow. It'll keep the nosey-parkers off the quay, I hope.'

'I suppose you're right,' de Vere grunted, shivering violently. 'No one in his right mind would be anywhere else today but in front of a roaring fire. My God, Dickie, how I could go a hot whisky toddy!'

Bird laughed sympathetically, his breath fogging the icy air in a grey cloud. 'And you shall have it, de Vere – as soon as we've got the skimmers unloaded and onto the goods train. I promise you that.'

'That's all well and good,' de Vere grumbled, wiping a melting snowflake off the end of his elegant long nose. 'But who's supposed to take care of that little bit of business? Neither you nor I can speak one solitary word of Finnish, and our Swedish is limited to "many thanks", "cheers" and "good-bye". Not exactly a sound basis for carrying out a business negotiation, eh?'

Bird grinned at de Vere's disgruntled look, as the Finnish coaster slowed down with a series of violent shakes, in order to enter a side channel. 'Never fear, de Vere. C took care of everything very efficiently in Stockholm – the transfer, and finding this old tub for us. So I have no doubt, his agent, whoever he is, will be waiting for us on the quay to do exactly the same here. Don't worry, you'll be wrapping yourself around your hot toddy soon enough.'

De Vere looked at the tall 18th century warehouses which now loomed up through the driving snow and grunted, 'P.D.Q., I hope. *P.D.Q.*!'

*

But ten minutes later as the coaster started to edge its way into its berth, it seemed to the anxious watchers on the deck that their leader's confident prediction was wrong. The cobbled quay now covered in hard-packed snow, stained yellow by the horses' droppings was empty save for a couple of leather-coated Finns sheltering under a crane, who might be dockers, and a slim man, with his back to them, next to a rickety pre-war Mercedes lorry, obviously disinterested in the coaster's arrival. Five minutes passed, and the coaster had tied up. The swarthy, dirty captain had ordered the engines stopped, which they did with a violent shudder, as if they were dead for good. Still no contact. Worried now, Bird walked to the other side of the ship. But the opposite quay was equally empty. Indeed the whole harbour, shrouded in a deep mantle of white, seemed abandoned.

In the end Bird made a decision. 'De Vere,' he said, 'I'm going down onto the quay to have a look-see myself. You and Bull and Ginger watch the skimmers.' He lowered his voice. 'Have you got your revolver handy?'

De Vere, his disgruntled look gone now, tapped the bulge in his pocket.

'Good. I'm off!'

Clattering down the gangplank, he set foot on Finnish soil for the first time and stared around in puzzlement. The two leather-coated dockers showed not the least interest in him. They were chattering away busily to one another in a totally incomprehensible language. He bit his lower lip and wondered what he should do.

Then he spotted the little wooden shed further up the quay, with a stove pipe poked through one dirty window emitting thick blue smoke.

He made up his mind. Bending his head against the driving snow, he set off towards it, hoping to find someone there who could help him.

He came level with the slim man poised with one foot on the lorry's splintered running board, obviously engaged in checking something in the cab. But in spite of the loud crunch of his nailed seaman's boots on the hard-packed stained snow, the man did not straighten up and look around at him.

Bird shrugged imperceptibly and wished the next moment he hadn't, as an icy-cold snowflake slid down the back of his neck. He shivered and plodded on. Suddenly the slim man spoke, in English. 'Welcome to Finland, Mr Bird . . . sorry we couldn't provide you with better weather.'

He spun round.

The 'slim man' was a girl, striking rather than beautiful in the conventional English fashion, her broad, bold face glowing with the cold, her dark eyes, the colour of polished chestnuts, sparkling with fun.

'Are you?'

'Yes,' she anticipated his question, 'London ordered me to meet you here.' The girl's accent was deliciously foreign, with a hint of difficulty with the r's.

For an instant, Bird studied her face and wondered whether he should ask her for any form of identification. But her next gesture confirmed she was a member of C's mysterious organization. She stuck out her hand and said, 'London wired you'd never been overseas before, Mr Bird. So you'd better get used to our funny continental habit of shaking hands every five minutes.'

'Of course,' he said and slipped off his wet mitten hastily. Her grip was firm and confident, just as her next words were, 'Now then Mr Bird, I think we should get down to business straightaway.'

'Yes, of course,' he agreed hastily, a little bewildered by C's

29

choice of agent. All the same the girl seemed to know what she was about. 'What do you suggest?'

'First thing, we must get your men ashore and into the back of the truck. We'll have to get you away from the harbour before our Red friends become too curious – and believe me, there are plenty of them about still.'

'Good, Miss – er?'

But the girl did not volunteer her name.

'Well, what about our skimmers – our crates up there?'

She nodded her understanding, as if she were fully informed about the skimmers. 'Don't worry about them, Mr Bird. I think my men are quite capable of handling that particular problem without difficulty.'

'Your men?'

She indicated the two dockers standing under the crane, their hard gazes fixed on them now, and their long, ankle-length coats thrown back to reveal the curiously shaped Finnish hunting knives they both wore at their belts.

Bird grinned. 'I see what you mean. Both of them look as if they would slit their own mothers' throats for a shilling.'

'Less – much less,' she agreed and there was no grin on her pretty face. 'Now come on, Mr Bird, let's get your poor freezing chaps off the deck of that old tub, eh?'

High above them in his look-out post in the crane's cab, the surly unshaven man with the permanently dripping red nose took his gaze off the mysterious crates on the Finnish coaster's deck and followed the man and the girl as they got into the Mercedes' cab. Then he made up his mind. He picked up the phone and whirled the wheel. The resident answered immediately. '*Da. Boris gavorit . . .*'

*

Thirty minutes later the four Navy men were squatting on the narrow wooden bench of the great green-tiled oven which reached to the ceiling of the shabby little kitchen in the wooden-frame house in the port's dirty industrial suburb, luxuriating in the warmth and sipping steamingly hot glasses of tea with rum.

The strange girl with the bold gleaming eyes and strong determined features let them enjoy the hot drink for a few

30

moments. Then she poised herself under the crucifix, the kitchen's sole decoration, save for a creased picture of Field Marshal von Mannerheim in full uniform. 'Let me introduce myself, gentlemen,' she announced somewhat formally. 'My name is Anna – Baroness von Klauwitz.'

Ginger Coates was the first to react, as always. 'Are you a Jerry – excuse me, Miss,' he corrected himself immediately, 'a German?' His sharp cockney eyes full of interest. 'I went through all the last bit of unpleasantness, but all the same, I never did get to meet one, a German, I mean.'

'No,' she answered, tossing back her chestnut-coloured hair proudly and displaying her admirable figure to its best advantage. '*Russian*! Though a long time ago, my ancestors did come from Prussia.'

'But Miss von Kl—' Bird stumbled badly over her name.

She laughed. 'Oh, please do call me Anna – all of you. I'm sure that Klauwitz is terribly difficult for your English tongues.'

'You speak excellent English,' de Vere said, his hands happily cradled around the glass of grog. 'I wish my German and French was as good.'

'Cheltenham,' she explained.

'Oh my God,' de Vere groaned, taking a hasty sip of the steaming hot mixture. 'Cheltenham Ladies College – that is a fate that no one should be allowed to suffer.'

She smiled and then her face grew serious again 'You were going to ask, Mr Bird, what I'm doing here, no doubt?'

Bird nodded, amazed at the girl's poise and style, although she was undoubtedly about his own age.

'My father was a Liberal, you see. Indeed he spent some time in his youth in exile on account of it and he was in the 1905 *Duma*. When Kerensky formed his Provisional Government in '17, he was an obvious choice. Perhaps he should have been more energetic – perhaps they all should have been,' she shrugged in the Continental fashion. 'But he wasn't. He let those traitors to the Revolution, the Bolsheviks, have their freedom to carry out their insidious work. And in the end he had to pay the price for it.' She hesitated for a moment, while they stared up at her expectantly.

'On the night of October 25th, 1917, the Bolsheviks seized

power in Petrograd. The soldiers took him to the Smolny Institute,[1] where he was tried,' she emphasized the word bitterly, 'by Soviet Military Council under the presidency of Lev Davidovitch Bronstein personally.'

'You mean Trotsky?' de Vere asked quietly.

'Yes, the present Soviet War Minister. That monster! According to our sources, the trial took all of five minutes. The verdict was obvious. *Death!* And the sentence was carried out equally quickly.' She hesitated, her dark eyes flooding with sudden tears. 'They took him outside into the courtyard, and systematically smashed his head in with a sledge-hammer.' She gulped and hurried on. 'Then they flung the remains out into the gutters of the Nevsky for the rats to gnaw.'

The four Navy men stared at her in shocked silence, broken only by the measured ticking of a clock in another room.

'I'm sorry,' Bird began.

She waved him to silence, the tears replaced by burning anger in her dark eyes. 'You asked five minutes ago what I am doing here? Well, Mr Bird, I shall tell you. It is your mission to take in the courier to link up with the R-Network, yes?'

Bird nodded his head numbly, wondering what the young aristocratic girl was leading up to. Next to him on the narrow bench, de Vere tensed, as if he already knew what was coming.

The girl pointed to herself and announced dramatically, '*I am that courier!*'

*

'You mean, you're going to go with us in the skimmers into Russia, Miss?' Ginger Coates asked incredulously.

'I am,' she replied firmly and Bird, still silenced by her revelation, could feel her iron determination.

'Crikey,' Ginger commented. 'That's a turn up for the book! What next?'

'I shall tell you what next, Mr Ginger Coates,' she said. 'You are all going to finish your grog, fill your pockets with that food over there,' indicating the squares of what looked like black plug tobacco which Bird knew to be pumpernickel sandwiches; 'and put these on.' She turned and opened the white painted

1. Headquarters of the Soviet Party.

door of the wall cupboard below the crucifix. A bundle of heavy furs rolled out onto the floor. 'Yours!' she announced. 'They are the best I could get on the black market. I hope they fit you all.'

Bull put down his glass and picked up the nearest coat, made of some heavy black fur. Curiously he draped it across his massive frame. 'Cor, Bull, you look like a ruddy great black Angus now!' Ginger remarked.

Bull ignored the comment, and looked down at the girl. 'But what do we need these for, Miss? We's got us coats already.'

'Pathetic things they are, too!' she said scornfully. 'They wouldn't even keep out the Finnish summer breeze. Where you're going, my dear Mr Bull, the cold will have the ears and nose off you in minutes if you're not careful. That's why you need fur – real fur. Now, let's get on with it. Nikonen will already have the train waiting for us at the goods yard and time is running out *fast*.'

Bird grinned, amused, as the other three rose obediently like schoolboys, responding to the command of a severe school marm. If he didn't watch it Baroness Anna von Klauwitz would be taking charge of the whole mission!

2

'Gentlemens, the locomotive!' Nikonen announced proudly. The tubby, unshaven engine-driver swept off his cap and looked at them as if he expected a round of applause.

'Gawd luv a duck!' Ginger exclaimed, staring in astonishment at the tall-funnelled, ancient, wood-burning engine. 'What is it – *Stephenson's Rocket*?'

'Shut up, Ginger,' Bird snapped, staring the length of their 'special', as Nikonen called it in the fractured English he'd picked up in the Pittsburg steel mills before the war. The tender, piled high with logs; the two flat cars which now bore the skimmers; and a small coach, its length pocked with machine gun bullets from the recent fighting.

'First class, gents,' the driver said, following the direction of his gaze. 'We're giving only the best for the English milords.'

He raised his black hand, beaming all over his chubby face and cried: 'God shave jolly old King George!'

'God shave jolly old King George, indeed!' de Vere groaned. 'Do you think that thing will even get us out of the yard, Anna?'

'Of course it will,' she said confidently, her face set under its rakishly tilted fur cap. 'And we're lucky to get it, I can tell you. It took a lot of convincing the officials.' She made the gesture of counting money with her thumb and forefinger. 'A lot!'

De Vere looked at her a little shocked. 'I say, you don't mean bribery, Anna?'

Bird and the girl laughed at the look on his horsey face. 'How naive you English are,' she said. 'How do you think I got you and your skimmers off the dock, without even as much as a sight of a policeman or customs official?'

With that she swung round and fired a stream of Finnish at the engine driver, who whipped off his cap again and bowed low, as if she were royalty, before scuttling off to his tender as quickly as his bandy legs would carry him.

'Now then,' she turned back to the four sailors standing shivering in the snowy goods yards among the rusting skeletons of engines knocked out by artillery during the Civil War. 'We're in for a long, slow trip. Nikonen's engine won't go much more than twenty miles an hour—'

'*Downhill*, I 'spect, Miss?' Ginger interrupted cheekily.

She gave him a fleeting smile. 'I imagine you're right, Ginger.' Her smile vanished. 'We could also be in for a dangerous trip. We'll be all right until we branch off for Lahti. There we'll be travelling mostly through cold farm areas.'

'*Cold* farm, Miss?' Bull, the Yorkshire ploughboy, asked in his ponderous way.

'Yes, that is what the Finns call them. Pioneer areas, which are re-named *warm* farms, once the land has been cleared of trees and a farmhouse erected.'

'Now, as you can imagine,' she went on, to the accompaniment of Nikonen throwing log after log through the engine's fire-door, 'it's pretty lonely country, solely inhabited by a few settlers, a handful of Lapp hunters – and the Reds.'

'*Reds?*' Bird queried quickly.

34

'Yes, worst luck. After the Battle of Tammerfors last year when Mannerheim beat the Red Finns and their Bolshevik allies, and crushed the Red Terror in Helsingfors, a lot of them fled into the forests up there and became nothing better than bandits. They live by raiding the villages, stealing the peasants' food and raping their women.'

De Vere blushed slightly at the word 'rape', but the girl did not seem to notice. 'Naturally they've got nothing to lose – their lives are forfeit anyway, if government troops ever catch up with them. So you see we could run into trouble once we get into that area.'

Bird nodded slowly, pondering her warning, a little bemused at the strange un-English world of bribery, banditry and worse, in which they suddenly found themselves. 'But we've only got our service revolvers to defend ourselves,' he said at last.

'No, we haven't sir.' It was Ginger Coates.

He looked at the grinning, red-faced cockney. 'What do you mean, Ginger?' he asked sharply.

'The Lewis guns, sir,' Ginger said, 'we could have 'em out of the crates in a brace of shakes, me and Bull here. They'd tickle the toes of any Bolshy trying to stop the Royal Mail – right sharpish!'

Bird's handsome young face broke into a smile. 'Right sharpish, indeed, Ginger! All right, break them out and let's get under way.'

'Ay, ay, sir,' Ginger cried and flung him a mock salute. 'Come on, Bull, you Yorkshire pudden. You heard what the officer said, didn't you?'

Ten minutes later the ancient train was on its way, with Bull and Ginger busily stripping the two machine guns on the dusty ripped plush of the first class coach, now heated by a glowing pot-bellied stove at the end of the gangway. The long journey eastwards had commenced . . .

*

The empty countryside lay weighed down with snow. Everywhere the firs, marching in silent ranks to the horizon, were deep in it, devoid of any life save that of crouching watchful hares, whose long ears quivered as the ancient train rumbled by, or hesitant stags, their steaming nostrils raised to the harsh, wintry sky.

But even in this wilderness there were a few villages, where the green-uniformed station-master would halt the train and enter their compartment, to ask their 'Honours' if they would give permission for the train to proceed. According to Anna the custom dated back to the Czarist days, when only aristocrats or high Imperial officials travelled first class. Hence their privileged treatment.

'Well, I'll go to our house,' Ginger exclaimed. 'Mrs Coates' lad has really gone up in the world since he went to foreign parts! First class on the railway, and now treated like royalty! What blooming next!'

But not all the station masters were so polite. Some fifty kilometres west of Lahti, just as the sun was beginning to sink covering the white waste with its blood-red hue, they had to stop at a tiny village for fresh logs. The station master entered their compartment, cap in hand, as in previous villages. He was a ruffianly figure, in contrast with the others, unshaven and unkempt, his head hung to one side, as if to conceal the expression in his dark, shifty eyes. Hastily Anna translated his words for them. 'He says,' she said, 'that he has orders not to let us proceed up the line till tomorrow morning. Apparently the Reds are on the rampage further up the line and the authorities have ordered all further traffic to Lahti stopped till the troops arrive. He wants us to move into the siding.' She indicated the rusty line behind the shabby wooden station, which ran to the handful of cottages, grouped round the onion-towered white church of the village.

Bird thought of the hundred sovereigns he had in his money belt under his shirt. 'Offer him money and tell him we'll chance the Reds. But we must get on.'

'I agree.' De Vere stared at the village in some apprehension. 'I don't fancy the prospect of staying in that one-horse place all night. They've probably got fleas – and worse.'

Anna translated Bird's offer. For an instant the station-master's eyes flickered greedily, then he shook his unkempt

36

head. They didn't need Anna's angry translation to know that he had refused the bribe.

'Can't we just go on, sir?' Ginger asked, 'whether old dogsbody here likes it or not?'

'No, gentlemens, we cannot.' It was Nikonen, his face black with smoke, wiping his greasy hands on a piece of cotton waste. 'This station-master bum, he have thrown the points against us. We gotta take the goddam sidetrack.'

Bird gave in. 'All right,' he sighed. 'Tell him, we'll spend the night here, Anna, and ask him if we can buy some food in the village.'

The station-master was transformed when Anna translated their decision. Bowing and scraping mightily, he backed his way out, promising that he, personally, would ensure they received the best salted cod the village could provide.

*

'I don't like it,' Anna said reflectively, five minutes later, when they were installed on the side line. 'I don't like it one little bit.'

'Neither do I, Anna?' de Vere sighed, as he slumped there in the dusty plush. 'Salted cod indeed!'

'Oh, do put a sock in it, de Vere, will you?' Bird protested, a worried frown on his face, as he warmed his hands at the glowing pot-bellied stove. 'This is serious, isn't it Anna?'

She nodded. 'Yes, why should he care what happens to us? And why didn't he accept the gold? After all, these petty officials will usually do anything for money. It's a survival from the Czarist days.'

'Yes, he could have told anyone who enquired, we hadn't stopped here. There were no witnesses to disprove him. Then he could have pocketed the gold and left us to take our chance, one way or the other.' Bird stuck his hands in his pockets and felt the comforting bulge of his revolver. 'I wonder just what that chappie's little game is?'

'I think I can tell you, sir.' It was Bull, who was staring grimly out of the portside window.

'What do you mean, Bull?' Bird snapped.

'Well, sir, there's somebody up on yon hill over there — and the beggar's watching us through a pair of field glasses . . .'

3

Just before the sun finally disappeared over the horizon and plunged the bitter landscape into a thick inky darkness, broken only by the flickering yellow lights of the oil lamps across in the village, they had decided they wouldn't stay the night there. The station-master, as greasy and as unctious as ever, had come and gone with his promised salted cod, which was stiff as a board (de Vere had promptly tossed it out of the window into the snow); and if the unknown man with the binoculars was still watching them, they could no longer see him. Now they grouped round the stove, their faces set and tense under the petroleum lamp which cast their monstrously magnified shadows on the wall of the coach, wondering how they could get away. Bull manned the portside Lewis gun ready for trouble.

'Couldn't we just bang the beggar over the back of his nut and make a run for it, sir?' Ginger suggested.

'No go, Joe,' Nikonen responded, as he chewed his pumpernickel sandwich. 'That bum – he got the key for the switch in the pocket of his bum pants.'

'Do you know what "bum" means in real English and not that Yankee lingo you—'

'Be quiet, Ginger,' Bird interrupted brusquely. 'Nikonen, do you mean that the switch for the points is not inside the station?' He indicated the yellow light burning in the station-master's private quarters.

Nikonen wiped the crumbs off his greasy red lips and belched happily. 'No, sir, you betcha! It's in that outhouse up the track. But the station-master bum, he got the key.'

Bird snapped his fingers excitedly. 'That's it! Of course, it is!'

De Vere straightened up quickly. 'What's what, Dickie? I say – do stop running off at the mouth like a raving lunatic and tell us.'

'Well, don't you see? We could turn the switch thing ourselves and change the points.'

38

'But that would mean "breaking and entering", Dickie!' De Vere protested. 'You can't do that.'

'But this isn't England, de Vere. You must have realized that by now, old chap.'

'Of course, it isn't,' Anna snapped angrily. 'My God, *you English*!' she clapped her hand to her temple, in despair. 'But listen, if you change the points, won't the Reds whom we know must be lurking in the forest outside the village, hear the train and be on to us before we can get away? They're bound to have horses.'

'No, gracious Miss,' Nikonen answered her question for them. 'Cock a gracious ear to that! We're gonna have a storm!'

But they didn't need to listen. As the first gust of the wind howling down straight from the Arctic Circle hit the coach, it rocked violently like a ship at sea.

'Of course,' Bird said. 'That wind should cover any noise we would make!'

'But listen Dickie. Let's assume that this station-master bird,' de Vere coughed abruptly. 'Excuse me Dickie for using your name in vain. But assuming he's in with the Reds and there are others of the same ilk along the line further up, couldn't he telegraph them that we're on our way, once we've departed so ungraciously?'

Bird's happy smile of enthusiasm vanished immediately. 'Of course, you're right. We've got to take care of those damned telegraph wires. But how?'

As usual it was Ginger Coates who had the bright idea. His smart cockney mind seemed to react the quickest under pressure. 'Well sir,' he said, indicating Nikonen, now busy with another sandwich, 'if his nibs has an hawser, we could sling it over the wires so that when the train moves off, it'd cut through 'em.'

'Right in one, Ginger!' Bird cried enthusiastically, his face brightening at once. 'Well, Nikonen, have you?'

'Sure boss,' he said easily, pausing in the middle of an enormous bite. 'Old Nikonen, he got everything.'

'Good! Now this is the way we'll do it. You Bull, you'll cover us from here, right?'

'Ay, ay, sir,' Bull replied, as unhurried as ever.

Bird turned to Coates. 'Ginger, you cut along with Lieutenant de Vere and see if you can get a wire over that telegraph line and then attach it to this coach. You, Nikonen, once you've given the sailor the hawser, you come with me. We're going to have a look at that shed. All right?'

Nikonen's dirty face lit up. 'You betcha, boss . . . a little bit of grab and smash, eh?'

'That's it, mate,' Ginger cried, 'a little bit of the old how's yer father "grab and smash".' He winked at Bird cheekily. 'Never thought I'd see the day, sir, when an officer of the Royal did a bit of tea-leaving.'

'Get on with you, you rogue,' de Vere cried. 'Let's get out into the cruel winter's night – *P.D.Q!*'

*

Heads bent against the howling wind, which pelted their faces with frozen snow, they fought their way closer and closer to the station-master's quarters; Bird with his revolver drawn and cocked. Behind them in the white flying gloom, de Vere and Ginger were busy trying to cast the heavy hawser up and across the telegraph wires thirty feet above the ground. Suddenly Nikonen grabbed Bird's arm. '*Attention!*' he whispered urgently.

The next instant, Bird saw the reason for the Finn's sudden alarm. The yellow light burning in the front-covered window had gone out abruptly.

'Do you think he's heard anything, Nikonen?'

'I don't know, boss,' the Finn hissed, swamping his nostrils with the foul odour of stale garlic and *aquavit.*

Bird hesitated. In spite of his three years of active sea service during the war, this was his first land action. What did one do in such a situation? Suddenly there was a faint but definite rhythmic squeaking noise, which he couldn't identify at once. 'What do you make of it, Nikonen?' he whispered urgently.

Beside him the Finn laughed softly and relaxed. 'Come on, boss, that bum in there is plenty busy now.'

'How do you mean?'

He chuckled again. 'He's busy getting up his old lady's drawers. That's what I mean, boss.'

Bird smiled at the engine driver's turn of phrase. 'Come on then you rogue, let's get on with it.'

The persistent rusty squeak-squeak of the bedsprings died away almost immediately as they edged past the station into the open once more, and received the full blast of the howling wind. Bird saw with relief that the little shed was in complete darkness. Obviously it wasn't occupied by the unknown enemy.

Swiftly Nikonen lit his stinking carbide lamp under cover of his ragged jacket and shielded the light while Bird inserted the wrench into the hasp of the padlock and heaved with all his strength. The padlock snapped almost at once. Hurriedly he flung open the door and held the hissing, white-glaring lantern, while Nikonen threw the switch and hammered a metal wedge underneath it, the noise drowned by the howl of the wind.

'He's all right now, boss,' the Finn grunted and straightened up. 'Now they can no move no more, the damn thing, I mean.'

Bird shook his head at the engine driver's impossible English. 'Yes, I understand. All right, Nikonen, come on. Let's hoof it smartish!'

*

Five minutes later, his teeth chattering with cold, he was standing in the cab next to Nikonen, who was throwing log after log into the fire box, which fortunately he had kept alight during their stop. Behind them, somewhere in the darkness, Bull and Ginger were manning the Lewis guns on the flat cars, ready to open fire at the slightest sign of trouble from the hill, while de Vere kept his eye on the hawser slung over the wires.

Finally the Finnish driver was ready. He straightened up and took a quick look at the green luminous dial of the pressure gauge. Apparently satisfied by what he saw there, he kicked the door of the fire-box closed. 'All right boss,' he announced. 'Hold on to your hat! Off *we are going*!'

Bird bit his lower lip and clutched his revolver more firmly. If any trouble were going to start, it would be now. In spite of the freezing cold, he found himself suddenly sweating. Gingerly, very gingerly, Nikonen opened the throttle. Bird jumped. The noise of the wheels beginning to move seemed tremendous. But nothing happened! Obviously the howl of the gale had drowned the sound. Bird swallowed hard with relief.

Nikonen eased the brass throttle open further. For a minute they seemed unable to move, as the train took the strain of the load behind it and the resistance of the wires. There was a loud clatter of wheels revolving furiously trying to get a grip. Across at the station-master's, the yellow light went on again abruptly.

'Come on, Nikonen!' Bird yelled, unable to contain his excitement any longer. *'Come on!'*

Somewhere in the darkness there was a faint cry in what Bird took to be Finnish. The alarm had been sounded! He raised his revolver. The cry had come from somewhere on the hill. Nikonen shoved the throttle further along the brass race. Steam exploded from the outlet in a great roar. The wheels chattered furiously.

On the hillside, a bright white light started to burn abruptly. There were more and more cries coming from that direction now. Bird could hear them even above the gale. He bit his bottom lip to prevent himself shouting out loud. The sweat was pouring down his forehead now.

Ping! The wires, hidden above their heads, parted with a sudden snap. In that same instant, the engine's wheels found the grip they sought. The train started to move forward in the darkness. Up above them on the hill, a slow machine gun began to chatter like an angry woodpecker. Slow white tracer zigzagged towards them, gaining speed with every second. Next moment the slugs struck the side of the engine like a tropical downpour on a tin roof.

Bird ducked instinctively, but Nikonen, a huge grin on his black sweating face, did not bat an eyelid. Nor did the two gunners hesitate. Almost immediately they opened up with their two Lewis guns. Like angry red hornets, the tracer sped towards the Reds hidden up in the trees above.

Suddenly a blob of white loomed up out of the darkness. A face, only ten yards away! Almost without thinking, Bird pressed the trigger of his revolver. The face screamed wildly and vanished immediately. 'Pretty damn hot shooting, boss!' Nikonen yelled above the ever increasing snap and crackle of small arms fire, grinning from ear to ear. 'Real Buffalo Billie—'

He ducked abruptly, as a burst of machine gun fire zipped

across the cab, shattering the pressure gauge and showering him with broken glass. 'S.O.B.!' he yelled angrily, shaking a hamlike fist at his unknown assailant. 'You break my train!'

For one moment, Bird thought the enraged driver was going to spring off the cab and strangle the unknown machine gunner. Fortunately, Nikonen controlled himself in time, and concentrated on the task in hand.

In front of them red lights were being waved frantically from one side to the other.

'Don't stop!' Bird yelled, and leaning out of the cab, the wind tearing at his clothes, he took a wild aim. He fired and quickly slipped behind the cover of the metal. There was a yell, and one of the lights went out abruptly. 'Don't stop!' he cried at Nikonen. 'Don't stop now!' whether the lights indicated some sort of obstacle or other, he didn't know. All he knew was that if they did, the obstacle must have been placed there by the Reds.

Nikonen did not hesitate. He pushed the throttle wide open. Wind, icy particles of snow, and flying ash, stung Bird's eyes as he tried to peer into the darkness ahead. As the train rattled on at its maximum speed, shaking violently, he could just make out some dark object lying across the line. But there was no stopping now.

The next moment the old wood-burner smashed into the object. There was a tremendous jerk. For one horrifying second, Bird thought she was not going to hold the track. And then she was plunging on into the night, with the vicious crackle of machine guns getting fainter and fainter by the instant. *They had done it* ...

*

Behind them, the leather-coated man with the binoculars watched the twin red tail lanterns disappear into the gloom. '*Yo tuoyu mat!*' he gave vent to his anger with the obscene Russian curse. Then he swung round and faced the shivering station-master, his gross frame clad only in a striped flannel nightshirt. 'You fornicating son of a bitch!' he yelled, 'you ought to have kept your damn lecherous Finnish eyes on them!' He raised his pistol.

'No . . . no, your Honour,' the staion-master cried in terror, falling to his bare knees in the snow, hands raised in the traditional gesture of supplication. 'Not that!'

The man with the binoculars did not hesitate. 'Bourgeois swine!' he cursed in his atrocious Finnish, and pressed the trigger. The big automatic jerked violently in his hand. The station-master was lifted clean off his feet by the impact at such close range. When he hit the snow again, his face was a gory red mess and he was dead.

The Russian did not even look down at him. 'Drop all that at once,' he ordered the ragged bandits who were already carrying out the station-master's poor possessions, pursued by a screaming fat woman with blonde plaits. He pressed the trigger of his pistol again to emphasize his order. A bullet kicked up a flurry of snow just in front of the leader's holed boots. 'Get back to your damn ponies immediately, *Davai*! . . . We've got a lot of hard riding in front of us this night!'

4

They spotted the Red cavalry an hour before dawn. Four kilometres east of Lahti, they had been forced to stop when the ancient engine ran out of fuel. Nikonen and Bull sawed at the firs lining the track to get the necessary logs for the engine's greedy and badly leaking boilers, while Ginger and Bird stood guard, covering their front with one of the Lewis guns. There, among the snow-heavy trees, Ginger, as sharp-eyed and alert as ever, nudged Bird. 'Sir,' he hissed urgently, 'up there!'

Bird forced open his sleep-heavy eyes. 'What?'

'On that ridge, next to the railway cutting. It's *them* all right – you can bet yer bottom dollar on that, sir.'

Ginger was right. About a mile away to their front, silent black specks were moving across the icy snow, which glittered in the silver-blue light of the moon. They were heading for the narrow cutting through which they had to pass to reach Lahti.

'Blast!' Bird cursed. 'I thought we'd seen the last of those devils!' Ginger laughed softly, but there was no mirth in his

44

laugh. 'Don't look like it, sir. Get a butchers of that!' The first of the riders, black against the silver light, had dismounted and was approaching the cutting in crouched caution. 'Yer don't need a crystal ball to know what that lot's up to, do you, sir?'

'No, you don't!' Bird answered grimly. 'All right, Ginger, you stay here and keep an eye on them. I'll double back and warn the others.'

'Ay, ay, sir,' Ginger sang out cheerfully, as if sudden night encounters with Red cavalry were commonplace, 'leave it to Mrs Coates' handsome son.'

Within minutes Bird had stopped the tree felling and gathered the rest of the crew, wide-eyed and a little apprehensive, in the darkness of the first class coach. Swiftly he explained what they had seen up ahead, while they listened in tense silence, broken only by the sound of Nikonen chewing heartily on yet another pumpernickel sandwich.

'So you can see their plan. They must have ridden like the devil cross-country for exactly this spot, because it is the easiest place in the world to stop us.'

'Yes, you're right, Dickie,' de Vere agreed grimly. 'I doubt whether that old engine could make more than ten miles an hour up that incline.'

Nikonen mumbled something through a mouthful of bread and sausage, but didn't disagree with de Vere's estimate.

Bird nodded, his face tense and drawn in the moonlight which was the coach's only illumination, now Anna had darkened the oil lamp. 'A determined man on the top of that cutting with a couple of Mills bombs, could settle our hash for us, I'm afraid.'

For a few moments, heavy silence descended on the little group, each one occupied with his own thoughts. Suddenly Bird started. Anna's cool white hand sought and found his.

Slowly he turned and stared at her. Her pale face showed fear for the very first time and he knew why. She was afraid – deadly afraid – of what might happen to her beautiful body if she fell into Red hands! Abruptly he realized that for a change, the normally daring Russian girl was relying on him!

He licked his dry lips and tried to force a smile. 'Now come on you lot,' he said in a voice which wasn't quite under control, 'stop looking like a wet weekend in Wigan! We're not beaten yet you know – not by a long chalk!'

'That's right, sir,' Bull agreed enthusiastically. 'Them foreigners'll have to get up a bit earlier to put one over on t'lads of the old Royal!'

'How do you mean, Dickie?' de Vere snapped.

'Look,' Bird explained swiftly. 'They obviously haven't spotted us yet. We're covered by the wood and we stopped the noise of the wood-chopping in time, all right?'

'*D'accord* – get on with it, old chap.'

'Well, it's obvious then that they're expecting us to come up the line. That's the direction they'll be concentrating on, won't they?'

Anna freed her hand from his, looking at him, as if he had suddenly gone crazy. 'But there *is* no other direction that we can come from!' she protested.

Bird winked at her conspiratorially. 'Isn't there?' he asked. 'Now listen, this is what we're going to do . . .'

*

'*Horosho!*' the Russian with the binoculars snapped. 'Your position is excellent, Arvid.' He took a last glance at the line of riflemen, dug in on both sides of the track running through the narrow cutting. Above him a couple of men crouched, their belts full of captured German stick grenades. 'If your firing line doesn't stop the train, the bombers will.'

Arvid, the cross-eyed Swedish-Finn leader of the Red troop, swung the Russian a caricature of a military salute. 'They won't escape us this time, Comrade Commissar,' he growled. 'We'll take care of that.'

'You'd better, Comrade,' the Commisar said in his atrocious Finnish, 'or you'll be a head shorter, sooner than you think . . . I shall leave it to you, and go back to the horses.' He indicated the dark mass of the wood, where they had hidden their animals.

'Yes, Comrade Commissar, it would be better if you did so.' In spite of his fear and dependence on the Commissar, who supplied the troop with most of their funds, he could not quite conceal his contempt for the Russian; the man was an abject coward in action.

Without another word, the Russian swung round and plodded swiftly through the snow towards the firs. Arvid wondered why he should set so much store on stopping the train to Lahti. After all it contained only a couple of flat cars, which didn't look too promising, and a handful of ragged passengers, who hardly seemed worth the effort.

Suddenly his thoughts were disturbed by a faint but familiar humming of the rails. He bent his head to them and crouched there momentarily. 'All right, comrades,' he cried straightening up, 'here it comes. And remember, don't miss this time, or you won't get that medal from Comrade Trotsky!'

There was a chorus of derisive laughter from the men crouched in their holes on both sides of the track, as their leader doubled swiftly for cover.

*

The ancient engine swung into sight. Behind it trailed a white flag of smoke. Scarlet flame stabbed the dark, from the open fire-box. Little blue sparks sprang from its wheels.

Arvid drew his machine pistol. In a moment the train would hit the incline and have to slow down to a virtual walk. Hastily he threw a glance at his men. They were tensed and ready. This time the foreign bastards would not get through. The rapid clatter of the ancient locomotive gave way to a strained chug-chug, as it took the start of the incline. Arvid clicked off his safety catch. It would all be over in a matter of minutes now. Above him on top of the cutting, the two bombers drew the china pins out of their potato masher grenades and prepared to throw.

Now Arvid could see the little train quite clearly, the dark shape of the driver, starkly outlined against the gleaming fire-box; the two flat cars and their mysterious precious load; and the yellow-lit coach at the rear, the train's passengers slumped in sleep next to the windows. It was obvious the foreigners suspected nothing.

Two hundred metres . . . one hundred and fifty . . . Great white clouds of smoke were streaming from the engine's tall ancient funnel, as it strained to master the incline . . . One

hundred . . . Another couple of seconds and it would be parallel with them . . . Arvid could hear the clang-clang of the
driver's shovel quite clearly now as he frantically shovelled
logs into the fire's ever-greedy maw . . . Fifty metres. The engine filled the night sky now . . . One more second . . . Arvid
raised his arm. All around him his men tensed . . . Thirty
metres.

'*NOW*—'

'*Brr!*' In that same instant, the two Lewis guns to their rear
opened up with a vicious high-pitched hysterical screech.

Arvid felt an excruciating burning pain in his guts. Involun-
tarily, he pressed the trigger of his automatic. As he fell screaming, flame stabbed the sky and before his eyes closed for good,
he glimpsed the locomotive squealing to a stop in a flurry of
hard blue sparks. Dying in the suddenly bloody snow, he dimly
heard the sounds of the massacre which had begun . . .

*

Crouched behind the snow-covered rocks on both sides of the
cutting, and sited so that they could enfilade the Reds, the two
crews poured a cruel stream of red and white tracer into the
trapped Reds. Now men were falling everywhere, and screaming in their death agonies. One of the bombers, wounded in
both legs, tried to throw his grenades from where he knelt.
Ginger, on Bird's gun did not even hesitate. 'Here, you Bolshy
beggar,' he grunted, his eyes gleaming with murderous pleasure, '*take this from Mrs Coates' son!*' He swung the gun
round and sliced a stream of slugs through the bomber's middle.
The man dropped the grenade. Next instant it exploded in
front of his knees. When the vicious ball of blue and yellow
flame subsided, the Red was no longer there, but his severed
head sailed through the silver half-light like a slow football.

On the other side of the cutting, Bull and de Vere had taken
their section of the Reds completely by surprise. They had
felled a good dozen with their first burst. Now the rest were trying to escape from their hellish fire, back to the horses hidden
in the forest a couple of hundred yards away. But de Vere
showed them no mercy. While Bull, his big body hung with
spare pans of ammunition, did the spotting for him, he potted

48

individual Reds, as if he were back on his father's estate, grouse-shooting on the 'Glorious Twelfth'.

'There's one, sir!' Bull would snap.

Up would go the heavy Lewis and de Vere would nonchalantly give the would-be escaper a short, sharp burst. Once, three of them, desperate and crazed by the cruel fire, rushed at the gun, knives upraised, screaming wildly as they pelted across the snow. De Vere gave them one well-aimed burst and they crumpled to the ground like discarded puppets. 'Three more for the bag,' de Vere commented coolly, while Bull looked a little shocked by the officer's disregard for human life.

A moment later the Lewis gun jammed. It was the opportunity the survivors had been waiting for. Screaming hysterically they rushed the gun. In an instant, they had overrun the two lone Englishmen. A bearded giant, stinking of sweat, horse, and garlic flung himself on de Vere, his hands grabbing frantically for the officer's throat. 'None o' that there!' Bull grunted and swung his big knee up swiftly. It caught the Red directly under the chin, and his head shot back with a dry crack. He fell to the snow without even a groan, his spine broken. The next instant, Bull himself was bowled over by two Finns, their knives gleaming wickedly as they raised them for the kill.

Desperately Bull writhed back and forth in the wildly flying snow, parrying off blow after blow. De Vere grappling with another assailant, bent on strangling him, could not come to his aid. One of the Finns slashed his knife down and hit an ammo pan on Bull's chest. Bull seized his chance, brought up his knee, and caught him in the groin. He screamed thickly, his mouth suddenly full of hot vomit and rolled over. Bull launched a wild punch at the other man. The Finn, dark and slight, avoided it easily, and Bull's fist hit the snow. 'Now die, foreigner!' he heard the Finn call in poor English. He caught a glimpse of Anna behind him, and heard her say, 'No, you die!'

Anna fired and flame stabbed the air. The Finn screamed, his spine arched and his hands clawed the air briefly before he hit the snow.

One second later, Anna bent down and placed her still smoking pistol almost tenderly, to the back of the other Finn's skull. Her face expressionless, she pressed the trigger. The Finn screamed. His head disappeared in a mess of red and white gore, spattering the pale gasping face of the nearby de Vere.

*

They looked down at the wounded Finn, the only survivor. He lay on the floor of the coach, surrounded by sacks which they'd stuck at the windows to make the ambushers believe they were in the coach. 'Well?' Anna snapped in Finnish.

The dying man stared up at her, his chest heaving as if he were running a race, his blue-tinged lips curled in a sneer even at the moment of his death. But he did not answer her question.

'I asked you something,' she said harshly. 'How did you know about us?' She rammed her booted foot cruelly into his skinny ribs.

The Finn groaned piteously. A thin trickle of dark blood ran out of the side of his mouth suddenly. De Vere stared at the hard-faced Russian girl with shocked eyes. 'It was the Commissar,' the Finn said weakly. 'He knew.'

'What Commissar?' she demanded and kicked him again.

'*Anna!*' de Vere cried, his young face white with horror. He stepped forward, as if to stop her. 'I don't mind killing someone in an honest fight, but this—'

Bird grabbed his arm in time. 'Leave her,' he hissed. 'This isn't England de Vere. They do things differently here.'

'But Dickie,' de Vere objected. 'She's torturing a dying man!'

'I know,' Bird replied, his face set and tense. 'But we need that information – and she's getting it for us, the only way she knows how.'

De Vere averted his eyes.

'Well?' Anna demanded. 'Who?'

'The Commissar from Petrograd,' the dying Finn stopped suddenly. His eyes rolled upwards until only the whites were visible. A moment later his head tilted to one side, a sudden flood of bright scarlet blood pouring from his lungs and swamping the floor. The Finn was dead.

Slowly Bird turned and stared at the girl in the yellow light of the little coach. 'Well,' he asked, 'what did he have to say?'

Anna von Klauwitz smoothed back a lock of dark hair from

her dirty, suddenly drawn face, her eyes blank of any emotion, as if all hate had been spent now. 'What did you say?' she asked tonelessly.

Lieutenant Bird repeated his question.

'Well,' she said, slumping down on the nearest seat. 'Not much. But one thing is certain.'

'What?'

'The Reds know we are coming . . . they know . . .'

5

Two hours later, in the middle of a raging snow storm, the ancient locomotive's engine gave out. There were no warning coughs, splutters, missed strokes. One moment there was the regular, reassuring puff-puff; the next, nothing but the sudden hiss of the wind, as the locomotive rolled slowly yet inevitably to a stop at the bottom of a snow-covered hill.

Bird was the first to react. He broke the sudden oppressive, foreboding silence with a curse. Next instant he had flung open the door and dropping into the soft new snow, was running heavily towards the now stationary locomotive.

'What the hell's going on, Nikonen?' his voice was sharp with anxiety.

Nikonen, his face flushed and sweaty, said something in Finnish, which didn't sound too pleasant and straightening up, turned to the young officer, looking up at him anxiously. 'Them bastards shot a hole in the stand-pipe.' There were genuine tears in his bloodshot eyes, as he indicated the rusty, holed pipe.

At any other time, Bird would have smiled at the little driver's concern for his locomotive, which had long been ripe for the scrap-heap, but not now. 'Is it serious?'

'*Serious*,' the Finn exploded, waving his dirty calloused hands excitedly. 'That ain't the word for it – it's . . . it's,' he searched his limited English vocabulary for a word to express the magnitude of the disaster, '*a catastrophony*!'

'A catastrophe,' Bird corrected him automatically.

'Yeah, that's what I said, boss – a catastrophony. The water cooler's gone, I can't make steam now. That means—'

'Can you repair it?' Bird cut in brutally.

Nikonen laughed bitterly. 'Sure, if I was back in the depot. But out here, boss!' He shrugged his shoulders helplessly. 'Couldn't even raise a fart out here. No siree, it don't go!'

*

They slumped despondently in the coach, which grew colder by the second, the snow belting against the windows with renewed fury. 'What now?' de Vere said miserably. 'Here we are in the middle of nowhere with that white stuff outside coming down as if it's never going to stop again. Two ten ton skimmers on our hands and no water within miles. What a mess!'

'We could change our minds and go home,' Ginger Coates said, but his voice lacked its usual humour.

'Oh shut up, Ginger,' Bird snapped. 'This is serious. For all we know there could be more of the beggars who ambushed us out there, just waiting to pounce again.'

Anna nodded her agreement. 'You are right there, Lieutenant. There are enough of the swine hiding out in the forests. For a handful of gold roubles that commissar who escaped could buy a whole army of the devils.'

'Did you say water, boss?'

Bird looked morosely at Nikonen. 'Yes, why?'

The Finnish engine-driver, who had now got over the shock of seeing his beloved locomotive knocked out of action, wet his thick lips. 'There is water, boss. Not far off from here. A small river. It is running into the Gulf.'

'*What?*' the four of them roared as one. 'What did you say, Nikonen?'

The Finn beamed. 'I am saying there is a river—'

'Yes, yes,' Bird interrupted hastily. 'I heard that. But where is the damn thing?'

Nikonen pointed ahead beyond the stationary locomotive. 'Up there, boss. In the valley on the other side of that hill.'

Bird's face fell, as Ginger expressed the thought which was flashing through his head at that very moment. 'Eh, up that hill? What the hellus do you think we are – a lot of ruddy mules? How do you think we're gonna get them skimmers up that hill? There are only four of us, yer know, yer Finnish dummy!'

But the 'Finnish dummy' had an answer for that question too. He beamed warmly at the sharp-faced cockney and pursing his lips spat neatly onto his calloused, dirty, big hands. 'That's how we're gonna to do it, sailor boy,' he announced almost happily. 'Graft – *by hard graft*!'

*

Momentarily Bird straightened up, trying – in vain – to ease the agony of the pincers which were clawing mercilessly at his back muscles. For the last two hours he had been bending, straightening, bending, straightening – over and over again – as they shoved the incredibly heavy wagon bearing the first skimmer up the hill. Now he had ordered a minute's break before they made the attempt to push it up the last fifty feet to the summit. At that moment it looked as far away as the summit of Mount Everest to a mountaineer standing at the base of the Himalayas.

He flung a quick glance at the others. They were in as bad a state as he was, except for Bull, who stood there upright and oblivious of the whirling snow, his sodden shirt moulded to his massive body, and his rolled up sleeves displaying his brawny, muscular arms. Bird drew a deep breath. The icy air rasped through his lungs. 'All right, Nikonen, stand by to take off the brake . . . The rest of you, get ready to push!'

'Cor,' Ginger croaked, his sharp face unnaturally pale from the almost unbearable strain, 'there never ain't no rest for the wicked is there?'

Sick at heart at the thought of the terrible punishment he was subjecting his men too, yet proud too of them, they were really a terrific bunch, he yelled hoarsely: 'Take the strain! All right, Nikonen, off with the brake! *HEAVE*!'

Nikonen let go. The wagon started to roll backwards. Bull's tremendous strength caught it just in time. Then they were all straining, shoving the heavy wagon up the hill by sheer effort of will.

Inch by inch. Keeping going at the expense of torn hands, shoulder muscles that blazed with agony, and lungs that rasped like punctured bellows as they gulped in great painful gasps of the icy air. Time and time, Bird was tempted to give up, simply to throw himself in the snow, forget the skimmers, the mission, everything as long as he could escape the back-breaking agony. And time and time again, the young officer forced his mind away from the burning pain in his body to listen to the stamp-stamp of their feet on the snow, as they fought the wagon up the hill.

Twenty feet to go! Bird flung a glance at the others. They were all at the end of their tether, their eyes blank, their faces ashen, their mouths open and gasping for air. Only Bull seemed capable of going on. Ceaselessly, tirelessly, he stamped through the snow with the metronomic regularity of a piston, his heavy jaw thrust out almost aggressively.

Ten feet to go! Through a waving red mist that threatened to engulf him at any moment, Bird could see the enamel sign at the top of the hill with the figure '13%' written on it in red. A warning to the drivers, he told himself. A steep descent. *Five feet!* Bird could no longer feel his legs. It was as if he were walking on jelly. The '13' wavered frighteningly in front of his eyes.

Suddenly the wagon came to an abrupt stop as Nikonen applied the brake and sat down in the snow. Bird caught himself just in time. Behind him de Vere and Ginger didn't react so quickly. They sprawled head-first in the snow and lay there, their bodies heaving with the strain, forgetting the icy cold in their gratitude for having been relieved from the unbearable pressure. For what seemed an age, Bird didn't react. He couldn't. All he could do was to lean weakly against the side of the wagon, his chest heaving frantically.

Finally he pulled himself together and staggered to where Nikonen, his head sunk on his chest, still sat absurdly in the snow. 'What . . . what . . . did you put the brake on for?' he croaked.

'Got an idea, boss,' Nikonen forced himself to lift his head.

'Idea?'

Nikonen picked up a handful of snow and smeared it across his sweat-streaked, crimson face. 'Down – thirteen per cent,' he gasped, having to force himself by an effort of will to produce each individual word. 'We get cable . . . from train.'

Bird nodded slowly, beginning to realize what the bow-legged Finn was hinting at. 'You mean, use this wagon to raise the other skimmer . . . from down there?'

Nikonen nodded numbly. 'If the cable . . . don't break, boss . . . we could do it . . . big drop.'

Bird's ashen, exhausted face broke into a slow smile. 'Of course,' he breathed. '*Of course*! Listen,' he turned and spoke to the others. 'Nikonen here has had a tremendous idea.'

Slowly, very slowly, de Vere and Ginger raised their heads and stared at him with dull, unbelievably weary eyes. 'What is it, sir?' Bull asked, wiping the sweat off his forehead with the back of his brawny arm.

'If we can get a cable attached to this wagon and link it to the other down there, once we push it over the summit, with a descent of thirteen per cent on the other side, it could pull the other one up of its own accord.' He looked at them in triumph. 'Now what do you say to that?'

'My Gawd,' Ginger croaked reverently, rising slowly to his feet, his frozen purple hands already outstretched to begin pushing again, 'ain't that bloody wonderful!'

*

The cable snapped twice – like everything else on Nikonen's train it was well rusted – but finally, thanks to the little Finn's ability at splicing, they got it attached between the two wagons and were ready to try. Nikonen stopped sucking his fingers which were bleeding from the steel wires. 'All right, gentlemens, I am crossing my thumbs for us.'

'You ain't the only one, mate,' Ginger replied and prepared to take the strain.

Bird said a quick prayer. If it didn't work, they'd never get the other skimmer up the hill. He flashed an anxious look at the gleaming splices and hoped to hell they would hold long enough to get the second wagon up to the summit. 'All right,' he ordered, 'on the brake Nikonen. The rest of you – get ready!' Anna flashed him a look of encouragement. He forced a smile and yelled. 'Brake off – *heave*!'

With renewed strength, the five of them shoved. The wagon

creaked and moved. For a moment it teetered on the summit. The cable hissed suddenly and straightened. *'PUSH!'* Bird yelled desperately, the sweat standing out on his forehead, the veins at his temples throbbing heavily.

They pushed. The wagon squeaked rustily. Still it did not move. Behind them the cable trembled like a live thing. Bull thrust his big shoulder at the wagon furiously, cursing wildly under his breath. Suddenly it began to edge forward. They renewed their frantic efforts, their eyes threatening to burst from their sockets at any moment with the strain. The wagon started to gather speed. The pressure eased. De Vere slipped and sat down abruptly in the snow.

'Let her roll!' Bird yelled delightedly.

They needed no urging, as the wagon bearing the skimmer started to work its way down the slope, rocking alarmingly. On the other side of the hill, the wheels of the second wagon screeched and grated in shrill cacophony, its bullet-splintered woodwork creaking and protesting like a ship ploughing its way through a heavy sea. But all the same it was moving – slowly but definitely – up the hill. *It was moving!*

But Bird had no eyes for the second wagon. His gaze was fixed hypnotically on the taut wire, now humming frighteningly, as if it were charged with electricity. 'Please God,' he whispered fervently to himself, 'please God, make it hold.'

The cable cracked alarmingly. Bird jumped. A gleaming sliver of wire had detached itself from the main cable, vibrating frighteningly like a crazy thing. The second skimmer was half way up the slope now. Next to him, Bull, the most experienced of them ducked instinctively. He had seen what happened when a cable broke in a ship's rigging and hissed frighteningly across a crowded deck, slicing through human flesh like a hot knife through butter. Bird bit his bottom lip and tensed. The second skimmer had almost reached the summit now. Would it make it?

'Look out, skipper!'

Bird caught a terrifying glimpse of the broken cable slicing through the air, then flung himself into the snow, as it whipped across the summit with a bone-chilling crack, snapping through a couple of firs there, as if they were matchwood. But before the resin-fragrant firs descended upon him, blotting out sound, he heard with joy a tremendous crash followed by another as the wagons containing the skimmers careered headlong off the tracks and smashed into the ice-covered river . . .

6

'Well, Nikonen?' Bird stretched out his hand, 'are you sure you don't want to come with us? We could use a good man like you, you know.'

The fat Finn, suddenly red and embarrassed, shook his head. 'No thanks, boss. Sure appreciate it – and the dough.' He touched his pocket, bulging with the sovereigns Bird had given him as a parting present. 'Got to think of my old woman and the kids, see.' He wiped the palm of his calloused hand on the leg of his trousers and grasped Bird's. 'All the same, I'm wishing you all the best of good wishes.'

Bird pressed the big hand firmly. They owed a lot to the little engine driver. 'And what are you going to do?' 'I'll mosey back to town, boss, and see if I can get somebody to come out and haul me back. You know.' He waved his hand at the locomotive.

Bird smiled. He knew. The Finn loved the ancient locomotive as much as he did the old woman and the kids, wherever they might be. 'All right then, the best of luck – *and thanks*!' Rapidly the Finn did the rounds of the rest of the crew and Anna before plodding down to the locomotive, outlined stark black on the snow against the red, setting sun. Bird watched him go. Then he dismissed him from his mind. He had problems enough. For a few seconds he stared at the two lean skimmers positioned in the middle of the great hole in the ice which the wagons had broken as they had plunged crazily into the river.

All afternoon they had worked in the freezing cold to free them from their crates, standing up to their waists in the icy water, working in ten minute shifts until they could bear it no longer and had been forced to hurry to the great fire to thaw out which Anna kept going at the side of the river. And now, both the skimmers' engines were throbbing throatily, as they

57

waited like two hunting dogs, impatient and expectant, to be let off their chains.

Bird crunched over the snow to de Vere, his trousers still steaming as he held them to the dying flames of the great fire. 'What do you think, de Vere? Should we chance it?' The Sub-Lieutenant knew what he meant, at once. 'As far as I can judge, Dickie, the ice isn't too thick. I imagine that the screws and the bow could stand it without too much damage.'

'And if it gets thicker?'

In spite of his exhaustion and strain de Vere grinned wearily. 'Then, old bean, we'll get out once again – and *push*!'

They were to be prophetic words.

*

The hours that followed seemed plucked from the darkest most horrifying nightmare that Lieutenant Bird could ever have imagined for himself. They were endless, numbing hours of springing wearily out and in of the frosted, sluggish skimmers, when the ice got too thick for the crafts' tough, yet paper-thin hulls. Stumbling and slipping on the ice, forcing their racked bodies and tortured muscles to crack through its iron-hard surface with their home-made staves, more often than not, sinking up to their waists in the freezing river as they did so.

But Bird tolerated no slacking. Deliberately he made his racked body forget its insistent demands for rest. Springing from boat to boat and in and out of the water, he bullied them, cursed them, threatened them, pleaded with them, forcing them ever onwards. He knew only too well that if the Reds ever caught up with them in their present position, they were as good as dead: very definitely sitting ducks on a frozen lake. 'Christ almighty!' Bull cursed, even his great strength beginning to peter out as a haggard, grey-faced Bird sprang in to the freezing water yet again and thrust his shoulder angrily against the side of the skimmer in front, 'that Lieutenant Bird . . . he's a real tough 'un, sir!' He shook his big head wonderingly.

And all that Sub-Lieutenant de Vere French could do was to breathe his leaden-lunged, desperate agreement. *Bird was as tough as they came!*

Steadily, under his bitter, driving leadership, while Anna

watched these desperate men with wide, awe-filled eyes, they chopped a path for themselves to the sea.

Some time during the night, the temperature eased and it started to snow once more. 'Hells bells and buckets of blood,' Ginger croaked bitterly, as if he might start sobbing at any moment, 'ain't it sodding well bad enough as it is!'

But nature was going to give them no respite. Heavy, wet and feathery, the snow swamped them in a blanketing curtain of white, drifting down their necks as they bent, working its way up their sleeves, grating against the red-raw flesh. It blocked their mouths and ears. It blinded them. It turned their gloveless hands into unfeeling lumps of ice. Numb, blinded, completely exhausted, they battled on towards the Gulf . . .

*

The weak, yellow sun peeped up above the green-swaying horizon, as Bird opened his eyes and shivered with the cold. Wearily he threw back the tarpaulin which covered him. He'd fallen into an exhausted sleep as soon as they reached the estuary at four that morning. Next to him, Ginger still snored on. A yard away, Anna was buried from view beneath her tarpaulin.

As quietly as he could, he crawled out from beneath the cover, stiff and hard with frost. Gasping with pain as his aching leg muscles sent out their message of warning, he rose to his feet, massaging his calves as he did so.

To left and right, the Gulf of Finland stretched out in a great green curve, cradled in the embrace of the white arms of the coast. Rubbing the sleep out of his eyes, Bird swept his gaze across the lonely, starkly beautiful panorama, breathing in the icy air in great gulps as he did so. Exhausted, stiff and cold as he was, he could not help but admire the beauty of the dawn scene. Suddenly the muted throbbing of a diesel motor cut into his reverie.

He swung his head round to the direction of the sound. A long lean shape was sliding into view from the east, the creamy bow wave dying away to a gentle ripple as the diesel muted to a distant murmur and the unknown craft came to a rest, perhaps half a mile away from their hiding place at the mouth of the estuary. A few moments later, a tense and anxious Bird could hear the rattle of the chain as the warship – for its low rakish shape definitely indicated that it was some kind of fighting ship – lowered its anchor. Their way out of the estuary into the Gulf was barred!

*

'Well, Ginger?' Bird hissed, as the five of them crouched in the snow-heavy firs, which covered the two skimmers from the Gulf. 'What do you make of her?'

Ginger, the Squadron's recognition expert, lowered Bird's binoculars slowly. His thin clever face was thoughtful. 'She's definitely Russkie, sir,' he said softly. 'A T-class torpedo boat, laid down in seventeen. Armed with two torpedo tubes, a six pounder and aft, one—'

'Skip the details,' Bird snapped, shivering a little with cold and added fear. 'Could you make out her flag?'

'She ain't flying one, sir,' Ginger answered promptly. 'Couldn't tell whether she's a Bolshy, or one of their ships which went over to us last year when we went into Estonia.'

Bird nodded his thanks. He knew that Admiral Cowan's Baltic Fleet was stationed further west in the Finnish Gulf of Bothnia, just outside territorial waters in order not to embarrass Field Marshal von Mannerheim too much. So if the strange torpedo boat did belong to Cowan's fleet, would it be likely to anchor well within Finnish waters, he asked himself, his brow creased. 'Ginger,' he ordered, 'give me the glasses. I'll see what I can make out.'

Hurriedly he focused and swept the torpedo boat's rakish length with them. As Ginger had said, she wasn't flying a flag and there was no indication on her deck whether she belonged to the Red Fleet stationed at Petrograd. Suddenly he caught his breath. A sailor had appeared on deck, his body swathed in heavy winter clothing, which could have belonged to any sailor of any fleet in the world. But then the man did something, which clearly identified him. He whipped open his flies and urinated on the deck in a great yellow stream of liquid. Bird dropped the glasses and looked at the others, who were staring at him expectantly, his face grim and determined. 'I'm afraid to say that she's a Bolshy,' he announced, one hundred per cent

60

sure that only in the Red Fleet would such conduct be tolerated.

'Are you sure?' de Vere queried.

'Quite,' he replied firmly.

Anna looked around their set, pale faces. 'But there are two of you and only one boat out there,' she said determinedly. 'You have got torpedoes too. Why—'

'We'd need more depth than we've got here to fire our torpedoes,' Bird interrupted her unceremoniously. 'It's too technical to explain, but we can't fire the fish – er, the torpedoes – from here. And we wouldn't have much of a chance with our Lewis guns against that six pound quick-firer of theirs. They'd blow us out of the water before we could even get out of the mouth of the estuary.'

'So?' she demanded impatiently.

'So, Anna, if we're ever going to get out of this nice little trap we've landed ourselves in, we'd better do some pretty damn swift thinking.'

*

'Stoi?' the Red sentry at the machine gun demanded as the strange looking craft with the makeshift sails came closer, appearing suddenly from nowhere in the evening gloom.

At the bow beneath the rough-and-ready sail, still carried forward by the momentum of the hurriedly switched-off Thorneycroft, Ginger gave a perfect imitation of some local sailor, failing to understand the challenge.

The Red sailor's finger tightened round the trigger of his machine gun. Down below there was the clatter of pans, as if the rest of the crew were having their evening meal. 'Stoi?' the Red rapped once more.

Ginger stared up at him blankly.

The Red made a gesture with the machine gun, a gesture which even some dim-witted fool of a Finnish fisherman could understand. It said, 'raise your hands and don't move, if you don't want a bullet through your stupid great head.' Slowly, Ginger, playing his role to perfection, began to put up his hands. Now the two craft were a matter of yards apart.

On the Russian vessel, the sailor carefully released one of his hands and took hold of the signal whistle which hung from around his neck. It was the last thing he was ever to do.

Before he could alert the rest of the crew, Bird sprang up from his hiding place at the camouflaged bridge. Coldly and precisely, he pressed the trigger of the Lewis gun. The sudden burst caught the sentry directly in the chest. An abrupt line of red holes appeared along its length, as he was flung backwards, slamming into the hatchway behind him, screaming wildly in his death agonies.

Swiftly Ginger hared to the tin box, filled with the grenades they had taken off their ambushers at the cutting. In frenzied haste, he crimped the three-second fuse. On the other craft, a sailor armed with an automatic rifle appeared in the hatchway. Bird pressed the trigger of his Lewis gun. The cruel burst caught him in the stomach, nearly sawing him in two. As he dropped his automatic chattered furiously, its slugs whining harmlessly into the darkening sky. And in that same instant, Ginger lobbed the glowing tin box into the Red torpedo boat's engine room. Somewhere in the gloom behind them, de Vere started the Thorneycroft up with a great roar. But even its tremendous noise was drowned by the explosion of the twelve grenades packed in the tin box.

Violent scarlet flame spurted up from the torpedo boat's engine room. The long craft heaved madly. Great chunks of debris flew through the air, followed by the howling hot wind of the concussion which struck Bird across the face. He gasped for air and shook his head, dazed by the ear-splitting proximity of the explosion.

Now screaming, fighting, panicked men, their uniforms smouldering bloody rags, were trying to mount the ladder from below as the torpedo boat began to sink fast. Bird seized the Lewis gun. It chattered into violent action once more. At the bow, a sweating, black-faced Ginger was lobbing grenade after grenade wildly at the stricken craft. Men flew overboard, screaming as they disappeared beneath the icy water. At that range neither he nor Ginger could miss. A brawny sailor tried to seize the machine gun located next to the shattered skeleton of the wheelhouse, the tiny greedy flames from the fire below already beginning to lick at his feet. He never made it. Ginger's stick grenade exploded at his chest and the sailor slammed against the suddenly grotesquely twisted machine gun, his head gone, his body a ghastly mangled caricature of a human being. To port, de Vere's craft hissed through the water, mercilessly over-running the bobbing heads there. Bull opened up at once, riddling the other side with lead, remorselessly mowing down the terrified Reds cowering there.

But now the Soviet torpedo boat was sinking fast, her flaming deck already tilting crazily to port, her bows awash. Bird pressed the engine button. The Thorneycroft started at once. Hastily he opened the throttle and shot forward, to get clear before the stricken Soviet craft went down. He was just in time. Suddenly there was a muffled roar of the torpedo boat's fuel tanks rupturing. A great flash of oil-tinged flame shot into the night air. Bird caught a last glimpse of the headless corpse at the machine gun, his shattered arms outstretched horribly as if he had been crucified on the burning wheelhouse. The Soviet craft gave up its vain struggle against the sea. With frightening suddenness, it slid vertically downwards to vanish beneath the wild, white churning water, carrying its dead and dying with it.

Abruptly there was a loud echoing silence, broken only by the obscene belches of the great air bubbles bursting on the littered surface of the sea, which was rapidly settling down again to its former calm as if the torpedo boat had never even existed.

Slowly and carefully, de Vere guided his lean skimmer through the charred debris and the bodies which floated face downwards, until he came alongside Bird's stationary craft.

'Well, we did it, Dickie, didn't we!' he cried, his hands cupped around his mouth. 'Congrats, old chap!' But there was no sound of triumph in his voice and his young face was very pale. As he waved his thanks, Bird could see that and he knew why. The sight of a ship going to its death violently – even an enemy craft – is a terrible one for any sailor. Still, he reflected, as he gave de Vere the signal to follow him out into the Gulf, the Sub. would see a lot more of them before he was finished with this particular mission.

Minutes later the two skimmers, like two hunting dogs let off the leash at last, were hissing across the surface of the sea at forty knots an hour, disappearing into the green gloom of the dying day within seconds . . .

THREE

THE PETROGRAD PLOY

'If I may be so bold, Lev Davidovitch, I would recommend that Comrade Lenin be brought here to Petrograd.'

1

A thin grey fog hung over Petrograd. The grey ribbon of the Nevsky Prospect, with the skinny-ribbed dead horses in the gutters, was splashed with grey pools. Even the smoky blue cupolas of the Smolny Institute, the Red HQ, seemed petalled grey by the low-hanging fog, with its grey opaque drops dripping miserably from the Imperial Arms, still carved insolently on its noble facade. It was a grey time in a grey year.

But if the grey fog and drizzle indicated that the spring thaw was not too far away in the stronghold of Red power, there was no let-up of the shootings which had been going on systematically throughout the winter, as the Bolsheviks destroyed their enemies with brutal persistence.

Down in the cobbled courtyard of the Smolny Institute, the Red Guards were already bringing in the prisoners to face the four machine guns, their ammunition belts hanging like deadly snakes from the breeches. *Mensheviki*, frock-coated, fat *Cadets*, newly captured *Junkers* and Whites. Even a couple of heavy-bosomed girls in trousers from a White Death Battalion, their pale faces still blue from the beating they had taken before they had been raped. They were all forced to squat on their knees on the wet cobbles, their backs to the machine guns.

Up above at his office window, the pale-faced bespectacled observer with the shock of black wavy hair nodded his approval, his dark eyes burning behind the pince-nez. Old Russia was breaking up rapidly. The Ukraine, Finland, the Baltic States, Poland had already gone. To the West, East and South, the white reactionaries were already massing their forces under the old Czarist generals, supported by Allied money and arms.

And within the new state itself, conditions were daily becoming more chaotic. Hundreds of thousands of his Red Army men were deserting from the front, wandering aimlessly over the ravaged countryside, burning, looting, raping, while the *Kulaks* hid their grain so that the men who remained at the front starved. The only answer was to fight terror with terror.

Down below the commander of the firing squad had raised his arm. The crowd of onlookers in their rough, dirt-coloured coats and squashed grey fur hats tensed. The man at the window licked his sensual lips expectantly.

'*DALOI!*' [1] the commander yelled and brought his arm down sharply. The four machine guns chattered into action as one. The stone courtyard echoed and re-echoed to their frantic noise. In an instant the prisoners were galvanized into violent staccato action as the bullets slammed into their bodies, their screams drowned by the cruel chatter of the guns.

At the window, the observer caught his breath, enraptured. Once in another life, he would have thought it unbelievable that the sight of writhing, falling, crawling, bleeding, dying human bodies could give him such an intense painful pleasure. Now he knew differently. In his loins something stirred which was almost sexual, at the violent way in which these men and women, who had tried to destroy his dream, were now dying in the courtyard below.

'*All power to the Soviets!*' they were screaming now as the firing started to die away, leaving behind it a loud echoing silence.

The man at the window watched mesmerized as the commander started to clamber over the heap of contorted bodies, placing his big automatic behind the head of those who still were not dead and blowing them to extinction, while the crowd roared hoarsely '*All power to the Soviets!*' Time and time again. Finally it was over and the commander, his boots red to the ankles, began to clear away the crowd, so that the bodies could be removed before the next batch of prisoners. The watcher knew he had had his pleasure for that morning. Terror had been met with terror. Now he must get down to the grim business of the day.

1. Down with them!

Slowly and reflectively, wiping his lips dry from the excitement of the executions, Comrade Lev Davidovitch Bronstein walked to his desk and rang the bell on it.

His little mouse of a secretary, a bourgeois who looked absurd in his Bolshevik blouse and riding breeches, appeared immediately, as if he had been listening and waiting apprehensively behind the door of Number Four, 'All power to the Soviets!'

'Yes, all power,' Trotsky snapped curtly. 'Now get me the comrade from the Cheka.'

'Immediately, Comrade Trotsky ... *most immediately.*' The timid, middle-class secretary disappeared hurriedly.

*

'Well, Comrade Rosenblum?' Trotsky rapped. 'You have exactly five minutes of my time.' He did not like the assistant head of the Petrograd Cheka, who had appeared from nowhere and like the typical Yid he was, had worked himself up to the top rank in a matter of a few weeks.

Rosenblum, dark-skinned and with piercing black eyes, elegant in spite of being clad in the earth-coloured blouse all Party members wore, shrugged. 'Information is scarce on them, Comrade. But this is what we know. Our source in London followed Cummins – the man they call C – to a naval base in the north of the country. Then on March 2nd, *their* calendar, men from that same base turned up in Abo.'

'You speak English?' Trotsky snapped. 'Or did you have someone translate this information for you? I must be sure you have it correct.' 'English, and seven other languages, Comrade,' Rosenblum said. Trotsky frowned angrily. The Cheka agent could not resist that typical Yid tendency to boast, which he had continually to repress in himself. One day, he realized suddenly, the Party would have to rid itself of its Jews; there were far too many of them. 'All right, go on.'

'The naval officer and his companions had two strange crates loaded on a train bound east. One of our agents with the Finns – Comrade Alexeyev – failed to ascertain what the crates contained, or unfortunately to stop the English. He did—'

Trotsky held up his hand for silence and with his other scribbled a swift note on the pad in front of him. 'He's no good,' he announced in his deep bass, 'He has already cost us twenty thousand roubles of foreign valuta. Liquidate him!'

'It will be done,' the Cheka agent said as coolly as if he were making a statement about the weather. 'Well, Comrade, we did obtain a little information from one last source. A Finn named Nikonen, who unfortunately passed away suddenly after – er – volunteering the information.'

Rosenblum grinned abruptly, but there was no answering light in his eyes. Suddenly Trotsky realized why the Petrograd Cheka was so feared. Rosenblum's long wolfish face bore the stamp of the cold-blooded killer, who would let nothing and nobody stand in his way. 'And that information was, Comrade Rosenblum?'

'The English and their mysterious crates arrived west of Viborg. There was an accident. They were heading for the coast. More our Finn did not know.' Rosenblum leaned forward, his dark eyes intent. 'But even the little bits and pieces we do have, Comrade, add up to something.'

'What?'

'That their Lloyd George is preparing to move against us, Comrade.'

'That bourgeois blow-hard with his eternal skirt-chasing!' Trotsky sneered. 'Why he's like a gambler playing bad roulette, scattering his chips on every number. He will never move against us as long as he has his forces in dribs and drabs all over Northern Europe.'

Rosenblum remained unmoved, watching Trotsky's face suddenly flush, with eyes that stayed as cold and as cunning as ever. 'I agree with you, Comrade. But we are not dealing with Lloyd George alone any more. We are dealing with that arch-reactionary Churchill, who has openly declared he will destroy our glorious socialist revolution.'

Trotsky did not accept the Cheka man's spurious revolutionary fervour. All the same he knew Rosenblum was right about the new English War Minister. Churchill was a bourgeois trickster – his whole political history had proved that. He *knew* his own mind. 'So, what do you think is the answer to this mystery, my so intelligent Comrade Rosenblum?'

The Cheka man ignored the irony. Confidently, he said: 'Well, Comrade, look at the general picture of our front in the North. The British Baltic Fleet has cut off the Baltic to us. That traitor Yudenich is at present in Helsingfors negotiating with Mannerheim – and now a party of English naval officers suddenly appear in Finland heading east, presumably to plant themselves on our own doorstep here at Petrograd. To my way of thinking, it all adds up to one thing.'

'And that is, Rosenblum?'

'The tail is wagging the dog,' Rosenblum announced, not quite able to conceal his delight at his own cleverness. 'Churchill has convinced Lloyd George he must launch a concentrated attack on the heart of the Revolution – our own Petrograd.' He hurried on before Trotsky interrupted. 'The Anglo-Americans will come down from the Murmansk–Archangel area, Yudenich will come up from Estonia.' He flashed Trotsky a cunning look, 'and – here is the reason for the English naval officers being close to our border – a combined Finnish–British land-and-sea attack will make up the third of the three-pronged attack. Obviously those men are there in order to find some way through our sea defences off Petrograd.' He stopped suddenly, took a deep breath and waited for Trotsky's reaction.

The Minister of War did not speak for what seemed a long time. Outside the commander of the firing squad was bellowing orders at a fresh group of prisoners.

'But that is directly contrary to what Comrade Lenin in Moscow anticipates,' he said at last, slowly. 'He feels that the Whites and their bourgeois allies will attack from the Urals. Kolchak, you know?'

Rosenblum nodded.

'With that old goat Denikin coming up from the Black Sea in support. Comrade Lenin is firmly convinced that the enemy's first objective is Moscow.' He looked at the other man's dark eyes, sycophant, yet calculating and all-knowing. 'You disagree?'

'Comrade Lenin is a great leader, Comrade,' Rosenblum replied easily, 'but he is no military commander – *as you are*,' he added hastily. 'After all, the nearest enemy force is three hundred versts from Moscow. Yudenich, on the other hand, is only one tenth of that distance from Petrograd. And what is Moscow in comparison to Petrograd? Here, not only have we our sole outlet to the sea, but also the most loyal supporters of the revolution – the Petrograd proletariat.'

Trotsky nodded, convinced in spite of his distrust of the Cheka man's ancestry. Hadn't Lenin telegraphed him only two days before that it was 'damnably important to finish off Yudenich at once,' even if he had to mobilize the whole of the Petrograd proletariat and throw them in to one last mass assault?

Rosenblum pressed home his advantage. 'If I may be so bold, Lev Davidovitch, I would recommend that Comrade Lenin should be brought here to Petrograd. His presence would immensely fortify the will of the workers and soldiers to crush the reactionaries.'

Trotsky bit his lip. 'But here he would be in danger. Could the Cheka protect him against assassins, who might well slip through the enemy lines? The Party cannot afford another Kaplan affair.[1] Comrade Lenin's life is too precious to be risked at the hands of such mad women.'

'The Petrograd Cheka will ensure that nothing of that kind could happen here.' Rosenblum allowed himself a smirk. 'In Petrograd our methods are not so effete as those of our – er – comrades in the capital.'

'Good,' Trotsky made his decision. 'I shall telegraph Comrade Lenin your suggestion. Now listen, I want all possible information you can obtain from Finland and Estonia on the moves of Yudenich, Gough, and the rest of that reactionary pack. I want to be informed immediately at the first sign of offensive action on their part. Understood?'

'Understood!'

Below the machine guns were beginning to chatter again and Trotsky waited till their sound and the agonized screams of the victims had begun to die away. 'I shall also put at your disposal,' he continued, 'torpedo boat units of the *Tsentroflot*[2] to discover what is going on in the Baltic and the Gulf of Finland, in particular.'

1. Dora Kaplan, a Jewish girl, who shot and wounded Lenin in 1918.
2. The Red Central Fleet, located in Petrograd.

The suggestion did not appeal to the Cheka man. 'I would prefer it, Lev Davidovitch,' he retorted hastily, his dark eyes showing sudden alarm for some reason known only to his devious mind, 'if we of the Cheka could be allowed to take care of that matter in our way.'

Trotsky shrugged. 'As you wish, Rosenblum, but remember this. I want to find out what those English are doing on our own doorstep – *and I want the information soon*!' The threat was obvious. 'Now you may go, Comrade Rosenblum.'

*

Outside it had stopped drizzling, but the sky was still pewter-coloured and the seagulls, wheeling whitely overhead, cried mournfully. Abraham Rosenblum halted and let a *troika* piled high with the steaming bodies of the newly dead to pass, their bloody limbs sprawled out in extravagant, abandoned postures. But his dark eyes did not see the most recent victims of the Revolution, which he hated. His mind was still on the conversation he had just had with the Red strongman. The *troika* rumbled by. His face suddenly contorted. Abraham Rosenblum spat into the gutter, already bubbling red with fresh blood. '*Jewish canaille!*' he cursed under his breath in absolute disgust.

Then he remembered who he was supposed to be. Hurriedly he pulled himself together, the look of blind hate replaced almost immediately by his usual one of cunning. A minute later he had disappeared into the drab crowd of pedestrians shuffling along the Nevsky Prospect in numb resignation . . .

2

'Well, de Vere, what do you think?' Bird asked, as they stood on the debris-littered terrace of the old Imperial Sailing Club at Seehafen and surveyed the tiny man-made bay, constructed over two centuries before by Peter the Great's German engineers, who had given the place its name.

'Absolutely ideal for a show of this kind, Dickie,' de Vere answered with unusual enthusiasm for him. He shared the typical Etonian's reserved attitude to everything in life, save blood sports and chats about the aristocracy. 'Far too shallow for anything but a small sailing boat or a skimmer, which will keep any nosey-parker from the waterside out, and well covered from land by the forest.' He indicated the thick fir forest, which ran round the stone Club building and the handful of red-roofed summer *datchas*, in a thick, spiked barrier. 'Again, a pretty effective means of keeping our activities concealed from prying eyes.'

'Yes, you're right enough there, de Vere,' Bird agreed slowly. They had been two days in Seehafen now and it had turned out exactly as C had predicted it would. The handful of Finnish peasant refugees, who had taken over the abandoned *datchas*, had been only too eager to help get the skimmers into the still dark-blue water in return for a sovereign apiece; 'the horseman of King George', as they called the coin, according to Anna. And for a further sovereign apiece, they had sworn eternal loyalty and secrecy, proving their gratitude with bountiful presents of fish, firewood and venison steaks. Yet for a worried Bird, everything had gone *too* well. It had all been too damned easy!

'But what if the Bolshies send over a plane, de Vere?' he objected. 'They'd spot our skimmers here in a flash.'

'Oh, do wrap up, Dickie! You know as well as I do the Bolshies haven't learnt to fly yet. My God, most of them still think the dashed earth is flat instead of round. Buck up, old lad – we've got a perfect base here for the job on hand. Once that chap C gets his people to send up our petrol from Viborg, there'll be nothing to stop us from running Anna into Petrograd, believe you me!'

Bird nodded slowly, his face, grown even leaner and harder from the events of the last few days, suddenly troubled by the mention of the mission they had come so far to accomplish. Yet it wasn't on account of the danger, but because of Anna. Over the last week, he had grown fond of the strong-minded Russian girl, who had shared their dangers as if she were a man. She was unlike the girls he had known back home, whose main concern was to 'land a likely fish' and settle into comfortable matrimonial sloth.

71

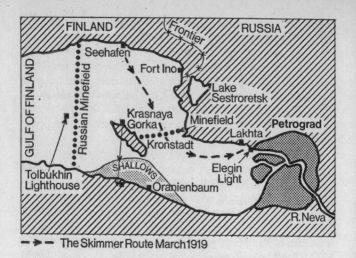

— ► — The Skimmer Route March 1919

The Petrograd Approaches

'A penny for your thoughts, Dickie?' de Vere cut into his reverie.

'Oh, it's nothing, de Vere. I was just thinking.' He pulled himself together. 'Come on, let's go over and see how they're getting on with the skimmers. We can have a better look at the Petrograd approaches from there, too.'

In silence they walked along the path through the firs, where the snow dripped monotonously, to where Bull and Ginger were busy re-mounting the Lewis guns. Pushing through the crowd of silent, gaping peasant children in fur hats, they walked across the plank to the long, lean, grey skimmers. 'Everything all right?' Bird queried.

'Ay, ay, sir,' Ginger sang out cheerfully, 'all ship-shape and Bristol-fashion.' He wiped the sweat off his brow, a spanner in his hand. 'Except for the audience. I wonder if I could pass the hat round?'

Bird laughed and turned to Bull. 'How are the Thorney-crofts'[1]

'Well,' Bull said in his slow ponderous way, 'I daren't test

1. The skimmers' engines.

72

'em out, sir – make too much noise. Happen they could hear them over there.' With a sweep of his oily, hamlike fist, he indicated the dark smudge of Kronstadt on the dark-blue horizon. 'But I don't doubt, sir, that they'll be up to scratch on the day. The Thorneycroft's a right good engine.'

'I hope your prognosis is correct,' de Vere said, wrinkling his long nose in his customary disapproval at Bull's broad Yorkshire. 'Because if it isn't, and they fail out there among those Bolshy forts, we'll be sitting very unpretty – very unpretty indeed!'

'Go on, sir,' Ginger butted in. 'Can't happen cos I'm a HO rating.[1] Besides them Russians are too slow to catch a cold.' The two young officers laughed and strolled to the skimmers' bow, which at full speed raised high out of the water so that the little lean craft seemed to skim across the surface like some mechanical waterbug. They raised their binoculars. Immediately the Petrograd approaches sprang into view, clearly outlined black against the setting sun. The Tolbukhin Lighthouse, which marked the line of mines guarding the harbour; the squat, grey, menacing outline of Krasnaya Gorka, covering Kronstadt, the fort's heavy guns clearly visible through the glasses; then to the right – beyond the long grey shapes of the Soviet fleet – Oranienbaum on the opposite shore.

'You can see by the colour of the water that the mud banks are just below the surface,' de Vere remarked, lowering his glasses. 'Otherwise that southern approach would be the easier route in, to my way of thinking.'

Bird nodded agreement. 'You're right, de Vere. But even the skimmers couldn't get across those shallows.'

For a moment the two men studied the problem of entering the most fortified and dangerous harbour in the whole of the Baltic with their two flimsy craft, armed only with a couple of torpedoes and a single machine gun.

'I'm a bit worried about the noise the Thorneycrofts'll make,' de Vere broke the silence. 'When they're going full out, the dashed things would wake the dead.'

'I agree. Of course we'll go in at night which will make it harder to locate the noise – in the same way Keyes did at Zee-

1. Hostilities Only, i.e. wartime service only.

brugge last year.[1] Besides,' he raised his voice, trying to convince himself that the noise of the 500 HP motors would not alarm the harbour, 'we'll not be able to get very close in to the shore. Once we're within rowing distance, we'll have to use one of those skiffs behind the clubhouse to take An – er – to take the courier in.'

'Yes, I see that. The skimmers are the devil to reverse in tight water.'[2]

Bird lowered his glasses and sucked his front teeth thoughtfully. The whole op. wouldn't be easy, he knew that. There were a lot of imponderables. But he had a grand crew. Even de Vere, the youngest and most inexperienced had proved himself at the railway cutting and later in the Gulf. He could rely on them all one hundred per cent. It was a comforting feeling.

'But what if the Bolshies are alerted while we're stuck there, just off shore?' de Vere cut into his reverie. 'What are we supposed to do then, Dickie?'

'Pray, de Vere – *pray*,' he chuckled.

'Oh, I say, Dickie, you are a—'

But de Vere did not finish his protest. Suddenly from the direction of the sandy track through the dripping fir forest, which was the only means of reaching Seehafen, there came the asthmatic choking rumble of a heavy, ancient truck. 'It's the lorry, sir,' Ginger yelled excitedly, 'with the juice, and a bit of fresh meat from Viborg too, I hope! I'm getting a bit sick of them steaks with antlers on.'

De Vere laughed. 'Well, old bean, there's the petrol we've been waiting for from your pal C. So, now it's on, I suppose – *PDQ*?'

Bird grinned. 'Yes, pretty damned quick now.'

Like excited schoolboys, scattering the solemn-faced Finnish children to all sides, they raced towards the lorry . . .

*

1. The famous raid to block Zeebrugge Harbour, Belgium, a German U-boat base during WWI.
2. For technical reasons, the CMBs had no reversing gear so that they couldn't be stopped by going astern. Normally when berthing, the skipper had to cut off the engine like a pilot landing and hope the CMB would stop before it hit the shore. Once berthed in a confined space, the CMB had to be turned round manually.

They began planning the operation that very evening. The four men crouched over the map of the approaches, illuminated by the flickering yellow oil lamp, munching the last of their cheese and biscuits supper. Anna sat back, smoking a long Russian cigarette, apparently withdrawn into herself. Outside all was silent now, save for the soft, sad lap-lap of the waves on the foreshore and the hoarse cry of a night bird.

'As we saw last night,' Bird commenced, finishing the last of the hard tack, 'the forts are all blacked-out after dark. After all the Bolshies are still at war in a way. So by way of a beacon, we'll have the lights of the Finnish Fort Imo here – and that of Tolbukhin Lighthouse here, just before the minefield.'

He took his eyes off the map and waited for the others' reaction. They all nodded their agreement, save Anna, who seemed completely uninterested in the map. Her dark eyes were fixed instead on his face, as if the plan which might decide her own fate were less important than something she sought in his features. Lieutenant Bird flushed slightly and bent his head to the map again. 'As I see it then, chaps, we'll orientate ourselves between the two lights,' he continued hurriedly, 'and head into the main channel – here. We'll keep our distance from Fort Krasnaya Gorka covering Kronstadt in the hope that the noise of our engines won't carry that far. Inevitably we'll reduce speed to about ten knots at that spot, because it's about there that we'll hit the minefield.'

'Oh, I say, Dickie,' de Vere interrupted hotly. 'Don't be so dashed provoking. *Hit the minefield*, indeed! I do wish you wouldn't use the King's English so loosely! You would never have got away with it at Eton.'

'Sorry, de Vere. All right we'll run into – oh, blast, there I go again!'

The others laughed at the officer's discomfiture, with the exception of Anna.

'Once we're through the minefield – five knots' speed at the most, de Vere – we'll open up and head into the harbour itself at top speed, in the hope that if the Bolshies hear us, we'll be gone before they can pin-point us.' He turned to the Russian girl. 'Now Anna, here is where you come in. Where would you suggest is a good spot to land you on the coast?'

She did not even hesitate. With seeming boredom, she pointed her slim finger, brown with nicotine, at a place just beyond the Elagin Lightship. 'There', she said unemotionally. 'It's a lonely spot, but close enough to the city for someone like me to disappear quickly.'

Then before any one of them could comment, she added with the decisiveness of an ultimatum, 'and we go tomorrow night!' Standing up suddenly, she nodded a curt goodnight and went out, leaving them staring at her disappearing back in a heavy silence.

*

The soft knock came at Bird's door well after midnight. He woke up immediately. As the door commenced to open, he grabbed hastily for his revolver underneath his rolled-up pants which served as a rough-and-ready pillow. Then he saw who it was and he lowered the weapon.

It was Anna, her coat thrown over her shift, her long chest-nut hair released from the severe bun she usually wore and hanging appealingly down over her shoulders. She explained her presence at this late hour in her usual direct manner. 'I couldn't sleep. Do you mind?'

He swept back his tousled blond hair with his hand. 'No, no, of course not. Please sit down.'

She sat down on the rough wooden bench under the window. 'I tossed and turned, but I couldn't get off. Tomorrow, you understand?' She looked at him in the silver-blue light of the moon shining through the window.

He nodded. 'Of course, I understand,' he said softly. 'But—'

She interrupted him, as if she already knew what he was going to say. 'No, I *must* go, Dickie. They need me over there,' she waved her hand vaguely in the direction of Petrograd across the bay.

'You mean the R-Network?'

'Yes.'

He leaned back on his pillow, his hands beneath his head. 'Anna, tell me a little about your Network.'

She shrugged. 'There is little to tell. It is made up of people like myself – from all classes naturally. Priests, poets, politicians, peasants,' she smiled wanly, 'anybody and everybody who is against that monster Lenin.'

'But why is it called the R-Network?'

She hesitated for a fraction of a second. 'Well, I suppose I can tell you, Dickie. After all you are going to risk your life to help us. It is named after our leader. I cannot tell you his name, I am afraid. That would be too dangerous. If they ever caught you—' she shuddered violently, her breasts trembling under the thin material of her shift.

Bird's throat was suddenly dry. 'What kind of a man is he?' he asked hastily. 'Is he Russian like you?'

'No, or at least I don't think so. He speaks flawless Russian, but somehow I don't think he is one of us.' She shrugged eloquently. '*He* could be anything. A bold man, a cunning man – his idol is Napoleon – but a man I do not altogether trust . . .'

'*What?*'

'He has great courage and he's a genius as an agent. But somehow,' her brow furrowed, as she sought for some way of expressing her doubts about her mysterious chief, 'there is something sinister about him, as if we are all mere pawns in some great game with our lives – a game known only to him.'

Time passed. The silver of the moon became a pale, ugly white and then the grey of the new day. Over at the *Datchas*, occupied by the Finnish refugees, the hens began to cackle and there was the soft persistent sound of an axe striking wood, as some housewife chopped the firewood to light the stove for breakfast. Dickie Bird smiled tiredly, 'Anna, what will the chaps think? We've talked all night, but they'll probably think something else. That Ginger's got a nasty mind, believe me.'

She laughed a little sadly and rose to her feet. 'I suppose so. Sorry for keeping you awake.'

'Oh, I probably wouldn't have been able to sleep before the op anyway,' he lied.

For a moment she stared out of the window. The sun, still hidden from view, was suffusing the eastern sky with a dull orange, outlining the harsh, black bulk of the massive Kronstadt forts. 'Russia,' she whispered, as if to herself. 'The new world, Dickie. The twentieth century in all its horror.' She swung round suddenly and faced him, her eyes full of sudden resolve. 'Understand, we're attempting to turn the clock back – and if we don't manage it, Dickie. God help us!'

Abruptly she crossed the room with her quick bold stride, bent down and pressed her lips against his surprised mouth and was gone . . .

3

The sun was already beginning to sink behind the circle of firs, as the three of them went down to the water. In the skimmers Bull and Ginger had started the great engines and the Thorneycrofts were now purring softly like dangerous big cats, held in restraint by force, eager to be let loose. Now, long sinister black shadows had begun to slide across the water, as the forest stilled, towards the forts of Kronstadt, now which were gradually disappearing into the violet gloom.

They walked in silence, Bird, Anna and de Vere. At first the young 1st Lieutenant had wanted to take her alone, but de Vere had insisted he must have cover while he ferried the girl to the shore. 'What if Ginger were caught out in the shallows by a Bolshy patrol?' de Vere had protested, with unusual vehemence for him. 'He would have to abandon you in order to save the skimmer!'

In the end Bird had given in to his friend's protests. Now as they walked through the resin-scented firs, he was glad he had done so. He had a strange uneasy feeling in his loins that something might go wrong – and he didn't want to be alone out there, in the heart of the enemy fortress.

On the wet shore, they stopped and looked at each other awkwardly, while the engines throbbed impatiently.

'Well Anna,' de Vere thrust out his hand. 'May I wish you the best of luck—'

Impulsively Anna seized him around the neck and cut short his words with two quick kisses to each side of his mouth in the Russian fashion.

'Oh, I say, Anna,' he stammered, suddenly flushing a deep embarrassed crimson, 'that's awfully nice of you.'

'Goodbye, de Vere,' she said, stepping onto the plank and

crossing over to a waiting Ginger. 'We shall meet again, never fear.' Bird waited until she was settled behind the protective windscreen of the cockpit. 'All right, de Vere, old chap. This is it. Keep in close behind me – and remember if we run into any trouble, it's each chap for himself. *Don't* try to win the V.C. this time, will you?'

'Never fancied the colour of the ribbbon, old chap,' de Vere replied airily, as they shook hands. 'Didn't think it matched the colour of my eyes, you know.'

The two of them took up their positions behind the controls, while Bull and Ginger undid the mooring ropes. Bird waited an instant and rang up 'dead slow'. Slowly and silently the long lean craft started to cleave through the dark, calm water, the faintest trace of white at her bows. De Vere followed a moment later.

They cleared the little bay. A cooler wind began to blow across the open sea. Behind them Seehafen started to disappear rapidly into the gloom. Bird, very professional now, with Anna crouching down out of the wind next to him forgotten, as he concentrated on the task in hand. Very carefully he corrected his course and steered slowly towards the winking light of Tolbukhin Lighthouse, which marked the minefield. Behind him de Vere's boat did the same.

Now they were in the open sea with the darkness increasing rapidly. Bird opened the throttle a little more and then even more. The girl gasped as the skimmer's bow rose at an angle and two wings of white water appeared at either side. He took one hand off the controls to reassure her. 'Don't worry,' he yelled above the increased noise of the engine, 'we're only doing twenty knots still!'

She nodded her thanks, her face paler than usual.

Bird concentrated on lining his boat up between the shore and the winking light of the Tolbukhin, knowing that de Vere would soon have to come up even closer if he were to follow Bird's skimmer by means of the white wake – the only guide he would have in the growing darkness.

Satisfied he was in the main channel, he swung his boat to the east and handed the controls over to a waiting Ginger. 'All right, Ginger, let her go! *Full speed ahead!*'

The red-haired cockney needed no urging. His hair streaming behind him, as if on fire, he thrust open the throttle. The skimmer responded immediately. Its nose reared up towards the dark sky. The stern disappeared in a sudden, threshing violent burst of white water. At thirty-six knots an hour, the long craft began to skim across the black water. They were on their way!

*

A high silver crescent moon hung over the Gulf casting a thin spectral light over the still water. Now, the wind had almost died and the two skimmers hissed softly through the dark velvet swell, the only sign of their presence the soft white wave at their stern.

Bird shivered a little. But it wasn't with the cold. It was with what he must soon face – the minefield. He dug his face deeper into his collar and stared at the ominous silent mass of the Fort, looming up ever nearer and signifying the start of the minefield. He cut down the speed to almost dead slow. A hundred or so yards behind him, de Vere did the same and brought his skimmer into direct line with Bird's wake. Bird laughed drily. 'What is it, Dickie?' Anna, crouching beside him, asked.

'Only de Vere,' he answered, not taking his eyes off his front. 'The beast is taking no chances. If I hit a mine, he'll have *his* channel cleared.'

Then he forgot the girl. Now they were in the minefield. Somewhere – a mere foot below their paper-thin hull – the deadly metal balls waited patiently to blow their victim sky high at the slightest contact. In spite of the cold, he found himself beginning to sweat, his hands clenched to sudden tense claws.

The seconds passed. Over on Kronstadt everything was black and silent, as if the garrison were fast asleep. Steadily they crept forward, the Thorneycroft just ticking over. Bird's hands, gripping the controls were wet with sweat. Cold sweat trickled down the small of his back and his breathing was quick and gasping. Beside him Ginger strained, his eyes searching the water's dark surface for the tell-tale horns of a loose mine.

Now, far, far ahead, he could just make out the faint lights of Petrograd's waterfront, obviously not blacked out. Surely they must be through. 'I think we've—' he began to the girl.

'Sir,' Ginger cut in, in sudden alarm, 'to port. *A mine!*'

Bird's heart missed a beat. Beside him Anna gasped. A dark, horned globe was bobbing up and down on the swell, only inches from the skimmer.

'*Blast!*' Bird exploded, giving vent to his tension. Then he controlled himself hastily. 'Stop engine,' he rapped. 'Ginger take over – and for God's sake, hold her steady man!'

'Ay, ay, sir,' Ginger answered smartly, as if he were back on the *Iron Duke*, 'steady it is!'

Bird sprang from behind the screen. Doubling along the wet sloping deck, he ripped the light boat hook from its clamps. Balanced at the bow against the gentle sway, the boat hook held across his body like a fighting stave, he peered at the mine. At any moment, it could be carried against the bow. The instant one of those deadly horns struck, the skimmer and the three of them, would disappear in one final violent burst of flame.

For a second he stared at its dark rusted dripping surface, his lips suddenly very dry, his heart pounding. Then gingerly – very gingerly – he reached for the mine with the long awkward boat hook. Behind him at the controls Ginger tensed and said a quick prayer. There was the scrape of metal against metal. Bird's heart leapt. But suddenly the hook slipped and went into the water so that if he had not caught himself in time he would have overbalanced and followed. Anna gasped with fear.

Momentarily the mine disappeared beneath the surface. An instant later, however, it bobbed to the surface again, as dark and as menacing as ever – *and even closer to their bow!*

Bird swallowed hard. The sweat was pouring down his brow now. Desperately he fought to control himself, as he raised the long pole once more. This time he must not fail. Otherwise – he dare not complete the thought.

Infinitely slowly he brought the gleaming brass hook closer and closer to the bobbing dripping ball of steel, packed with five hundred pounds of deadly explosive. Metal touched metal. He sucked in a deep breath, praying that the hook wouldn't slip this time. Gingerly he began to draw the hook between the horns, tracing the mine's slippery wet surface for a firm hold.

Even the slightest pressure on one of the horns would activate the mine's infernal mechanism. Hadn't it been just a glancing blow against one of them which had sunk the *Hampshire* in 1916 and killed his own father?[1] Suddenly the hook grated against rough metal. *Rust*! He had found the hold he sought!

Lieutenant Bird counted to three. Behind him de Vere's boat had come to a stop now. At the controls Anna and Ginger stared with wide anxious eyes at his dark slim figure poised as if about to do some circus balancing act, hardly daring to breathe.

Slowly, he took the strain. The pole trembled. *Was the hook going to slip?* The question ran through his mind alarmingly. The trembling stopped. The hook had lodged in some rust-eaten crack. He breathed a sigh of relief. Next moment he took the full strain, leaning against the pole with as much weight as he dare, almost as if he were punting on a lazy summer's day. The mine did not move. The veins standing out on his damp forehead, he exerted more pressure. Suddenly the damn thing moved!

'Ginger,' he called urgently, forgetting the fortress only half a mile away, 'Take her forward – dead slow!'

'Ay, ay, sir – dead slow!' Ginger's voice had lost its usual cockney cheerfulness.

Gritting his teeth with effort, feeling the pole dig cruelly into his shoulder, as the skimmer eased forward, Lieutenant Bird began to walk the deadly mine to the stern. Behind him de Vere crept towards the first skimmer, now well aware what was happening.

Yard by yard, the boat pushed forward. In all it must have taken only seconds before Bird had accomplished his task, but to the sweating young officer, gasping for breath, it seemed like a whole life-time. Then suddenly the mine ducked. Bird just stopped himself overbalancing. A moment later, the deadly object appeared on the surface some twenty feet away, bobbing up and down in wait for another, less lucky prey.

'*Phew!*' Bird breathed out in heartfelt exhausted relief. 'We've done it, by George!'

1. Sunk on its way to Russia, as it carried the Minister of War, Lord Kitchener.

His hands trembling wildly and his voice slightly out of control, he called: 'Ginger, take her away. *Full speed ahead!*'

The skimmer's tremendous motor burst into full life, shaking the light-metal craft as if it might fall apart at any moment. Almost joyously, it sprang forward, a huge white wave springing from both sides, its prow high in the air.

They were through the minefield!

*

'*Dead slow, Ginger!*'

The skimmer slowed down, and Bird raised his night glasses to scrutinize the shore. Now they were positioned between the flashing light of the Elagin Lighthouse to their right and the faint yellow glow of the town of Lakhta to their left. But to the centre the coast was black and without any sign of life. A mysterious stillness brooded over the coast which Anna had selected for the landing.

For a moment he stood there, glasses to his eyes, deep in thought; then, suddenly, he made up his mind as de Vere's skimmer closed up on his. 'All right, Ginger, take her in – dead slow.'

'Ay, ay, sir,' Ginger replied in whisper, aware of the danger now. 'Dead slow it is.'

Slowly the skimmer began to crawl towards the silent shore, while de Vere's followed at a hundred yards' distance. Now they were about three hundred yards away, and beyond the luminous white of the breakers, Bird could see a ragged, uneven shore outline, indicating that it was covered with reeds or bushes. He sighed sadly and went to the port torpedo discharger now emptied of its weapon and accommodating the skiff they had found at the Seehafen club. Swiftly he untied the leather straps which held it there and ran an expert eye along its length to check that it was all right.

His face set and glum, he went back to the controls. The shore was only a hundred and fifty yards away now. He couldn't go in much fur'· ·r, there might be sandbanks. 'All right, Ginger,' he ordered. 'Stop her!'

Ginger kept silent, as if he did not want to destroy whatever existed between his skipper and the pale-faced Russian girl, by speaking. The purr of the great engine died away. The skimmer started to slow down. Now they could hear the soft, gravelly noise of the breakers on the beach.

'Anna,' he said softly.

'Yes.'

'We must be getting on – in two hours it'll be dawn.' He didn't wait for her answer. Instead he picked up the suitcase containing the portable radio with which C had supplied her.

Anna looked at Ginger.

'Happy landings, miss,' he whispered, the bounce gone out of him. 'And . . . and, see you soon.'

'See you soon, Ginger.'

Ten minutes later the skiff hit the red bank of reeds. Instantly Bird let go of the oars and grasping his revolver sprang into the soft wet sand beyond the reeds. He crouched there, revolver at the ready. But the beach was empty and there was no sound save the cry of some night-bird.

'All right, Anna,' he whispered, not taking his gaze off his front. 'You can come now.'

Grasping her scruffy brown case, she stepped ashore, while he tied up the skiff.

Finally he straightened up and looked at her, his face gaunt and tense in the pale glow of the sickled moon, 'Anna,' he said urgently. 'This is—'

She put her cold hand up to his lips. 'Don't,' she commanded. 'I have to go.'

He pushed away her hand. 'But—'

'There are no buts,' she interrupted, almost brutally. 'I must make the station at Razdielnaya before dawn. There I can catch the first train with the work people going in to Petrograd. My appearance won't be noticed among that crowd.'

Suddenly she stretched out her hand, her manner of doing almost masculine in its directness. 'Dickie, won't you wish me goodbye?'

'Of course, Anna,' he said, pulling himself together swiftly. 'But God, I don't like to see you go like this!'

She did not respond to his urgent statement. Thus they stood there for one long moment, hands clasped together, staring at each other in silence, the only sound the soft lap-lap of the waves. Then she broke his grasp. 'All right, Lieutenant Bird, off you go, *now*.'

Sadly Dickie Bird turned and began to trail back to the little skiff.

*

She waited until she could no longer hear the stiff, regular squeak of the skiff's rowlocks, then she picked up the heavy case and started to slog her way through the wet sand.

One hour later she was walking up the dirty, wet cobbled road that led to the little station. Already the peasants in their fur hats, and the black-smocked workers were plodding towards the same destination, smoking their little clay pipes in stolid, early morning silence. Once she had bought her ticket, she told herself, she would disappear into the lavatory and wait there until the first train came; she wouldn't chance being asked for her pass by some curious Red Guard.

She bought her ticket from the bored sleepy clerk without difficulty and passed through the barrier. The Red Guard, who would be posted there in a couple of hours' time, was probably still asleep in one of the wrecked goods wagons across the rusting tracks. She sighed with relief and began dragging the heavy case towards the lavatory, pushing her way through a group of heavy-bosomed, kerchiefed *Babuskas*. They clutched great baskets of vegetables for Petrograd against their massive breasts, as if they were frightened someone might steal them at any moment.

But Anna von Klauwitz was not fated to reach the safety of the lavatory. Suddenly a dark figure detached itself from the shadows. Before she could react, the slim elegant man had seized her arm, almost cruelly. She started with fear; then she caught a glimpse of those well-remembered dark eyes and that swarthy, cunning Jewish face. '*You*,' she gasped . . .

4

With dramatic suddenness the searchlight cut the darkness, two hundred yards ahead of Bird's skimmer. Abruptly a white fence of harsh light barred their way home. Frighteningly!

'Cor stone the crows!' Ginger cried. 'Now we're in for it, skipper!'

Bird reacted instantly. 'Stop engine!' he yelled. '*Quick!*' Behind him de Vere, equally alert to the sudden danger, cut his motor too. Silently, their speed reduced to nil immediately, they drifted towards the light which had appeared with such frightening suddenness.

'Stand by the Lewis gun, Ginger,' Bird ordered, handling the controls, as if they had abruptly become red-hot. 'When I give the order, fire at that searchlight!'

'Ay, ay, sir,' Ginger sang out and doubled over to the machine gun. In a second, he had cocked it and swung its thick deadly muzzle round to bear on the Kronstadt Fort.

Slowly but inevitably they came closer to the menacing beam. Still it did not go out, or sweep away. It was almost as if the unknown searchlight operators were waiting for them to drift into the blinding white light, while behind them the gunners tensed at their batteries, greedy fingers crooked around their firing levers, ready to pour the whole weight of their deadly fire on the frail craft.

One hundred yards to go!

Still the beam of harsh white light barred their way. Soon Bird knew he would have to make a decision. Suddenly and frighteningly, the beam moved. But not upwards. Instead the beam started to probe the surface of the sea. Now it would be only a matter of moments before it drowned the skimmers in its all-exposing light, revealing them like sitting ducks to the waiting gunners. Hastily he fired the engine.

It started up with what seemed an ear-splitting roar. To their right a flare hissed into the sky, bathing the sea blood-red. Instantly, three other searchlights clicked on, their beams parting the darkness suddenly. Bird threw open the throttle. The skimmer surged forward. Hastily he grabbed hold and swung the boat to the left, then rapidly to the right. A great white S of water swished high into the air, obscuring them from view for a moment.

Frantically the four searchlights swept right and left over the water trying to find them. For a fleeting second they were blinded. '*Fire!*' Bird yelled frenziedly, as the beam submerged them in its cruel light. Ginger needed no urging. The Lewis tucked well into his shoulder, he pressed the trigger. A savage stream of tracer zipped through the night towards the searchlight. With startling abruptness it went out and they were in the blessed darkness again.

But the Russian gunners had had sufficient time to locate them. Red lights flashed on the shore. There was a low roll as if of distant thunder. The night sky was ripped apart violently. With the sound of a red-hot poker being plunged in ice-cold water, a salvo of three shells plummeted out of the sky in front of them.

The skimmer heeled violently. For one awful moment, Bird thought she might go over altogether. But the skimmer's Hampton Thames builders did not fail the two young men at that crucial moment. In a flash she righted herself, just as a tremendous rush of water swamped them making them fight wildly to keep their feet.

Struggling valiantly, Ginger resumed his fire, while Bird swung the boat desperately from side to side, plunging in and out of the white beams which criss-crossed their front. Again the guns roared. With the sound of canvas being ripped apart violently, the monstrous shells tore through the night towards them. Again Bird avoided them by a matter of yards, noting the red-hot, fist-sized pieces of shrapnel which hissed past their heeling boat on all sides. Behind him de Vere fought desperately to do the same.

The sweat pouring down his face, his shoulder muscles screaming out with the strain, the young officer plunged through the heaving sea, his mind racing wildly as he tried to find some way out of the trap in which they found themselves.

Then fate took a hand. Without warning a searchlight fixed

on de Vere's boat, pinioning the skimmer in a harsh-white, eye-searing glare. While de Vere twisted and turned frantically to throw off the pitiless light, Bird was left in peace, the gunners turning their furious attention to the other skimmer. It was the moment of respite Bird needed to carry out his sudden plan.

Furiously he swung the skimmer round. Behind him de Vere's boat seemed to be fixed by the beam, as if held stationary at the end of a white pillar. 'Ginger,' he screamed, 'over here – *quick*!'

Hastily Ginger scrambled across the heeling deck towards the wind-shield. Behind them, de Vere's boat was the centre of a red-and-white maelstrom of flying steel and angry red tracer. Bullets were systematically whipping up pieces of deck woodwork. But de Vere would have to take his chance now.

'Ginger, grab the controls – and straight as we go!' he gasped.

'What, sir, we'll be heading right on for the beggars!' he protested.

'Straight ahead, I said,' he yelled harshly. '*And full speed!*'

Not waiting for any further protests, he doubled towards their sole torpedo. Trying to control his trembling fingers, he fumbled frantically with the firing mechanism, concentrating every fibre of his body to shut out the horror behind him. Beneath him the deck tilted violently, as Ginger gave the skimmer full power.

In a flash, the Kronstadt Fort leapt up, black, squat and brutal, red lights winking along its length as the guns poured their merciless fire at de Vere's helpless craft. One thousand yards . . . seven hundred and fifty . . . five hundred yards. The Fort seemed to fill the whole horizon. It was now or never! Jutting his jaw, he took a deep breath and pulled the trigger.

The skimmer heeled and lurched crazily at the two ton 'fish' shot into the water, hissing below the surface in a flash. A ripple of bright flashing bubbles and it was gone. Hastily Bird sprang to his feet and pelted up the sloping deck to the shield. Roughly he pushed Ginger from the controls and swung the boat round in a great white heaving curve. A beam deluged them with bright light.

Too late!

'Drop the smoke floats, Ginger!' he screamed in a frenzied anxiety. 'We need—'

His words were drowned in a thunderous explosion just in front of the fort. A blinding blue flame seared into the darkness, blotting out everything else. In an instant the massed search-lights flicked from de Vere's trapped boat. Like great white staring eyes they flashed to the fort, just as Bird had hoped they would.

Behind their heeling skimmer the smoke flares exploded with soft plops. Dense white smoke started to pour upwards at once. The searchlights, aware that they had been tricked, clicked back.

In vain they tried to penetrate the thick white smoke, which hung ghostlike over the churning sea. But a sweat-lathered Lieutenant Bird knew they weren't out of danger yet. Hoping that de Vere would have the sense to follow him, he swung the boat to port and at thirty-five knots skimmed straight for the Soviet fort on the northern shore, the last before the border with Finland. Almost immediately de Vere tumbled to what he was up to and swung his battered skimmer round in a white, whirling cloud of thrashing water.

Like two tremendous white arrows they flew towards the opposite shore. Behind them, the Kronstadt fortress's search-lights clicked off, one by one, frustrated by the smoke barrier. But not those of the other fort. Almost immediately two harsh white beams spun in their direction, trying to connect and hold the speeding craft in their light. But now, as Bird had calcu-lated, it was more difficult than before; then the two skimmers advancing directly on them presented a much larger target.

At the top of his voice, Bird, his whole body tense with strain, yelled: 'Ginger, get on the Lewis! . . . Give 'em trouble, for God's sake!'

'Ay, ay, sir!'

In a flash, Ginger was swinging the heavy machine gun from side to side, sending a wild hail of white-and-red tracer the whole length of the fort. Almost parallel with Bird's skimmer now, de Vere's gunner joined in.

The Red gunners reacted as Bird had expected they would. Violent lights blinked from the fort. Like some primeval monster exhaling, the guns erupted. In an instant the sea churned and boiled horrifyingly and they were engulfed in the monster's vast hot breath, which seared their faces and tore at their retching throats. Their tiny craft rocked crazily from side to side. The water hissed with falling fragments of steel. But the vast red columns of burning liquid which towered above the heeling boats were *behind* them, just as Bird had calculated. The Red gunners were rattled!

The fort grew nearer and nearer. Soon he would have to break and make a run for it to Finnish waters. He flashed a look over his shoulder at de Vere's skimmer, its black nose rearing high out of the water, its stern hidden by the racing white waves. Did de Vere understand his crazy plan? Would he react correctly? The sweat pouring down his face, Bird said a quick prayer that he would.

When the fort was only five hundred yards away, de Vere reacted. *Correctly!* Suddenly his skimmer shuddered violently. Once . . . twice. '*He's used his fish!*' Bird yelled excitedly, and in that same instant, flung the boat round in a wild curve, sending Ginger grabbing for support.

With a monstrous roar, the four tons of explosive crashed into the rocky shore just below the fort. The horizon erupted in a blinding white flash, which for one long moment must have blinded the Red gunners. A second later it had gone, leaving behind it only the scarlet carpet of burning underbrush and reeds. But that second was sufficient for the two skimmers. Engines all out, they were roaring away into the darkness, racing joyfully for Finland and base . . .

*

Wearily Bird raised his glasses and surveyed their little harbour in the first grey light of the dawn. The Red torpedo boats, he'd half expected to be there, had not preceded them. The bay lay still, calm – and empty. With a yawn he lowered his glasses and said to Ginger, 'All right, you cockney rogue, take her in.'

Ginger forced his dirty, strained face into a weary grin. 'Ay, ay, sir. Home is the sailor home from the sea.'

Behind him de Vere did the same with his battered boat. Together they limped into the silent harbour and tied up to the little jetty. The Thorneycrofts stopped with a faint sigh, almost like a gasp of relief. Bird slumped behind the controls, red-rimmed eyes fixed on the hard grey line of the horizon, as the new day gradually broke. Then slowly he turned his tired gaze on de Vere's craft.

It was a mess! The control windshield peppered with holes, the deck blackened and littered with debris, a nasty hole in her bow which a shell had ripped.

'Pretty, ain't she?' de Vere's voice cut into his reverie.

'A face only a mother could love, sir,' Ginger cut in cheekily.

'Ay,' Bull chimed in, dabbing the nasty gash on his forehead with a piece of cotton waste, 'but them Russians'll have to get their skates on if they want to catch us skimmers, all the same.'

Bird smiled slowly at their dirty, weary faces. They were a damn good team; he knew now that he could rely upon them to the death. With an effort of will, he reached out his hand to de Vere, who had somehow lost the sleeve of his coat in the battle. 'Well old lad,' he said, 'we did it, didn't we?'

De Vere, for once allowing his emotions to triumph over his old school reserve, pressed his hand firmly. 'By God, didn't we just, what! Dickie, that was a show and a half!' He grinned suddenly and shook his head, as if in wonder that they had ever managed to pull it off.

For one fleeting moment Lieutenant Bird thought of Anna, wondering where she was at that moment and what dangers she might be facing alone, in an enemy land with every man's hand against her. But almost instantly he forced himself to banish the thought from his mind. It wouldn't be fair on the others in this moment of their triumph. 'Come on chaps,' he said with false gaiety, 'I think we've all earned a drop of Nelson's blood [1] for this one, and then some shut-eye. In fact a *lot of* shut-eye.'

'Now that's what I call a fair offer, sir,' Ginger agreed enthusiastically, at the thought of the fiery undiluted alcohol. 'Let's get at it!'

As they began to trail wearily to the stone club-house, the cockney broke spontaneously into Marie Lloyd's famous pre-war ballad:

1. Issue rum.

91

'Show me the way to go home,

I'm tired and I want to go to bed . . .'

Next to him the two officers, dragging their feet along the path, as if each foot weighed a ton, joined in softly. Only Bull, the big stolid Yorkshire giant, remained standing on the jetty, not infected by their sudden mood of happy, relaxed relief at having reached base safely. For a long moment he stared at the harsh dawn horizon across the Gulf. 'Next time,' he announced slowly to himself, with absolute conviction, 'the beggars'll be waiting for us when we come in.'

Then he was lumbering hastily after the singing trio, apparently afraid to remain alone any longer with that frightening prediction . . .

BOOK TWO

THE RED-TRACK APPROACH

*'There it is, the Red Track. Three foot deep, unless
the shallows have changed in the last five years. And
that's the way you are going to enter Petrograd,
gentlemen. By the Red Track Approach.'*

Admiral Walter Cowan,
C-in-C Baltic Fleet, 1919.

ONE

THE DECISION

'Happen we'll get a medal for this one, Ginger'

1

Just across the Riva Neva, Lenin himself was to speak to Petrograd workers, and as they pushed their way through the clamorous mob at the entrance to the great hall, the workers already inside were waiting for his appearance with wild exultation. With the aid of his Cheka pass, the two of them found a place near the dirty wall and leaning there, waited too.

There was no heat in the hall, but the stifling heat of unwashed stale bodies, packed together in dense rows sufficed. Heavy blue smoke from the stinking *marchoka* cigarettes most of the workers favoured rose from the black-smocked sweating mass and hung in a heavy cloud under the roof. Every now and again, an official with a red armband would mount the platform and plead with the 'comrades' not to smoke, but no one took any notice of the plea; the situation at the front was too grave and they needed the tobacco to calm their strained nerves.

Finally the bearded chairman rang his bell for order and almost immediately a short, squat figure with an enormous dome of a head and high cheek-bones, which gave a contemptuous look to his Tartar eyes, entered, followed by Trotsky in uniform. The Cheka man nudged Anna urgently. 'It's him,' he said above the tremendous roar of the workers.

Anna did not need to be told who the undersized civilian in the old-fashioned, double-breasted blue suit was. He looked ordinary but he was the most dangerous man in the world. While Lenin waited for the mob to be quiet, he surveyed their hysterical sweating faces with that quizzing, half-contemptuous, half-smiling look of his which spoke of limitless, conscious superiority. Anna watched the man who had ruined her own life and killed her beloved father. So this was V. I. Lenin!

'I told you he would come,' the Cheka man whispered urgently, as the frenzied roar died down. 'Fix his face on your mind – *fix it well*!' He gave her a flash of those dark hard Jewish eyes of his and then joined in the tremendous burst of applause as the Soviet leader began to talk. Trotsky, his vanity insulted as always when he was out of the limelight, sulked behind him on the platform.

'Comrades,' Lenin said, hands in his pockets, speaking as always with an entire absence of that hysterical arm waving used by so many Russian speakers, 'we are in a state of acute danger. That is why I am here in Petrograd. On all sides we are menaced. Massed against us are the reactionaries from half the world as well as our own White renegades.'

'*Deloie boorjoie* – down with the bourgeoisie!' the great cry rang out. '*All power to the Soviets!*'

Unmoved, his face set in a look of contempt at this mob who were his most ardent followers, Lenin waited for the roar to die down. 'And what do they want, these reactionaries and renegades? I shall tell you what they want.' He leaned forward, short stubbly brown beard thrust out aggressively. 'They want to bring back the Czar, the *Okhrana*,[1] the Cossack whip and those thrice-damned Siberian chains.'

'*Never . . . never!*' the mob screamed hysterically, rising to their feet and overturning their chairs in their passion.

'We do not want war. What do we gain from it? It is the capitalists and those powdered diplomats who make war,' his sneer of contempt at the word revealed what he thought of diplomats. 'Not the people. The capitalists get rich and we, the people, get killed. But workers of Petrograd, this war, which we will soon have to fight against the reactionaries and representatives of the old regime, will be the workers' war. So if you have to suffer, even die, in the days to come, it will not be for some blood-sucking capitalist boss, it will be for your own state – the workers' and peasants' Soviet. *For yourselves!*' He paused and waited.

The great rallying cry came as expected: '*All power to the Soviets!*' It echoed and re-echoed through the great hall, so that it seemed to go on for ever . . .

*

1. Feared Czarist secret police.

For a while they walked in silence, as they crossed the Neva and headed for the Smolny Institute. The cold April night was edgy. Patrols everywhere and Red Guards huddled around bonfires at every street corner, demanding passes and asking eagerly even before they had looked at them, for the latest news and what 'Comrade Lenin' had said at the great meeting. Somehow Anna had the feeling that the city must soon explode into some kind of wild frenzied action. What, she didn't know. They passed a great house broken into and looted months before. In the moonlight, she could see that the walls were pocked with bullet holes, the floors a mess of broken plates, bottles and human excrement. '*All power to the Soviets,*' her companion grunted cynically, breaking the silence. 'Pigs, the lot of them! Pigs in human clothing!'

She nodded numbly and they walked on towards the dark mass of Peter and Paul, from whence came drunken shouts and the sound of glass being smashed, as if the Red Guards there were looting again. 'Now the reason Kaplan failed,' her companion continued, 'was because she was impetuous, undisciplined. Her action in front of that factory last year was spontaneous.' He shrugged contemptuously. 'A typical Jewess, she had no self-discipline. But you are different, Anna. You are descended from a long line of soldiers. You know what discipline is. You are cool and contained, with the fire controlled, eh?' He looked at her with those dark shrewd eyes of his and reaching out, tried to take her hand.

She avoided it swiftly. She knew his reputation with the women. According to some who should know, in the network, he was currently running a stable of eight mistresses in Petrograd alone; she wasn't going to be number nine, if she could help it. 'But how are we going to know where he will be exactly – when the time comes?' she asked, as they turned into the well-remembered street that led to the Smolny Institute.

Her companion was businesslike again. 'I know what you mean. Lenin is here, there and everywhere, always on the move. Some would say that his movements are unpredictable.' His eyes flashed triumphantly. 'But I think I can safely say that I know where he will be on the night of April 20th, 1919.'

Coldly, begrudging him his triumph, she asked: 'And where will that be?'

'There,' he exclaimed. 'The Smolny Institute. Come – let me show you where exactly.' Taking her by the arm, he hurried her to the door of the institution, which only eight short years before, in what now seemed another life-time, had been her own school.

*

Now the old convent school, which had catered for the daughters of the Russian nobility and had been patronized by the Czarina herself, was thronged with the hurrying shapes of dirty, unshaven soldiers and workmen. On the old classroom doors which she remembered so well, the signs of the new order were pinned, announcing boldly that this was the power-house of the Petrograd Soviet. 'Bureau of Foreign Affairs' . . . Central Committee of Pan-Russian Trade Unions . . . Soviet of Factory-Shop Committees.'

They passed through the great ex-ballroom of the Institute, lit by great white chandeliers, where once she had danced in white lace and learned the rules of etiquette under Madame Dupont, with her incipient moustache. But Madame Dupont was long gone now, as was the gold-framed Imperial portrait; and on the dais, which on festive occasions had been banked by brilliant military uniforms and robes of bejewelled Grand Duchesses, ragged, dirty Red Guards snored happily, oblivious to their surroundings. Carefully her companion led her up to the second floor, showing his Cheka pass time and time again, as soldiers in mud-stained boots, leather dispatch pouches slung over their shoulders, came and went to the front with their messages of alarm.

Suddenly he stopped and gripped her arm almost painfully. 'Here,' he whispered.

The enamelled plaque on it still informed the passer-by that it was 'Ladies Classroom Number Four'. But hanging from a rusty nail hammered into the door, a new crudely-lettered sign announced 'Bureau of Defence'.

'Trotsky's office,' he explained in a hurried whisper. 'We

can't hang around here, it would look too suspicious. But on that night, *he* will be behind that door.'

'You mean . . .?'

He completed the question for her. 'Yes, you will do it in there!'

*

'But how can you be sure?' she asked just before they parted near the Neva to go their various ways. He was always very careful that even the members of the Network never knew where he was living at any time. 'Sure that he will be there on April 20th?'

He smiled at her enigmatically. 'Because some friends of yours will be taking offensive action that will occasion Trotsky to alarm that monster Lenin. The result? Lenin will hurry immediately to Ladies' Classroom Number Four. More I cannot tell you, my dear Anna. But, if you cared to—' he laid his hands on hers.

She shook herself free. 'No,' she said firmly. In these last years, she had done many things – terrible things – for the cause, but she was not prepared to satisfy his greedy desires for him. 'I must go,' she said.

He shrugged. 'As you wish. There are others available. Good-night.' Without another word, he turned and within seconds had disappeared into the night.

She watched him go in silence and wondered again who he really was and what his real motives were. But she could come to no real conclusion, except that he was a highly dangerous man who would stop at nothing to achieve his real aims, whatever they might be.

She turned and stared reflectively across the Neva's dark waters and out to the sea beyond. What had he meant by 'friends of hers?' Did he mean Dickie? For a moment her face softened, as she thought of the last night she had spent together with the handsome young officer, who had been so nice, so English. Then her face hardened again. *She* had no time for such things. Her whole life must be dominated by one great overruling passion – the desire for revenge.

Suddenly she turned, her face aflame, all doubts resolved,

all hesitation gone. Boldly she set off into the night, striding out for her lodgings in the Ochta district. Now, in one little week, it would be all over and come what may she would have the long-awaited revenge . . .

2

'You may smoke, gentlemen,' the Flag Captain, in the high stiff wing-collar affected by officers in the pre-war Navy, said generously, 'the Admiral does not object to his junior officers indulging.'

There was an immediate bustle as the young, fresh-faced mishipmen and sub-lieutenants, who had appeared so suddenly in the Baltic Fleet, busied themselves with their pipes and cigarettes.

Bird, who did not smoke, took the opportunity to glance round the operations room of the Admiral's flagship, now anchored in the Gulf of Biorko with the Finns' permission.

He did not know the eager, noisy young men crowded in all around him, but something told him they weren't the usual types one found in a cruiser like the Admiral's flagship, HMS *Caledon*. They were hardly like the sedate, big-ship officers like the Flag Captain, with his wing collar and starched linen handkerchief peering out from his gold-cuffed right shirt-sleeve. They were too scruffy, too noisy, too high-spirited.

'You know what, de Vere,' he whispered to his companion, as the dapper little Admiral himself came into the operations room in his usual brisk way, 'I think they're our types – skimmer chaps.'

De Vere nodded sagely, puffing at his gold-tipped De Reske Special. 'From the general sloppiness of their appearance, old boy,' he answered, 'I have the distinct impression that you are right. But why, eh?'

'All right, chaps,' Cowan barked, as if he were still on the quarter deck, roaring into a north-easterly, 'remain sitting, no time to waste on idle formalities.'

There was a murmur of approval from the eager young men

whom Churchill had sent to him after scouring naval depots all over England.

For an instant, Admiral Cowan, the Commander of the Baltic Fleet, stared around the room, taking in each individual officer's face with his clear, steady gaze, as if he wished to imprint its features on his mind's eye for ever. Then he spoke in the harsh, chopped-off manner of his, getting to the point straight away. 'Gentlemen, I've asked you here to discuss an offensive operation against the Russkies, which I am calling RK.'

There was an immediate excited buzz of chatter, but he silenced it at once with an uplifted eyebrow.

'Why RK? Because I've named it after my good friend Sir Roger Keyes who put up such a splendid show at Zeebrugge last St George's Day. Without putting in troops as he did, I want the same sort of swift surprise raid on a Russian port.'

This time the little Admiral allowed his young men a moment's chatter before snapping at the Flag Officer. 'Wingy, the pointer!'

The white pointer appeared as if by magic and swinging round, Admiral Cowan tapped the big map of the Gulf of Finland with it to draw their attention. 'Petrograd, the centre of the Bolshy revolution,' he rasped. 'Bloody awful place. Was there in fourteen before the last show started. All pox, prostitutes and pricey firewater!'

He didn't give the young officers time to laugh, but continued without pause. 'All the same a devil of a place to take. Now I'm prepared to take on the Bolshy fleet any day, with one eye closed and my right arm tied behind my back. But on the open sea. *Not* behind such formidable defences as they have in Petrograd. That's why you lot of young bloods have been sent over to the Baltic Fleet from England. Operation RK is going to be *your* show. Do you understand? *A completely CMB show?*'

De Vere looked at Bird swiftly, a look of absolute unadulterated joy on his long face; and his companion knew exactly what must be going through the ex-Etonian's mind at the moment. They were going into action again after four weeks of twiddling their thumbs at Seehafen, with nothing to do but fish and wait for the transmission from Anna, which never came.

'Now,' the Admiral went on again, 'I think it's very much of an open secret that we are going to launch an all-out attack by land on Petrograd in the very near future. Even dozey Johnson, my man,' he indicated the wooden-faced Marine corporal at the door, who was in constant attendance on the little Admiral, whom he admired with slavish devotion, 'knows that. And I always thought Marines had tin ears.'

He allowed the young men a moment's laughter at the expense of the Royal Marines, who were usually the butt of wardroom humour.

'But before the foot-sloggers can move, we must destroy the Bolshies' naval power. Otherwise, it wouldn't be too difficult for that chap Trotsky to launch a combined sea-land operation to our flanks. Now,' he tapped the map again with his white pointer, 'the Russkies have their Central Fleet bottled up behind the protective screen of their forts and minefields, here and there. And like most chaps who dig themselves in a nice deep ditch and think they're safe, they haven't realized that they have dug their own grave. Because,' he paused significantly, 'once anyone penetrates those mine and fort defences, the Russkies are trapped in their hole. In other words, their ships have no room to manoeuvre. They are bloody sitting ducks.' Suddenly he pointed his stick at the attentive young officers, 'and you are the lucky chaps who are going to pot those same ducks off – in double quick time!'

*

The little Admiral's blue eyes glinted with delight at the excited look on their eager young faces which had greeted his announcement. There was not a trace of fear in any one of them; just excitement at the prospect of violent action. Here there was none of the war-weariness, none of the cynicism, none of the disbelief that one commonly found on the faces of those who had been through the trenches in the last show, he thought. These chaps, he realized suddenly, were the best the Old Country had in the grey year of 1919. *They still believed!*

'Well, then,' he resumed his exposition, 'I can see that you chaps are not exactly disinclined eh?'

'You're right there, sir,' several of them answered enthusiastically.

'Good. But let me not delude you on the dangers. As you can see from the detailed map of the approaches – there on the left of the main chart – Petrograd harbour is decidedly well protected, with the north channel defended by a minefield and the southern one by the shallows off Oranienbaum. A sub would have difficulty getting through, not to mention my surface craft. The only thing that has a chance of getting through is your CMBs.'

He paused and looked at them grimly, as if he himself were only just realizing the difficulties facing them in their task. 'Now,' he said, raising his voice a little, 'the first problem facing your CMBs is the damn noise they make. Sometimes I wish the Navy had never abandoned sailing boats.

'But no matter. With the row you lot will make full out, you'd wake even the sleepiest sentry. So we've got to ensure that you don't.' The most decorated officer in the Royal Navy tugged the end of his nose. 'Now I've fought in China, the Sudan and South Africa in land operations and it's been my experience that it's always between one and three in the morning that the morale of sentries and look-out men is at its lowest. So at roughly that time you'll go in, covered by an aerial bombardment from the *Vindictive*. I should imagine the eggs the Fleet Air Arm boys will lay'll keep the Russkies' heads down, what.'

The young officers grinned at his reference to bombs as eggs, and nodded their agreement.

'Now the problem of noise is easily solved, that of how to get into the place is not so easy, however. We've already run one sally into Petrograd on – er – a rather unconventional mission. So the Russkies know about your skimmers by now and the fact they are in the Gulf. Don't they Bird?'

'Yessir.'

Everyone turned to look at the hard-faced young officer with the ribbon of the D.S.C. on his chest as he stood up to explain how they had taken in the two skimmers through the northern channel, and the reception they had received from the Russian forts. 'So you see,' he concluded, 'the Russians could well be waiting for us on any second trip or conversely they might have prepared some sort of special anti-CMB devices – cables, anti-sub netting, surface mines or even—'

'All right, Lieutenant Bird,' Cowan cut in, 'that's enough or you'll have the lot of them wetting their breeches. You may sit down.' Bird sat down, grinning, while the little Admiral smiled at him, his bright eyes twinkling roguishly.

'In brief then,' Cowan summed up, 'the northern channel might well be prepared for the likes of you. But the Russkies haven't reckoned with ageing boy scouts like me who are always prepared, as BP maintains they should be . . . Now back in fourteen we visited Petrograd. The rest of the fleet was lodged in the Russian knocking shops and various other dens of ill-repute, behaving in the usual disgraceful manner of sailors on shore, but young Walter Cowan and his faithful man, Johnson, tirelessly devoted to duty as always, decided to have a look at Petrograd's defences. Who knows, we thought, the Royal might want to know something about them one day.' He winked conspiratorially. 'So with Johnson, the brawn, rowing and Cowan, the brain steering, we rowed the length of the southern channel and – wait for it – *took soundings*.' He stopped suddenly and let them have the full impact of his last two words.

Bird breathed out hard. Next to him de Vere whistled softly through his teeth, impressed.

The little Admiral indicated the southern channel with his pointer again. 'There it is, the Red Track. Three foot deep, unless the shallows have changed in the last five years. And that's the way you are going to enter Petrograd, gentlemen. *By the Red Track approach!*'

*

Swiftly the Admiral detailed his rough-and-ready plan, cutting out all technicalities in his usual down-to-earth fashion. In essence, Bird and de Vere would cross the shallows first, following the red line of the Red Track Approach, as he called it, dropping sounding buoys behind them for the remaining four boats. These would follow through the marked channels at five minute intervals, the noise of their motors drowned with luck by the

Naval Air Service's bombing attack on Oranienbaum. 'Now once you're in the basin,' the little Admiral said, continuing easily as if the operation were already half won, ('*Once*,' de Vere breathed next to Bird. 'Oh my holy Uncle – *once*!'), 'you'll face the problem of six boats swanning around at high speed, probably under gunfire and in the dark. Could be an awful ballsup – excuse me – I must watch my language. I am not used to addressing ladies' colleges.'

They grinned.

'Unfortunately you chaps can't fire your torpedoes if you're not travelling at high speed.[1] So you stand a good chance of knocking into your silly selves. What are we going to do then? We're going to do this. Each of you will be allotted a particular ship to attack and you'll have exactly twenty minutes to carry out that attack. When that time has passed, gentlemen, Bird and de Vere here will attack – and sink – the heavy battleship *Spartak*. That will be the signal for a hurried departure home. Naturally you others are going to have to take your medicine too, but I'm afraid it's going to be you two,' he looked grimly at the two of them, 'who will really have to face the music. The Russkies will have recovered by then and they'll offer you the whole weight of their guns, I'm afraid.'

'Don't worry, sir,' de Vere said, 'We know the basin better than the other chaps. We're prepared to take that risk.'

The Admiral beamed suddenly, 'Well spoken, young fellow, well spoken indeed.' He fumbled in his pocket and brought out a slim gold cigarette case. He opened it and produced a thin piece of paper, which he unfolded with great care before looking up at them again. 'Gentlemen,' he said gazing round their curious faces, 'I have carried this piece of paper around with me for the last five years of war. It's something the great Nelson himself wrote. If you will bear with me for an instant, I'd like to read it to you.'

He cleared his throat then read the long dead Admiral's words: 'In close actions at sea and hazardous operations on shore, something must always be left to chance.' He hesitated a moment, as if to let the words 'left to chance' sink in. 'But in

1. At slow speed, the torpedo might strike the bottom and explode underneath the CMB.

case signals can neither be seen nor perfectly understood, no captain can do wrong, if he places his ship alongside one of the enemy.' '*Alongside the enemy, gentlemen,* that is all I ask of you.'

A long profound silence greeted his last words, as a solemn, almost funereal hush descended upon the young men assembled in the operations room. A silence, which Bird finally broke with his last question: 'And when will this operation take place, sir?'

'Take place?' Admiral Cowan barked almost harshly. 'Why on the night of April 20th, in the year of our Lord, 1919 . . .'

3

Slowly Rosenblum rose from the rumpled bed. For a second he gazed down at the naked countess, who now lay in an exhausted sleep on the silken sheet, her exciting white body sprawled in voluptuous carelessness.

His dark eyes glittered momentarily with pleasure at the warm memory of her hectic abandon as he had taken her for the first time; and how her passion had run away with her in the end, so that she willingly did the perverted things he needed to have done to him to achieve his satisfaction.

A week ago the countess had come to his office, offering her beautiful body to him without beating about the bush, in return for the protection that the powerful deputy head of the Petrograd Cheka could give to a member of the hated old aristocracy. But now she was his, *not* for the security he could offer, but because he had shown her this night what real physical passion was. Turning away and walking to the dressing-room, he told himself with his customary overweening vanity: 'She is my slave now, for as long as I need her.'

Carefully he began to dress in the dull Cheka uniform, which he hated, gazing as he did so at the Chalgrin sketch of the Arc de Triomphe, with its handwritten comments on the margin by his idol, Napoleon, himself.

It was the last piece of his treasured collection of Napoleana, which he had begun after he'd returned from Brazil. Now it was all gone to pay those who would play a key part in the counter-revolution.

Buttoning up the tight collar of his tunic, he began combing his hair, wondering whether Anna, too, was preparing for the night's work now. He would dearly have liked to bed her. She had an intriguing iciness about her, which he knew he could have thawed with his talents between the sheets. But it was too late for that. If she pulled it off this night, the whole rotten structure of the Bolshevik state would fall apart and he would have other things to do than concern himself with chasing skirts. Then *he* would be Russia's grey eminence. Yudenich, he would make the head of the Russian Army. His old friend Grammati-koff, he would appoint Minister of Interior, a key post. Then there was the Ministry of Communications, also vital in a state like Russia. Perhaps his old friend Chubersky might fit that slot?

He stopped suddenly and stared at his dark artful face in the mirror. Could he really pull it off? One obscure man against a nation of over a hundred million? What if the English failed to penetrate the harbour? Or if the girl lost her nerve at the very last moment? Naturally he was prepared to get out with no danger to himself. That was why the countess's apartment, directly opposite the Smolny Institute was so vital to him as an escape route.

He grunted, angry at his own sudden doubts. Of course nothing would go wrong! The British wouldn't fail and the girl, who was as hard as nails in the way only an aristocrat could be, would carry out her task to the bitter end. All that was needed, after so many months of careful planning, was faith and boldness. Wasn't it his own idol, the little Lieutenant from Corsica, who had started from nothing and conquered a whole world, who always maintained '*L'audace, encore l'audace, toujours l'audace!*' Of course boldness would succeed, as it always had done throughout the history of the world.

Dismissing his doubts contemptuously, he buckled on his revolver before going into her room. Gently he bent down and kissed her left breast. Her scarlet lips parted with a sigh of pleasure. 'Wake up, Fleur,' he whispered.

She half opened her dark sensuous eyes, under the heavy

black lids which indicated that she had some Georgian blood in her background. 'Is it time?' she asked lazily and yawned, stretching up her long white arms and thrusting her breasts towards him in delicious invitation.

'Yes, I must go now.'

Outside, the great clock in the Peter and Paul began to chime the hour. He glanced hastily at his watch. 'It's ten o'clock. You will wait for me, won't you?'

'Of course, my little dove,' she sighed with faked passion. 'For you always.'

He allowed himself a smile of triumph. Her statement was confirmation that no woman could resist him, even though some of his current mistresses were – like the countess – half his age. Softly he touched his lips to her outstretched hand. '*Dosvedanya* – God be with you.'

A minute later, Abraham Rosenblum was outside in the grey foggy street. It was now exactly five minutes after ten on the 20th April. *The operation had started!*

*

In her cheerless hotel room in the Ochta slum quarter, Anna knelt in front of the cheap ikon and waited till the clanging reverberations of the tram below had passed, before she prayed in a manner such as she had never prayed since she had left school in that terrible autumn of 1917. In the next room, the bedsprings creaked wildly, as the whore who lived there let some Red Guard or sailor from the Fleet have his way with her diseased body for a handful of kopecks. Slowly she rose to her feet and crossed herself, her mind at rest at last. She touched the second pistol tucked away beneath her Cheka blouse, and looked around the shabby room with its brass bedstead, as if she already knew she would never see it again. Then she went out. She did not look back.

The streets were cheerless. There was a faint unearthly pallor beginning to steal over them, dimming the watchfires and muting the clatter of the blue-yellow tramcars and the rumbling lorries heading for the front, as if heralding the terrible dawn which would soon sweep over Russia.

She halted at a tea-stall, its waxcloth counter littered with black bread crusts and wet with the tea dripping from the samovar, to allow a column of Red Guards to march by under red flags, embroidered with the words 'PEACE' and 'LAND' in gold. The soldiers were mostly young and they marched without music. The expression on their faces was that of men who knew they were going to die soon.

Up the Nevsky in the sour light, crowds of clerks in stiff collars were battling for the latest papers. A little one-legged newspaper seller, offering the illegal *Rabotchaya Gazata* for sale, was battling with a couple of sailors, burly chests strung with belts of machine-gun ammunition, who were trying to take his bundle of papers from him. 'But comrades,' he was bleating as she passed, 'It says that Lenin has betrayed the people of Petrograd . . . the streets will run with blood yet!' One of the sailors from the Central Fleet spat a stream of sunflower seeds into the man's face and grunted, 'the only blood that'll flow this night, little brother, is yours. Now will you give me those damned papers?'

An armoured car rattled by slowly, its machine gun turning from side to side like the snout of some primeval monster sniffing out its prey. Hastily a group of deserters in Red Army uniform, who were selling tobacco and sunflower seeds on the black market, pocketed their wares and fled into the grey darkness, like great rats disturbed in their scavenging.

She pushed her way through a group of squat men in dirty frock-coats and thigh-boots, their women in yellow wigs, suckling drowsy children at their big dangling exposed breasts, and chattering away in a language she could not recognize for a minute. Then she had it. Yiddish! She wrinkled her nose at their smell of herring and cabbage. Polish Jews abandoning the city, as if they could already sense that on the morrow the enraged populace might well take their revenge on the Jews. After all the Russians always had – for century after century.

She turned a corner, the cold mud under foot already soaking through the Cheka knee-boots, with which he had supplied her. A tram clattered past, carrying black-smocked workers, clerks in bowlers, and Red Guards, whose long bayonetted rifles, hung from its sides. They shouted wildly at passers-by, happy that they were not having to walk to their destination this one night.

Then it was gone, its bell clanging behind it and she was looking at the great grey edifice of the Smolny Institute, with its blazing lights and faint hum as if it were some great human hive.

She looked at the cheap nickel American watch he had given her, craning her head to one side to see the hands and as she did so feeling the second pistol stick coldly into her naked flesh.

It was ten thirty exactly.

*

A thin grey mist hung everywhere in Seehafen. It clung in wet patches about the rocks of the harbour so that they looked like bearded giants. Now a mysterious stillness brooded over the little bay and muffled the cries of the nightbirds. All the same they could still hear the plaintive, monotonous singing of the mechanic with the injured hand whom they were going to have to leave behind. Over and over again the wind blew faint snatches of the old wartime ditty to them, as they shivered there on the skimmers' dripping decks and waited for the agreed time of departure.

'Don't cryee . . . sighee . . .
There's a silver lining in the skyee . . .
Cheerio, chin-chin, napoo . . . tootle-lo . . .
Wipe the tear, baby dear, from your eyee . . .
Goodbyee . . .'

'Oh, for Gawd's sake!' Ginger cursed to Bull, 'why don't he put a sock in it! Him and his ruddy good-bye! If I was up there, I'd soon put something ruddy else in his eyee!'

'Happen, he's sad,' Bull said, 'that he's got to stay behind like.'

'Go on, yer silly daft Yorkshire pudden,' Ginger exploded scornfully. 'You ain't got the sense you was born with. Sad to stay behind! Nobody in his right mind would be out on a night like this and gonna have a go at that lot up there!' Bull grinned, in no way offended, and wiped the damp off his big, red face. 'Happen we'll get a medal for this one, Ginger.'

'Yer,' the cockney replied dourly. 'A ruddy putty one no doubt – and posthumous at that, I'll be ruddy well bound!' Bird grinned as he listened to the two of them. Let them grumble, he told himself, but when the chips were down, he knew that he would be able to rely on both of them implicitly. He flashed yet another glance at the green-glowing dial of his service wristwatch – at least the tenth time he had done so in the last five minutes.

'Well, de Vere,' he broke the silence, 'I suppose this is where we go again.'

De Vere started, and recovered himself an instant later. 'I say, old chap, you'll have to give me prior notice when you're going to speak to me on nights like this. The old ticker's dicky enough. I just might turn up me toes on you, you know.' He laughed, but there was no humour in it. 'The old nerves are going like a banjo as it is.'

Bird stuck out his hand. 'Oh do stop being such an ass, Sub-Lieutenant French!' he said with an attempt at formality. Then with a sudden burst of affection. 'Well de Vere, best of luck, old chap and happy landings!'

'And happy landings to you, Dickie!'

Bird pressed the starter. The Thorneycroft came to life with a deafening roar. Suddenly the damp night air stank with the fumes of high-octane fuel. White smoke enveloped the skimmer for an instant. Behind it CMB skippers along the whole jetty started their engines. The night was hideous with their noise.

Hastily Bird throttled back and while Ginger swallowed the rest of his corned-beef and pickled onion sandwich, wound a white silk scarf round his neck. This time he was in uniform and he wanted to look the part of a dashing young skimmer skipper.

Across from him, de Vere gave him the thumbs up sign and grinned.

He grinned back and shouted to Ginger. 'Stand by to slip the ropes, Ginger.'

'Ay, ay, sir.'

Bird threw a last glance round the green-glowing controls. Everything was all right.

'All right, slip her!'

Hastily Ginger loosed the wet rope and doubled back along the slippy deck to the control shield. Bird opened the throttle.

The skimmer started to move, an ever-increasing shudder running her length as he raised the speed. Swiftly the jetty began to fall away behind him. The craft cleared the entrance to the little harbour. A sudden keen wind struck him squarely across the face. He shuddered and opened the throttle wide. The engine took up the challenge eagerly. With a mighty flurry of foam, it thrust the skimmer forward. Twin waves of surging white sprang up on both sides. The skimmer's bow tilted towards the night sky. At thirty-five knots an hour, the skimmer, followed by the rest of that wild pack, tore into the night like a vicious grey avenger.

It was now eleven o'clock. Already the de Havilands would have left the *Vindictive* at Biorko, winging their way steadily eastwards to their silent brooding target, intent upon the kill.

*

Anna peered up at the dark, still back of the Smolny Institute and counted off the windows. Three was Trotsky's bedroom and four belonged to the Head of the Cheka, who, as she knew from Rosenblum, was ill with enteritis at the Tzarskoe-Selo Hospital in the suburbs. Number Four was her target!

She crouched as a military lorry rumbled by slowly, her heart beating fearfully for an instant. Then it was gone and all was silence again, save for the faint rustle of the wind through the dripping dank trees.

Once as a girl she had climbed this selfsame facade in broad daylight to the delight of her fellow pupils and the horror of the bespectacled, corsetted Principal. She had tweaked her ear, told her she would come to a bad end, and then asked her what she had done with her stays, as if that were very important in a venture when she could have well broken her neck.

But that had been during the day. Now it was night and the facade was wet and slippy with fog. Still it had to be done, if she were to carry out her task. Taking a deep breath, she reached up and took hold of the two wrought-iron flower baskets jutting out of the wall above her. They were cold and wet, but when she put her weight on them experimentally, they held.

A moment later she was scrambling upwards, her feet astride on the flower baskets, reaching up for the next ledge, which ran around the whole facade just below the second floor. Gingerly she reached up and took hold of it, first with one hand and then with the other. Satisfied, she started to heave herself upwards. Suddenly her right hand slipped. In a flash the rough stone had torn her fingernails away. Red-hot needles of pain shot into her fingers. Just in time she stiffled her yelp of agony, as she felt her feet connect once more with the ledge below.

For what seemed an age she balanced there, trembling violently, her body pressed against the wet surface of the wall, while she sucked her bloody fingers, which felt as if they were on fire. Then she pulled herself together, as that iron will of hers triumphed again. Once more she reached upwards and took hold. This time it held. Slowly – very slowly – she started to raise herself onto the ornamental ledge. A second later she had done it, her body soaked in a cold sweat, her heart beating furiously. She breathed out hard and rested for a little while, her gaze kept firmly at the level of the ledge, knowing she wouldn't be able to move another step if she ever looked down. Somewhere far off, a dog was barking in hoarse persistent hysteria, but the bedrooms behind the offices were silent, as if the Bolshevik murderers to whom they belonged were already deep in a dreamless, contented sleep.

Now she began to wriggle sideways along the wet dripping ledge to the shadowy outline of the number four window. Foot after foot, bleeding aching fingers scraping the rough wall for the least little bit of support. Once there was a soft shower of stucco breaking away. But it was behind her and after she had overcome her initial shock, she was able to continue without difficulty. Then finally she had made it and was balanced there twenty metres above the ground, her body turned to face the thickly curtained window of the Cheka Chief's room.

She hesitated a moment and turned her head slightly to the wind to catch the least sound. Nothing! The room was empty, then who dare occupy the feared secret police chief's bed? Balancing the best she could, she brought out the package slowly, which he had prepared for her: a small roll of thick brown packing paper, smeared with a thin coating of treacle.

Carefully she unrolled it and pasted it on the thick pane of glass next to the window catch. Far off the dog was still barking, but it did not distract her. Satisfied with her handiwork, she took a deep breath and doubled the fist of her uninjured hand. 'Now,' she said to herself and smashed it against the brown paper. The pane gave and cracked with only the slightest of noise. A moment later she had opened the catch and climbed inside.

Her nostrils were assailed by a strong and sickly perfume. Jasmine and rose, she told herself in disgust; the kind used by street-women, gigolos, and worse. But she had no time to concern herself with the Cheka Chief's perverted tastes. Feeling her way through the over-furnished bedroom, she sought and found his tooth-glass on the washbasin in the corner. Hastily she placed it against the wall to Trotsky's bedroom, and listened.

A deep rhythmic breathing! As Rosenblum had promised her, the Minister of War had retired early and was fast asleep, as was his habit. She put the glass down and tip-toeing to the connecting door, slipped the key in.

Again Rosenblum's prediction was correct. The key fitted perfectly. Breathing out deeply, she dropped on the Cheka Chief's overstuffed bed, her nostrils assailed once more by that disgusting perfume. She had done it! She was in place. Faintly, far off to the west, she could hear the first of the air-raid sirens beginning to sound its warning of death and destruction. But to her it seemed to herald the start of a new age for Russia . . .

*

Rosenblum showed his Cheka pass to the Red Guards at the door, their bodies hung with machine gun ammunition, and stick grenades thrust into their belts. They looked at it in their usual surly manner and an unshaved giant, in a Cossack cap, muttered something about 'these damned upstart Yids'. But at that particular moment, he didn't mind. The plan was running one hundred per cent on schedule and he was happy, or as happy as *he* ever could be. They let him pass and he started to thread his way through the loud echoing corridors, thronged with the hurrying shapes of workmen and soldiers, carrying printed propaganda of all sorts to distribute to the uneasy population of the great city outside.

He would have dearly loved to go upstairs to check whether she was already in position, but knew he couldn't do that. If anything went wrong and she was arrested, he did not want any alert guard to remember that Petrograd's deputy head of Cheka had been prowling along the office corridor just prior to the event. Although at that moment he was supremely confident that his plan would succeed, his long years in espionage had taught him never to take unnecessary risks.

Thus, instead of going upstairs, he wended his way to the Institute's low-ceilinged refectory, which now served the hundreds of Red Army soldiers and black-smocked workmen, who stood in a patient line waiting for a meal. He paid his two roubles and joined them, edging his way slowly to the great serving tables, where sweating men and women ladled out great scoops of steaming cabbage soup and thrust hunks of black bread and horsemeat at the hungry men.

But as he threaded his way through the eating Bolsheviks who lined the dirty, littered wooden tables, towards the far end which was reserved for the Cheka, his mind was not on the cabbage soup or even the grey cold horsemeat, a delicacy in starving Petrograd. It was on his great plan.

Flopping into one of the stained benches he began to eat his food mechanically, not even aware of what he was eating.

At first, the year before, his reaction to the Bolshevik Revolution had been simply one of horror; horror at the rape of the 10-year-old daughters of the aristocracy; at the Czarist officers with their testicles cut off and their shoulder straps nailed to their naked shoulders; at the murder of the elderly ministers, whose beards were torn from their faces with the flesh still attached before they were pushed into slag-heaps to die of suffocation.

But that had been in the beginning, and after all he had seen comparable suffering among Brazilian *Indios*, at the hands of their white masters. Later he had come to realize that here was the opportunity he had always sought – the opportunity for greatness!

But what a back-breaking, frustrating task it had been to start the train of events which would bring him that greatness. The anti-Bolsheviks – Yudenich and the rest – were all good at talking, but seemingly quite incapable of putting a plan into operation. How much time and how much money had he been forced to spend to get them organized! Then there had been the British. How slow, how careful, how hesitant these men had become, whose ancesters had once gone out boldly from their grey little island to conquer half the world! But in the end he had even managed to convince them – or at least *some* of them – that his great plan would work.

And now, after what seemed centuries, but in reality was only months, the moment of truth had arrived. He swallowed the last of his black bread without even noticing that he had done so, taken up completely by his thoughts. In the end he had managed to pull it off. The pawns were all in their appointed places; C; the young British naval officer; Yudenich; *the girl*. He sighed happily and pushed his soup away from him. Now the great game could begin.

As the first bombs began to drop and excited shouts and cries of alarm went up on all sides, Abraham Rosenblum, the head of the R-Network, leaned back against the wall and waited for what must soon happen . . .

TWO

THE SKIMMER ATTACK

'Oh, my gawd, they've got Mr de Vere and that poor old Yorkshire pudden, Bull!'

1

At a dead slow crawl, the Thorneycrofts purring softly, as the lean grey shapes of the skimmers approached the shallows in a wide V formation. To their right the inky sky was stabbed scarlet time and time again, as the Russian guns fired at the Navy biplanes from the *Vindictive*. Bird stood very erect at the shield, eyes glued on the green-glowing compass, his body shrouded in his British warm, while Ginger tensed with the first buoy. What was going through the officer's head, the Lord only knew, Ginger thought. All he knew was that he was ruddy well scared. He shivered violently and stamped his icy feet on the throbbing deck. On the shore another group of fifty pound bombs thudded home and there was a sudden angry red glare behind the line of squat forts. The fly-boys were really giving the Russkies some stick!

'Stop engine!' Bird ordered suddenly.

Hastily Ginger dropped the buoy and did as he was ordered. The boat lapsed into silence. Behind them the little flotilla did the same. One after another, the slap-slap of the waves on their sides decreasing in strength by the instant.

Bird frowned and stared at the compass once more, while the Russian searchlights swung wildly to and fro across the sky, searching in vain for the Navy planes which had now flown off to the east, prior to roaring in for another attack. He narrowed his eyes and tried to penetrate the murk. Then he spotted it in the light reflected from the searchlights' beams. A thick patch of brown. There for an instant and gone the next. But it was enough for him. They had reached the shallows. 'All right, Ginger,' he cried, 'drop the first buoy!'

Ginger reacted at once. With a soft splash the bulky wooden buoy went overboard to be followed a second later by de Vere's to the right. The entrance to the channel was marked.

He started the engine once more. Carefully he began to move forward in line with de Vere's skimmer, while the noise of the Bolshy ack-ack died away to their right. But now Bird had no time to worry about any noise they might be making; his whole being was concentrated on the green glowing needle of the compass and the Red Track Approach Admiral Cowan had mapped out so many years before. For he knew if he failed to find the channel or alarmed the enemy before the little flotilla had passed the guns of the forts, only half a mile away, the whole operation would come to a sudden and deadly end.

Crawling forward through the dark brown sluggish water, his eyes, ears and every muscle strained, Lieutenant Dickie Bird felt his nerves begin to sing out in protest. But he knew he could not afford any let-up. After their next attack, the Navy biplanes would have to return to the *Vindictive* and then they would be on their own, with no aerial diversion to cover the noise they were making going through the shallows.

Without warning a sharp white light poked its way through the darkness ahead. Bird tensed, his heart suddenly beating furiously. The light wavered, as if the operator had thought he had heard something and yet was not quite sure whether his ears were playing tricks upon him. 'Cor luv a duck,' Ginger breathed, clutching the fat buoy to his wet uniform almost protectively, 'the beggar'll spot us in half a ruddy tick!'

Slowly the terrible white beam started to advance upon them across the still surface of the water, ready to pinion them in eye-searing glare. Desperately Bird sprang to the Lewis. At the very moment it drowned them in its merciless light, he would let the beam have a full burst. He licked his dry lips and prepared to fire.

Suddenly there was a great, frightening crash. A terrifying orange flash shot into the sky. In an instant the whole coastline was illuminated a dramatic, blazing red, and the little craft trembled with the impact. A hot blast of air hit Bird in the face, and as the first stick of bombs began to explode along the length of the fortifications, the white beam swung upwards searching for the new attackers.

Bird breathed out hard, his body suddenly drenched in a cold sweat. As he took his hands off the wooden butt of the Lewis, he could feel them trembling violently. Forcing himself to remain calm, he ordered: 'Ginger, drop the next buoy overboard.'

'Ay, ay, sir,' Ginger sang out, but the usual forceful note was absent from his cheeky cockney voice.

*

Time passed. To their right the second flight of biplanes were coming in for their last attack. Red and white tracer hissed into the dark sky to meet them like a flight of angry hornets. Down on the ground, dull orange flames leaping up higher and higher in greedy profusion testified to the accuracy of the naval aviators. But Bird had no eyes for what was going on ashore. They had approached the half-way mark through the shallows. Already the first of the remaining four skimmers would be nosing its way into the Red Track Approach, to be followed at five minute intervals by the others. He knew they were approaching the most dangerous part of the Oranienbaum Shallows, where they reached out almost as far as the Island of Kronstadt itself. At this spot they would have at the most some three hundred yards of water between the sandbanks and Kronstadt. One slip-up here and they would be sitting-ducks at the mercy of the Russian guns.

Bird reduced speed even more so that the Thorneycroft was just ticking over on this side of stalling. To starboard, de Vere steered his skimmer even closer. They were perhaps twenty-five yards apart now. 'Ginger,' he called, 'drop that buoy and get up on the stern with the boat-hook!'

With a soft splash the sounding buoy went overboard – the signal to those who were following them that here they were now approaching the toughest stretch of the Red Track. Picking up the boat-hook, Ginger poised himself at the bow, ready for the skipper's orders.

Gingerly Bird pressed on, fighting each yard in anxious, nerve-racking apprehension of what might happen if he slipped up, feeling the sweat standing out on his brow in great beads despite the coolness of the breeze.

'Sound her, Ginger!' he yelled.

Immediately the cockney mechanic plunged his pole into the suddenly sluggish muddy water. 'All right, skipper,' he yelled back. 'Half a pole. Still got clearage!'

And now Bird could hear the lap-lap of waves breaking on the sandbank, perhaps a hundred yards ahead. He breathed a sigh of relief. The soft sound indicated deeper water; they were nearly through!

'All right, Ginger,' he began, 'get back to—'

He never finished the order. Suddenly the skimmer received a frightening bump. There was a horrible rending sound. Caught off guard, Bird was slammed against the windshield. And as his mouth filled suddenly with the salty taste of blood from his split lip, the skimmer came to an abrupt halt.

'Gor, ruddy beggar it!' Ginger yelled in disgust, as Bird spat out a mouthful of blood, *we've gorn and hit the bleeding sandbank!*

*

In the twenty-odd years of life still remaining to him, Lieutenant Bird would never again experience a moment worse than that on that night of April 20th, 1919, when after the first benumbing shock, he realized the full seriousness of their plight. Stuck on a sandbank, a mere couple of hundred yards away from enemy territory, and somewhere in the darkness behind him the whole attacking force heading for the same fate, if he couldn't do something about it *quickly*.

'Ginger,' he swallowed hard and tried to control the note of panic in his voice, 'jump to it! Check the rudder and the skin. Get on with it man!'

The sharpness of his words seemed to galvanize Ginger into frenzied activity. While Bird waited at the controls, ready to rev the engine, he ran the length of the forty-footer, zig-zagging from side to side to check whether the skin above water had been holed; then dropping on his knees, peered over the side at the rudder.

'Well?' Bird demanded, mentally saying a rapid prayer that

Ginger's answer would be positive.

'No holes above the waterline, sir. And both the rudder and prop seem all right.'

Bird breathed a sigh of relief. 'Good show, Ginger,' he forced himself to say in as casual a voice as he could manage. 'Stand by – I'm going to try to get her off.'

The next instant, he opened the throttle. There was a terrible roar. At the stern the muddy water was threshed into an angry white frenzy. *Nothing happened!* Desperately he increased the pressure on the throttle. Now the night was hideous with the noise the trapped boat was making, drowning even the sound of the last bombs exploding on the shore beyond. Still nothing happened. Sobbing with rage and despair, Bird threw the throttle wide open. The roar was ear-splitting, as the 500HP engine threshed crazily only a foot beneath the surface of the wild white water.

'*Sir . . . sir!*' It was Ginger, his hands cupped around his mouth, his eyes wide and wild with fear, as he shouted above the tremendous noise of the racing engine. '*It's no bleeding good, skipper!*'

'What do you mean?' Bird yelled at him savagely.

'*The prop's half out of the ruddy water . . . we're not gonna get off that way, skipper!*'

For one long moment, his hand still jammed hard against the throttle, the whole craft vibrating crazily under his feet with the motor's purposeless fury, Lieutenant Bird stood there, desperately not wanting to believe him. Then he knew he must. Reluctantly, he eased back the throttle, knowing as he did so they were irrevocably trapped on the sandbank . . .

*

In the next room the phone shrilled suddenly.

She started, alert at once. It must be the call she had been expecting to come this last hour. Hastily she knelt on the Cheka man's bed and pressed the glass to the wall. The ringing seemed to go on for ever. Finally, when she was beginning to despair that Trotsky would ever pick up the receiver, the ringing stopped and a sleepy voice said 'what?'

Suddenly the voice lost its sleepiness. '*What?*' it demanded with abrupt urgency. '*Where?*'

In the silence that followed as his questions were answered, she could imagine what his unknown informant at the other end was telling the War Minister.

His next words confirmed her guess. 'Good, I understand . . . do not yield an inch of ground if they attack in force . . . And listen Comrade Commandant.' Trotsky's voice was suddenly coldly venomous. 'You can expect to be a head shorter if you do!'

Anna heard the receiver crashed down, as if in rage. She tensed. Now was the moment. *Would he?*

Her swift prayer ended abruptly, as Trotsky picked up the receiver again and started rattling the bar for the operator. She sighed with relief, as his voice rapped. 'Vladimir Ilyich – *Vladamir Ilyich, at once!*'

The connection was almost immediate and swiftly he put the man at the other end in the picture. 'Vladimir Ilyich,' he snapped. 'Trouble! They're bombing Kronstadt, Oranienbaum, Krasnaya Gorka, the whole coast.'

A pause.

'No, we don't know yet, but I assume it's the British . . . and sentries report suspicious noises out in the approaches. So far we haven't been able to identify them. But I'm not taking any chances. Whether it's the start of an all-out Imperialist attack or not, I've ordered a general stand-to in Petrograd. I suggest—' Trotsky broke off suddenly, as if the man at the other end had asked a question.

'Good, good, I agree it would be better if you came to the Smolny Institute yourself. You'd be safer here as well . . .'

Another pause.

'Very well, Vladimir Ilyich, I shall send an armoured car to collect you. I'll expect you here in thirty minutes' time. *Dosvedanye!*'

The phone went dead suddenly and she sat back on the bed, her heart beating wildly. It was all working out as Rosenblum had predicted so confidently. *He was coming!*

For what seemed an age she slumped there, staring blankly at the white-painted wall as she had done in that very room seven years before. Here the Principal had finally dismissed her from the Institute and she had been sent to Cheltenham for the 'traditional English discipline' as her dead Father sternly described it. Outside the night was suddenly full of confused sound, as Trotsky went to work with his usual energy. Car-horns, orders, excited shouts, distant rifle shots. With electric suddenness Petrograd was coming to frightened life again. Down below in the park, the Red Guards were already drag-ging up an howitzer into position, to place it behind a barricade made from the chairs and packing cases being thrown out of the Institute's upper windows.

'Revolutionary discipline!' a hoarse voice protested from below. 'It is the property of the people!'

'*All power to the Soviets!*' a drunk bellowed from above and laughed coarsely, as the sound of smashing glass went on.

Slowly she dragged herself out of her reverie. *He was com-ing! . . . he was coming . . .'*

With fingers that were trembling violently, she unbuttoned the flap of the big holster and drew out the Cheka revolver Rosenblum had given her. It would be a matter of mere minutes now.

*

Like a black-grey river the Red Guards and the Workers Mili-tia were pouring down the corridors of the Institute, grabbing the ammunition and weapons handed to them at the door and disappearing into the night, already alive with the wild snap-and-crackle of small arms fire.

Rosenblum let himself be dragged along with the hysterical, screaming mob. A couple of burly sailors from the Central Fleet pushed in front of him and dumped a bearded young mate on one of the vacated couches, then turning, disappeared with the rest.

It was the opportunity Rosenblum had been waiting for. A look of fake concern on his dark hawklike face he bent over the young sailor, who was dying from a shrapnel hole in his chest, from which fresh bright blood welled at each breath. In this way he could post himself near the door without arousing sus-picion.

'What is it, little Brother?' he asked and stroked his damp

brow. The sailor's eyes flickered open momentarily. '*Mir boudit,*' he gasped. '*Peace is coming, brother!*'

'*Peace is coming!*' he sneered under his breath, gazing down at the dying sailor. Somehow the boy represented for him at that moment the silliness of the human soul, the complete absurdity of human creatures.

And then the door was flung open. In an instant the burly, sour-faced Lettish bodyguards in their leather uniforms had pushed the excited Red Guards to both sides to allow *him* to enter. A second later he came through the door himself and took in the excited scene with a flash of his dark Tartar eyes.

Rosenblum looked at him as he posed there at the door in his shabby blue suit. The man looked like a provincial grocer, a corner shop-keeper, a suburban clerk; and yet he commanded the destiny of a hundred million people.

'Clear this rabble out of the way!' he commanded imperiously. Raising their rifle butts, the Lettish guards advanced up the corridor clearing it with cold-blooded brutality. Rosenblum pressed himself against the wall, quickly repressing the flush of absolute triumph which had flashed to his dark face. Next moment, the Soviet dictator swept by him, hurrying to take command of the confused situation.

Vladimir Ilyich Lenin had arrived ...

*

Bull took a deep breath and flexing his massive body, he raised the heavy wire hawser above his head.

Bird licked his salt-dry lips. If de Vere's courageous attempt to drag him off the sandbank failed, he would have to abandon the skimmer and suffer the awful humiliation of being a mere passenger and spectator of the action, on de Vere's craft.

Bull, some twenty feet away now, poised himself more steadily on the other skimmer's heaving bow and whirling the hawser end round his head like a cowboy with his lasso, hurled it through the air. It crashed onto Bird's deck and snaked out across the wet dripping planks.

'Get it, Ginger!' Bird yelled desperately.

Ginger dived full length on it and caught it just as it was about to disappear over the side. Hastily Bird ran to aid him.

Panting furiously they secured it to the metal towing ring, while Bull grinned across at them with pleasure at the success of his suggestion.

'Go on,' Ginger panted. 'You ain't that smart, yer big Yorkshire pudden! And what yer standing there for, like a ruddy fish and chip supper waitin' fer vinegar? Get that line secured!'

Bull woke up to his duty. 'Aye, yer right, Ginger lad!' With only the slightest of grunts, he picked up the heavy metal hawser, as if it were made of string and attached it to his skimmer's hook. 'Us end is fixed on, skipper,' he yelled at an impatient de Vere, who was surveying the still burning horizon anxiously.

'Must you shout your damn, silly head off like that, Bull?' de Vere protested in alarm. 'You must have alarmed every Bolshy between here and Timbuctoo!'

Bull hung his head in shame. 'Sorry, sir,' he mumbled, 'I wasn't thinking like.'

'Well, *do* next time,' de Vere snapped, but the rancour had gone out of his voice. Without Bull their scheme to get Dickie's boat off the sandbank before it was too late would not have been possible. 'Come on, let's be getting on with it.' He cupped his hands around his mouth and called as loudly as he dared. 'All right, stand by with your boat-hooks! I'm going to take the strain.' Swiftly the two men on the stricken skimmer poised their long poles on both sides of the craft. De Vere nodded his approval and turning to his controls, gently eased the throttle forward.

The hawser snapped taut. A sudden flurry of white water appeared at the bows of de Vere's boat as it took the strain, the frame shaking in abrupt protest. Nothing happened!

'Blast and damn!' de Vere cursed. Time was running out rapidly. If he couldn't get the skimmer free soon, Dickie and Ginger would have to abandon it. The other skimmers couldn't be more than a quarter of a mile behind and the biplanes were long gone. The Bolshies might discover the lot of them at any moment. 'All right,' he called across the water, 'I'm going to have another go and please – for the sake of the old school – let's have a bit of effort this time, what?'

'What old school?' Ginger quipped daringly, but all the

same he gripped the boat-hook intently; he knew, too, that there wasn't much time left.

De Vere eased the throttle forward once again. The hawser sliced the top of the water as it snapped taut. On the other boat, Ginger and Bird took the strain, their faces crimson, the veins standing out starkly at their temples as they pushed their poles against the sand below with all their might. The Thorney-croft raced wildly. White water shot high into the air. The stricken skimmer creaked loudly. Suddenly its deck yawed violently. Bird and Ginger caught themselves just in time. De Vere upped the pressure, praying desperately that the hawser wouldn't burst. On Kronstadt the first searchlight clicked on alarmingly. De Vere, sweat dripping from his brow, increased the revs. The whole boat seemed about to shake itself apart in violent fury at being restrained thus. Still Bird's skimmer did not move.

'Damn this for a lark!' Bull yelled in a sudden rage. Before anyone could stop him, the big Yorkshireman plunged over the side into the icy water. Swimming awkwardly under the wildly shivering cable he collided with Bird's boat.

Gasping with the shock of the icy water, he looked at the two men straining on the poles above him in the darkness. 'All right, this time does it. *NOW!*'

With all his bull-like strength, he rammed his shoulder into the skimmer's side, as the other two heaved. The skimmer moved.

'*ONCE AGAIN!*' the gigantic Yorkshireman yelled in triumph, as the craft kept moving, '*COME ON!*'

They needed no urging. Across at Kronstadt, the searchlights were flicking on alarmingly everywhere. While de Vere threw the Thorneycroft wide open with an ear-splitting roar, they heaved with their last remaining strength.

A minute later she was clear and floating in deeper water, apparently undamaged and not shipping water. Bull was swimming hurriedly back to his own skimmer as the searchlights grew closer and closer.

'Slip the tow!' de Vere yelled urgently. 'Slip the beastly tow!' Hastily Ginger complied with his order. The heavy metal hawser splashed and disappeared below the surface, while

Bird cupped his hands and cried gleefully, 'thank you for the assistance, de Vere. I'll stand you a noggin for this one.'

'Never mind the noggin, old man, here they come! Let's get underway,' he thrust open the throttle hastily, a laugh on his sweating face, 'P.D.Q.!'

And with that he was gone, in a sudden fury of water, leaving the absurd catch-phrase trailing behind him like an epitaph . . .

2

In that same instant the veil of mist over the port split. With dramatic suddenness, the whole of the Soviet Fleet was revealed, silhouetted a stark black against Petrograd's lights. Ship after ship lying in their berths like sheep in their pens, waiting to be slaughtered. And even as the aldis lamp began to clatter its urgent white message of alarm and warning, the other four skimmers leapt forward like savage grey hunting dogs released from the leash at last.

As the first wild star shell exploded above them in the dark sky and bathed their twisting, turning shapes in its brilliant icy light, the first skimmer released its fish.

One! Two! A great clanging sound of metal striking metal. A sheet of scarlet flame rent the night. 'Cor blimey!' Ginger cried in awe as a searing light struck his eyes. He closed them hurriedly, as the Red cruiser exploded, its masts tumbling to the heaving deck, metal debris flying through the air everywhere, coal dust and smoke spurting from sudden great holes.

'*A hit . . . a hit!*' Bird cried joyously. '*They've made a hit!*'

Now number two skimmer was going in, according to the plan worked out by the little Admiral. Everywhere the Red machine guns were beginning to wake up to the mortal danger, clacking slowly like rusty typewriters. Green and red tracer zig-zagged slowly through the air, growing ever faster as it approached the boat twisting and turning crazily at high speed, its two wings of water simulating flight over the churning sea. A pom-pom opened up with a steady thump-thump. Lead started to strike the water just in front of the number two skimmer. Bird dug his nails into the palms of his hands. The Bolshy fire was damned accurate now. Would skimmer number two do it? Suddenly the craft lurched violently. For one frightening instant, Bird thought she had been hit. But no! She was swinging round in a great wild curve, the spray flashing twenty feet into air, as she broke off. She had fired her fish!

Seconds later, the torpedoes struck home. Bird cringed with shock at the tremendous explosions. A terrifying orange flame shot into the sky. The Soviet cruiser's deck dissolved into a mass of writhing flame. Even half a mile away as they were, he could feel the sudden heat strike him in the face a physical blow. He opened his mouth and gasped for breath. And as he did so the cruiser started to keel over, the violent flames searing the paint off her buckled plates so that they bubbled and writhed, as if with an independent life of their own. With majestic slowness she began to sink beneath the glowing water. Men sprang screaming overboard, their uniforms aflame. Explosion after explosion ripped her apart below the waterline. Then with frightening suddenness, she disappeared in a great shriek of escaping steam.

'Good grief, sir, did you just get a butcher's hook at that!' Ginger breathed in awe, in the sudden echoing silence that followed. 'I'd never believe it possible, if I hadn't seen it with me own eyes.' Bird nodded, his eyes wide and staring with shock, unable to find the words necessary to express his own awe.

But now the Reds had recovered from their initial shock. Every ship in the fleet, trapped as it was, opened up. Abruptly the sky was criss-crossed brilliantly with red, white and green tracer. At the far end of the harbour a twelve-pounder had opened up. Now, abruptly, skimmers number three and four faced a tremendous barrage, just as Admiral Cowan had predicted they might.

Their young skippers, eager for some desperate glory, did not hesitate a moment. At thirty knots an hour, they hurtled to the attack. In an instant the whole weight of the Red fire concentrated on them. The sea in front of them was ripped apart. It churned and boiled as the gunners peppered it with lead. Still the two skimmers came on. Now it appeared to the watchers in the shadows that a solid burning wall of fire had been suddenly built in front of the two tiny boats. Bird gulped. Surely they would never be able to penetrate it? Repelled yet fascinated, as one is by some terrible nightmare, he watched as they went in for the final kill.

Then in the violent red glare, he saw their objective, the great 10,000 ton fleet tanker. Against the burning background, her every detail was sketched in stark black – derricks, bridge, four smoke stacks, lifeboats and the tiny figures scurrying about her decks in sudden frenzied alarm, as the deadly skimmers got closer and closer.

Skimmer three lurched violently. With a cough of thick yellow smoke, the fish shot from the tubes, ungainly and ugly until they struck the water. Then they were in their element. Remorselessly, gathering speed at every moment, they shot towards their target. In that same second, number four fired its torpedoes. Instantly both were heeling to left and right in a mad flurry of water, as they swung out of danger.

Not a moment too soon. At that distance it was impossible to miss. All four fish struck home, ripping the guts out of the great tanker. The aft fuel tank immediately erupted into a violent searing sheet of flame. Burning oil spilled out over the deck. As the tanker started to tilt, the flaming mass swamped the men crouching there, turning them at once into blazing torches. Sailor after sailor sprang overboard, trailing flames behind them like dying rockets. But now the very water was on fire as a hundred-foot blow-torch hissed terrifyingly across the sea, burning up everything that lay in its path.

Ginger buried his ears in his hands to try to shut out the noise of the drowning, burning men's screams. 'It's 'orrible . . . 'orrible, skipper!' he moaned.

But there was worse to come. As the great glowing carcass of the tanker slowly began to sink to the awful sound of tearing metal, which drowned the horrifying screams of its crew still trapped below, the skipper of number three skimmer was suddenly blinded by a searchlight. Desperately he threw his fast-moving craft from side to side, trying to throw off the blinding light. In vain. And then it happened.

At thirty knots, his skimmer rammed number four at right angles. '*Oh no!*' Bird screamed. '*No, not that!*'

But the skipper of number four kept his head. He stopped his engine instantly and Bird could see him as he waved his hands frantically at the other skipper. He reacted at once. Opening his throttle as far as it would go, both boats locked together at a crazy angle, with number four taking in water at every second, he forced the craft towards the exit of the anchorage and possible safety. Foot by foot, with his Thorneycroft protesting wildly at the impossible strain being placed upon it. The watchers hardly dared breathe.

But the Red gunners were not going to be cheated of their prey. Now every gun in the harbour concentrated its fire on the hopelessly slow, crippled enemy craft. Tracer clawed towards them. A flurry of splashes churned the water around them into a wild heaving fury. Red ripples ran along their decks, tearing them apart. But still the skipper of number three kept the skimmers going.

Now the exit to the anchorage was a matter of yards away. Once they had cleared it, they could gain the protection of the mole. Perhaps there, Bird told himself desperately, they could release the sinking craft and escape in the seaworthy one. After all the Finnish shore was only fifteen miles away.

But that was not to be. Just as the skimmers reached the exit, the whole weight of a salvo from the *Spartak* descended upon them. Whether the great 12-inch shells struck the boats themselves, Bird couldn't see. But when the violet flame and huge burst of yellow smoke had disappeared, the skimmers had gone, vanished from the face of the sea, with only a few planks tossing up and down on the heaving water to mark their passing.

In the loud echoing sound that followed, Bird raised his hand slowly in salute to the brave young men who had died for England far from their Motherland; and as he did so, he realized with an abrupt sense of fear that now it was their turn . . .

*

Hastily Anna finished her prayer and crossed herself in the elaborate Russian fashion. For an instant she glanced upwards, as if that gentle, old man who had been so brutally slaughtered outside two years before were up there observing her. 'Pray for me, Father,' she whispered, 'give me courage to do what I have to do!'

Then with sudden resolve, the past forgotten, she reached out and turned the key. The door to Trotsky's bedroom opened noiselessly. Passing through, she tip-toed to the door of his office, her heart beating furiously, her hand gripping the heavy Cheka revolver, its chamber filled with dum-dum bullets to cause the maximum possible damage.

But in spite of her inner tension, she did not forget the final precaution that he had drilled into her when they had planned the attempt together. With her free hand she took out the small service detectascope, which he had given her.

Carefully, very carefully, she inserted the little device into a small crack in one of the panels of the ancient door and began to turn the fish-eye lens, of the latest globular type, until the dim shadowy outlines of the office came into view. Hastily she adjusted the double globe refractor to ninety degrees. Trotsky's office took on clear sharp contours. It was lofty and well-lit and its floor, unlike every other floor in the Smolny Institute, was cleanly swept and free from the cigarette ends and bread crusts. Still she could not see the men she had come to deal with.

She turned the refractor to a hundred and ten degrees. Two figures, grotesquely distorted by the diminishing properties of the refractor, sprang into view, bent over what might be a map. Hastily she upped it another twenty degrees and then, there they were the two men who had ruined her life. Trotsky, with his great mane of unruly black hair, framing his deathly pale face, and Lenin, his face red and pugnacious under the great domed intellectual forehead. *They were there!*

Gently, taking care to make no noise, she withdrew the little instrument, satisfied they were alone and unarmed, unless they carried hidden revolvers. But by the time they had dragged them out, it would be too late anyway.

Carefully she clicked off the safety catch. 'God, please forgive me,' she whispered to herself. Then taking a deep breath, she gripped the door-knob and began to open the door slowly . . .

*

'All right, Ginger, stand by,' Bird roared as the Thorneycroft burst into full fury, *'Here we go!'* He threw the silk muffler over his right shoulder and let the skimmer have full throttle.

It lurched forward. The roar of the great engine was tremendous, ear splitting. Bird grabbed the rail with his free hand, as the nose suddenly reared upwards violently, while Ginger hung on frantically to the torpedo gear. They were going in for the final attack.

Two hundred yards away to port, de Vere thrust home his throttle. His skimmer roared into action, following Bird's as it raced towards the dark hulk of the 25,000 ton Red battleship. Almost immediately they were spotted by the enemy gunners. White tracer sliced the darkness viciously, as both the land and ship gunners poured a furious fire at the two boats racing for the helpless *Spartak*, tethered in her berth like a doomed animal.

One thousand five hundred yards ... One thousand ... seven hundred and fifty ... The enemy fire was coming at them in a solid red-and-white flaming wall. Shrapnel and slugs were hissing into the foaming water on both sides. But they seemed to bear a charmed life. Nothing could stop them now.

All fear vanished, his eyes gleaming crazily, Bird swung the little craft from side to side in bold zig-zags, laughing uproariously as the tracer zipped harmlessly over his bare head.

Seven hundred yards! The skimmer was hitting the waves at forty knots, like striking a series of solid stone walls. Six hundred yards. *'Stand by tubes!'* he screamed above the crazy roar of the Thorneycroft. Now the *Spartak* filled the horizon, black, massive, seemingly impregnable, violet angry lights flickering the whole length of her armoured upper deck.

Six hundred yards! It was now or never. *'Fire,'* he yelled. *'One – two!'*

The skimmer shuddered violently. There was a cough of yellow smoke. The two deadly fish pounced from the gaping mouths of the tubes. *Splash ... splash!* Angrily they cleaved the water. There was a ripple of bubbles. Their sharp fins dug into their natural element and like two vicious sharks heading for their helpless prey they cut through the water towards the *Spartak*. There was no saving the Soviet heavy battleship now!

As Bird broke to the right in a great wide exhilarating curve that almost swung a gaping Ginger overboard, the fish exploded as one. The night was torn apart. A great white whirling mass of water rushed into the sky, higher than the *Spartak*'s mast. An instant later it was followed by a vivid orange flash. The mast crashed down. A high anguished metal groan drowned even the roar of their motor, as the deck started to take on an angle. Suddenly frightened, crazed men were springing overboard from the stricken ship everywhere. A man dived from one of the control towers, missed his distance, hit the side of the *Spartak* and crumpled into the heaving, already burning water like a sack of wet cement.

But the *Spartak*'s agony was not finished yet. Beaten in the race to hit the enemy first, de Vere brought his wildly racing craft ever closer to deliver the death blow. Six hundred yards – five hundred – four hundred . . .

Crouched over the tubes, a sweating, crimson-faced Bull could see every detail of the stricken battleship – the ever increasing list to port, the great ghostly clouds of steam escaping from her galleys, the panic-stricken Russkie tars, tossing overboard lifebelts, benches, rafts, anything that would float – and felt pity and a sense of loss at the death of this fine ship and her crew.

'*Fire-one!*' de Vere's high-faluting voice (as he called it) cut into his consciousness.

He ripped back the firing-mechanism. The skimmer lurched violently, and relieved of the two ton weight, hissed forward at an ever increasing speed.

'*Fire-two!*'

Bull grunted with the effort. The fish shot into the water with a tremendous splash; and in that same instant, the burst of tracer caught the skipper full in the face, ripping great bloody holes where his eyes had once been and slamming him brutally against the windshield.

Blinded he lay there for a moment, feeling his strength ebb rapidly from him as if someone had opened a tap, and knowing at the same time that he must swing the skimmer round before it crashed head-first into the massive steel side of the sinking battleship.

'*Sir!*' Bull's great howl penetrated into his red blurred consciousness '*Mr de Vere, sir*, we're gonna 'it 'er!'

Blindly he fumbled for the controls, sobbing with pain, the thick hot blood pouring down his ruined young face in twin streams. Desperately he tried to find the steering column. In vain. His fumbling bleeding fingers couldn't locate them.

'*SIR!*' Bull screamed and flung up his hands in front of his face in order to ward off the horror.

'*P.D.Q!*' de Vere gasped weakly, sinking to his knees, '*P.D.Q., old Chap!*'

Then at forty knots they crashed headfirst into the side of the sinking iron monster. They were dead in an instant.

*

'Oh, my gawd!' Ginger cried aghast. 'They got Mr de Vere and that poor old Yorkshire pudden, Bull!'

Instantly Bird throttled back in spite of the searchlights probing the boiling, red water of the harbour everywhere for them.

'*What!*'

'Head-on, skipper – right into the side of that rotten Russkie battleship.'

Ignoring the danger, Bird swung the skimmer round in a great heeling curve of white against the red-hued water. The *Spartak* was rolling over like a gigantic metal whale making a gurgling sound like water escaping from some enormous drain. Around it the sea was covered with bobbing frantic heads. But there was no sign of de Vere or Bull, just a crumpled burning mess of wreckage which might have been their skimmer.

For one long moment, Bird hesitated while the enemy guns hammered away unheard and unnoticed. Should he go in and try to find de Vere's horsey face or Bull's broad ploughboy features among the hundreds of heads bobbing up and down in the water, yelling frantically for help? Or should he turn and make his escape while he still had time?

But then the decision was made for him. A great underwater explosion ripped the keel off the *Spartak*. Blazing oil poured out of her in a scarlet frightening stream, engulfing the men struggling panic-stricken in the water in a flash. Slowly, majestically, the battleship completed the full circle, her propellers dripping and gleaming in the blood-red glare. For a few seconds she was poised there, her inside being torn apart with an awful rending sound by the inrushing water, as the metal carcass glowed a dull red. Another explosion. With a great sigh, what was left of her crashed to the bottom to disappear in a fury of white spray, burning oil and black, vainly struggling sailors. The *Spartak*, the pride of the Soviet Navy, had gone, taking with her all who had survived the initial attack.

Ginger's voice broke the shocked silence that followed. 'Skipper.' Hesitantly he touched Bird's arm. 'Skipper.'

Bird swung round, his face hollowed into a death's head by the dying glare. He stared at Ginger, as if he were seeing him for the very first time. 'What?' he croaked.

Gently, as if he were talking to a small and timid child, and had all the time in the world, the red-haired cockney said: 'Skipper, I think we ought to be making a B-line soon. The Russkies'll be opening up again in half a mo. And there's no use hanging on here any more, is there, sir?'

Lieutenant Bird choked back the hot fury which welled up within him at the terrible waste of the two young lives in this, their moment of absolute triumph. But it was no good. Ginger was right. There should be no more killing. Numbly, he nodded.

Without a word, he took the controls and swung the skimmer round for the last time. Not seeing anything, not hearing, not feeling, he flung the throttle wide open. In a desperate burst of speed, the skimmer shot forward pursued by the angry fire. In a matter of seconds it had disappeared into the night, leaving the burning desolate harbour behind it. The raid was over.

*

A single shot rang out from upstairs.

In an instant the Institute was in a mad turmoil. Suddenly wild-eyed, frightened, Red Guards and workers were blundering up and down the corridors everywhere, screaming, '*counter-revolutionaries . . . murderers!*'

Pressed next to the dying mate, Rosenblum tensed expectantly, his heart beating furiously, his dark eyes fixed on the stairs, as he waited for those three simple words, which would signify that his great plan had succeeded: '*Lenin is dead!*'

But they were not to come.

Suddenly a great roar went up from the mob, as a slight shabby figure appeared at the head of the stairs, his face deathly pale, a blood-stained handkerchief wrapped round his right wrist. 'Comrades,' he cried. '*Comrades listen to me!*'

The roar died down.

Rosenblum felt the grey bitterness of defeat sweep through his crouched body in an almost tangible wave. The back of his mouth was sour with bile. The girl had failed. Her shot – if it were hers? – *had missed the Red Dictator.*

'There has been an attempt on my life. But it failed. Comrade Trotsky was too quick for the assassin. Look!' Lenin commanded. Two of his leather-coated bodyguards dragged an unconscious, bleeding Anna to the head of the stairs so that the mob could see her quite clearly.

'This is what we will do with all those who try to sabotage the Workers' and Peasants' Republic!' Lenin yelled triumphantly.

'*A miracle . . . he has been saved . . . a miracle!*' the words flew from mouth to mouth.

Rosenblum waited no longer. Swinging round, he forced his way through the excited throng. Nobody tried to stop him until he was almost at the door. Then suddenly the big exit was flooded with the special, leather-clad troops, the Lettish Guard Battalion, whose only loyalty was to Lenin himself. '*Bumagi* – papers,' they were demanding from the Red Guards and civilians crowding there in their attempt to leave the Institute.

Rosenblum hesitated. His Cheka pass usually opened any door for him. Even the leather-coated Letts were afraid of the secret police. But what if the girl had already talked? Were they searching for him.

'Hey you,' a giant Lett pushed his way through the crowd, his face dark with suspicion. 'What you hanging around there for?' he asked in his atrocious Russian. '*Bumagi!*' He thrust out a huge paw for the pass.

Rosenblum made a play of fumbling in his pocket, lowering his head so that the giant towering above him did not see the sudden look of determination in his dark, shifty eyes. 'Here you are,' he said and in that same moment, brought up his knee sharply – right into the Lett's crotch.

The giant's scream of sheer agony was choked in the surge of vomit which welled up in his throat. His hands clutching frantically for his injured groin, he sank helplessly to his knees vomit trickling out of his gaping mouth.

'What's going on?' a voice suddenly alarmed called behind him as he swung round and began to run. A whistle blew shrilly. '*Sabotazhniki!*' someone yelled in alarm. '*Provocatori!*' A revolver cracked and a slug whined off the plaster a foot above his head, showering him with white dust. A bespectacled clerk thrust out his foot. Rosenblum sprang over it easily. In that same instant, he slammed his fist into the man's pale face. He staggered back, blood spurting from his smashed nose. Rosenblum ran on. Desperately he tried to find some way out of the trap he found himself in as he doubled down the corridor. Now they would be alerting the guards everywhere. For a moment he thought of one of the big windows. But a second later he abandoned the idea. They would be waiting for him with machine guns outside. Then he had it – the big kitchens below the former refectory down in the basement.

He pelted down the steps. The sudden alarm had emptied the place of its guests. Now it was occupied only by a couple of cooks, squatting at one of the littered tables eating their own food in lazy, silent contemplation. They started as he clattered through. One of them shouted something. He ran on. A man in a dirty white apron tried to stop him at the door of the kitchen. Still running, he shot him from the waist. The man's knees started to buckle underneath him, his eyes wide with pain and surprise, blood seeping through the dirty fingers clasped to his stomach. Rosenblum blundered by and into the steaming kitchen.

He slammed the door behind him. Fortunately no one had stolen the bolt as they had stolen everything else in the Institute. He rammed it home. Outside the cries of rage and alarm were getting louder. There was no time to be lost. His chest heaving wildly, he threw his gaze round the room frantically, searching in desperate haste for the means of escape. Then he spotted it. The trap that led to the sewer. Because Peter the Great had built his city on a marsh in close proximity to the sea, the sewers in Petrograd were as high as man to allow for the great volume of water that swirled under the city at high tide. Desperately he began to claw at the catch.

Outside, heavy shoulders were being launched at the door. It started to splinter. He yelped with pain as one of his nails was torn off by the stubborn trap. He struggled on, his nerves jingling with fear. 'Get out of the way,' a gruff voice commanded. 'I'll shoot the rotten lock off!' A shot rang out. The wood splintered. But the door still did not give. 'It hasn't got a lock,' another voice protested. 'It's bolted!'

'Why in three devils' name didn't you say so,' someone cursed, as shoulders rammed the door once more.

In that same moment, the trap came up. Rosenblum gave a great gasp of relief. He had done it.

A nauseating smell of fetid waste assailed his nostrils. Taking a swift breath, he dropped neatly into the sewer below, just as the door was smashed open and the Letts stumbled into the kitchen.

*

The first shot crashed into the sewer, the muzzle flash like a bursting scarlet flower. He started to run, staggering down the round tunnel by the faint light that came in from outside. Behind him heavy feet dropped onto the concrete. 'Which way did he go?' someone demanded.

'If you'd shut your great trap, we might be able to hear,' another voice answered angrily.

Rosenblum ran wildly on, not knowing where he was going, aware only that he had to put as much distance as he could between him and them before they took up the pursuit. All around him there was a confusion of pipes and tubes, covered in dirt and ugly white fungi, all dripping in the stench and slime of centuries.

Behind him they too were running now. He could hear the clatter of heavy nailed boots. Twisting and turning desperately in and out of the stinking corridors, the running green walls rushing by in a wild phantasmagoria, the desperate man tried to throw them off. In vain. The sound of their boots were getting ever closer! In another couple of moments they would be on him.

And then Rosenblum had a stroke of luck. Running blindly into another corridor, his feet stepped into space and in an instant, screaming in panic, he was falling.

With a hellish splash he plunged into the stinking, stagnant water of the drainage pool. Fighting desperately, gasping for air, he sank and rose again, striking the green scummy surface with wild flailing arms. And then he controlled himself. Of course this was it!

Just as the heavy nailed boots came level with him, he took a deep breath and ducked his head under the stinking water. The boots hesitated. There was a distorted mumble of many voices. A torch flashed across the still surface of the pool. He could see its beam gleaming through the green scum. A second later it flicked away and they were running on up the corridor. He counted to twenty and plunged to the surface, gasping for air, his lungs threatening to burst at any moment.

*

Fighting off the waves of nausea caused by the fumes, Rosenblum staggered down the main sewer, blundering blindly against the dripping brick walls, driven on by unreasoning terror that he might never escape from the underground chambers again. Now he had forgotten his pursuers, wherever they might be; his sole concern was to get out of this nightmarish world of dank, dripping desolation.

Time passed leadenly. He fought his way through a foaming, evil-smelling cascade of water, which told him he couldn't be too far from the surface. Still the air was foul and close. That meant he was not yet near any exit from the frightening, confusing rabbit warren of sewers. He blundered on, fighting off the heavy lassitude which threatened to overcome him at any moment. Once he stopped, he knew the sewer gas would kill him; he would die alone and untended, lost to the world for ever. Stark atavistic fear forced him on. *He must find an exit!*

Suddenly his stumbling progress through the endless corridors came to a shocked halt. In the dim halflight, he could just make out two vague figures crouched there strangely, in silent, almost animal expectation.

He let his shoulders sink despondently and waited for them to arrest him. But the two figures did not move. What seemed an age, passed. Nothing happened. Hoarsely, his spirit broken at last, he croaked: 'Well – come on you devils!'

Still they did not move.

Hesitantly he moved forward a little. He gasped with a thrill of horror. They could not move because they were dead! Slowly, his boots echoing hollowly in the still chamber, his whole body tense with horror, he advanced upon them.

They were a man and woman – peasants by the look of their thick hands. But it was not their hands which drew his attention. It was their bare knees! Limp like broken puppets, they crouched on barbed hooks, which had been driven into them from behind so that the hooks skewering the kneecaps had forced them to crouch in this horrifying fashion, as they had bleated out their pain-racked answers to their torturers' harsh questions.

Now the sight of their terrible mutilations no longer horrified Rosenblum. Instead, they made his heart leap with joy, for he recognized their origin; they were the work of the Cheka torturers, who he had watched often enough at work in the cellars above his head. *He was directly below the Cheka Headquarters – and that house of terror was only twenty metres away from the banks of the River Neva!*

*

Ten minutes later, he was stumbling crazily in the direction from which the blessed cold air was coming, fervently sucking in great lungfuls of it. Wildly he crashed his body against the rotten wood of the door which barred his way. It gave instantly and next moment he was falling wildly onto the wet sand, sobbing madly like a little child woken from a bad dream.

Five minutes later, he had clambered up the embankment and, head tucked deeply into the collar of his soaked greatcoat, was hurrying through the now silent streets to the Countess' home and escape . . .

THREE

THE RESCUE

'She will have another forty-eight hours, yes that would be it, Lieutenant Bird, two days!'

1

Moodily Bird lay on his rough bed, hands beneath his head, staring at the peeling ceiling of his little room. Outside they were having a noisy party, celebrating their success at the Red Track Approach, drowning their losses in the captured Red firewater which Cowan, together with his telegram of congratulations, had sent up for the survivors. But Dickie Bird had not been able to stand the forced gaiety for long. His mind was too full still of de Vere's and Bull's death – and Anna's disappearance without the slightest trace. He had wound up the horn gramophone for a last time and excused himself.

Now he lay in sad contemplation on his bunk, thinking of all which had happened since they had left England so confidently, so full of hope, only a few weeks before. Beyond his window the spring day began to give way to the soft stillness of the Finnish night.

Cowan's long signal had hinted at decorations for gallantry for all of them, including the dead. But the knowledge that he might one day be presented to the King himself to receive his Distinguished Service Order, a thought which would have enthralled him only a matter of days before, left him strangely cold and apathetic. What did it matter now that they were gone? Outside that sad little song about the roses 'which bloom in Picardy', which had been so popular in the last years of the war had begun on the old scratchy gramophone record yet again. He closed his eyes, utterly weary and despondent. Slowly, as the harsh northern light outside started to fade away, to be replaced by a faint restful violet, he drifted off into an uneasy, exhausted sleep.

*

'Dickie . . . Bird . . . Dickie Bird,' the excited voices seemed to come from miles away. 'Wakey-wakey . . . come on now, rise and shine. Show a leg there!' Rough hands shook him.

The urgent drunken voices did the trick. He opened his eyes to find Shaw and the Colonial, an Australian volunteer for the skimmers, staring down at him, red-faced and excited.

'What is it?' he stuttered, licking his scummed dry lips.

'We've got a turn-up for the book,' Shaw said drunkenly, swaying violently.

'Eh?' Bird sat up suddenly,

'Yer,' the Colonial drawled, 'there's some civvie bloke out there, wanting to see you, Dickie . . . Said he's just come over the frontier from Bolshy-land. Asked for you by name, he did. Lieutenant Horatio Bird, as I live and breathe.' He stared triumphantly at Bird.

'What did you say?'

'You heard me – or have all you Pommies got cloth-ears? Asked for you by name.' He hiccuped suddenly and clapped his hand to his mouth. 'Excuse me, must have been those dog biscuits we had for supper.'

'More likely all that *aquavit* you've been swigging,' Shaw replied.

'Where is this chap?' Bird cut in urgently, swinging himself off the bed.

'In there, feeding his face, as if he'd not eaten anything in a month of Sundays! I told him—'

Bird did not wait to hear more. Leaving them standing there, he flung open the door to the main room and stopping abruptly, stared at the ragged, dark-looking man with a bloody bandage round his left hand, who was wolfing down thick corned-beef and hard tack sandwiches under the admiring gaze of a red-faced Ginger and the rest of the ratings. 'Strewth, skipper,' Ginger said, seeing him there so suddenly, 'the beggar's already polished off three of 'em. Must have a jaw like a nut-cracker!'

Bird held up his hand for silence, as the ragged civilian lowered the sandwich slowly. 'You are Bird – Lieutenant Horatio Bird – I suppose?' he said with only a trace of an accent, his dark eyes sizing up the young officer's face.

'Yes. But what is this? How did you know my name? What do you wish to speak to me about—'

The strange civilian touched his lips with his bandaged hand for silence. It was a curious gesture, reminding Bird of his nanny in the nursery. It worked. Bird stopped his flow of eager questions, although a little voice within him was screaming: '*Do you know Anna? ... do you know where she is?*'

Slowly the civilian got to his feet and clicked his heels together, as if he were some grand foreign swell. 'May I introduce myself,' he said. 'My name is Reilly – Sidney Reilly.' At the door Shaw tittered drunkenly. '*Reilly* – with that accent! Go on will you, pull the other one – it's got bells on it. You'll be telling us next you're from Dublin!' There was a ripple of laughter from the others.

The civilian's dark hawklike face displayed no emotion, neither amusement nor anger. 'No,' he said carefully. 'Not from Dublin, Lieutenant, but from Tipperary.'

Suddenly something clicked in Bird's head. The man's English was immaculate; he knew all about the skimmer base – hadn't he asked for him by name – and the first letter of his surname was 'R'. Hadn't Anna said that was how the spy network over the water in Petrograd had received its code-name?

Bird swallowed hard. 'Then, you must be the head of the R-Network, C told me about?'

The other man nodded gravely. 'That is correct. *Sidney Reilly, alias Abraham Rosenblum!*' And there was no mistaking the pride with which he said the words.

*

Hastily Bird thrust a mug of the fiery Finnish *aquavit* under the hooked nose of the mysterious stranger. 'Listen Mr Reilly,' he said almost desperately, while the others stared at him, their drunken smiles frozen in surprise now, 'I must know what has happened to Anna von Klauwitz. You were the head of the R-Network – her chief – you *must* know!'

'My whole network is probably destroyed by now – or will be within the next forty-eight hours.' He took a sip of the *aquavit* and coughed. 'The Cheka works swiftly.'

'*But Anna?*' Bird persisted. 'What has happened to Anna?'

'Calm yourself, Lieutenant, please. I shall tell you what happened to Anna.' He shrugged suddenly, a gesture strangely foreign to that carefully cultivated English accent of his. 'I warned her, I ordered her not to, I pleaded with her. But she wouldn't listen to me. Her desire for vengeance was too—'

'What the devil did she do, man?' Bird roared, beside himself at the agent's procrastination. 'Spit it out for God's sake. *What*?'

'She tried to assassinate Lenin,' Reilly announced, as if he were making a casual statement about the weather, in no way moved by the young officer's anger.

There was a shocked gasp from the others. 'Cor, chase me up a blooming gum tree!' Ginger whispered, his bright blue eyes suddenly filled with shocked awe. 'What did she go and do that for?'

'It was all part of the plot, you see,' Reilly explained easily. 'If the Bolshevik dictator had died, the whole rotten Red house of cards would have fallen apart just like that,' he clicked his thumb and finger together contemptuously. 'Then your General Gough could have co-ordinated a three-pronged attack on Petrograd from south and north, with a seaborne landing somewhere here in the Gulf. With your destruction of the Central Fleet, nothing would have been able to stop that. But the main thing on which everything hinged was her assassination of Lenin.' He shrugged again. 'Unfortunately that attempt failed. Now we will have to commence once again from the start. That is why I am here – you must get me to General Gough's headquarters in Helsingfors immediately. I must inform him of the situation . . .'

Lieutenant Bird was not listening any more. Now all the pieces clicked into place, and suddenly he realized that they had been dupes – de Vere, Bull, himself, *Anna*. Innocents abroad, manipulated like living puppets by cunning, devious, skilled puppeteers such as Reilly, C and whoever his chief might be. Their youth, their patriotism, their absurd enthusiasm had been shamefully abused. But there was no time now for recriminations, for the past. Suddenly he knew that it was the future that counted.

'Reilly,' he interrupted the civilian's flow of words, his rage

144

still there, but absolutely under control now, 'you say that Anna made an attempt on Lenin's life and failed. Did they – kill her?'

'No, Lieutenant, they didn't kill her. They arrested her. Just before I made my escape, I saw Lenin's bodyguard bring her out of Trotsky's office where the attempt was made . . . She was alive *then*.'

'I see,' Bird said carefully, banishing the look of contempt from his eyes at Reilly's cowardly abandonment of his key agent. He needed the man; he mustn't rub him up the wrong way. 'Now, Mr Reilly, what will they do with her – if she's still alive at this moment?'

'Last August they shot Dora Kaplan the morning after she had made her attempt on Lenin's life. You recall?'

Bird nodded. 'But Anna?'

'No, she will still be alive,' he answered, his eyes thoughtful. 'Kaplan was killed because Lenin was not expected to live. Her killing was a spontaneous reaction on the part of the Cheka, an expression of pure rage and desire for revenge. In this case, dear Comrade Lenin,' he sneered over the words, 'was unfortunately uninjured. Hence the Cheka will want to wring everything they can out of her; her contacts, the members of her network, and so on. My guess is that they must have started working on her this morning, as soon as she recovered consciousness—'

'Consciousness?' Bird asked hurriedly.

'Yes, when I last saw her yesterday, they had – er – beaten her unconscious. So let us assume they have started questioning her early today, the gentlemen from the Cheka; they will have already got her to betray her comrades within the network. Oh, yes, my dear Lieutenant, they all talk sooner or later when the Cheka has them in its clutches! I could tell you stories, but no matter. Now she will have another forty-eight hours of life while they find those she has betrayed in order to check that she has been speaking the truth.' He wet his thick sensual lips with the fiery spirits and coughed delicately behind an upraised hand. 'My guess is she has two days to live . . . yes, that would be it, Lieutenant Bird, *two days*!'

*

Bird paced his little room, its wooden floor squeaking regularly under his slow stride, while outside the suddenly sober sailors plied their unexpected visitor with curious questions about the happenings in Petrograd. He paused every now and again, his face creased in a thoughtful frown, to peer out of the little window at the sea, smooth-sparkling and silent in the silver light of the spring moon.

'*Only fifteen miles off,*' he whispered to himself during these pauses. '*Fifteen lousy miles.*'

Suddenly he remembered the pictures of Dora Kaplan they had published in the paper the previous summer with the accounts of her assassination attempt. She had had a dark placid face with emotionless, unnaturally calm eyes, as if she had known what her fate was to be right from the start, and had accepted it with apathetic resignation.

He paused again and looked out of the window at the faint pink glow in the middle of the horizon, which was Petrograd. '*Fifteen miles,*' he whispered to himself once more; then with sudden resolve, he hammered his fist against the sill and snarled, his face contorted violently, 'but damn me, *she* won't die! *I won't let her!*'

He strode over to his bunk and dropped on it, his mind racing as a rough-and-ready plan began to form there. For another twenty-four hours or so, the three remaining skimmers were under his direct control until Admiral Cowan decided to withdraw them to his own base in the Gulf of Biorko. In essence he was in command and he did not anticipate any trouble from Shaw and the Colonial; after all they had joined the CMB Service for adventure – and he would give them that, by God, he would! Thus, once he had committed his skimmers, it would be too late for any superior officer to do anything about it. They could court-martial him if they liked, but he didn't care, as long as he could save Anna.

His mind made up, suddenly for the first time in a life dominated by his father, the Admiral, the harsh restrictions and inhibitions he had learned at Dartmouth and the stifling traditions of the Royal Navy, he was in full command of himself and the situation. He opened the door to the other room. For once, he was going to run his own show.

'Reilly,' he snapped, 'I'd like to speak to you.'

The spymaster spun round and stared at the pale-faced, determined young man framed in the door. 'Yes – *Lieutenant* Bird, what can I do for you?'

'Answer a few simple questions.'

'With pleasure.' He shrugged cynically, 'but whether my answers will be so simple – that is something else.'

Bird ignored the comment. 'According to you, Anna is imprisoned by the Cheka. Now where is the Cheka Prison in Petrograd?' He stepped briskly to the table and spread his own map of the city and its approaches across the littered surface. 'Point it out to me would you, please?'

'It is here on the River Neva, not far from the Winter Palace at the *Ulitsa Gogala*.'

'I see. And it is a regular prison? With heavy fortifications and so on?'

Reilly looked at him incredulously. 'You don't mean that you intend—'

'Please just answer my questions?' Bird cut him short, coldly.

'Well, no, it is a former *Okrana* – the old Czarist Secret Police headquarters, and they didn't want to advertise their presence by such things. You understand, hm?'

Bird nodded and relapsed into a thoughtful silence for an instant while Reilly and the rest stared at him in bewildered curiosity. He remembered catching a glimpse of the Neva delta the night he had landed Anna. It had been fringed with high dense rushes, in which it would not be too difficult to hide a boat, close enough in to reach the shore without trouble but far enough out to prevent it being seen by some curious passer-by. 'So if we landed here between Lissy Nos Point and—'

'*Lissy's nose*, sir, did you say?' Ginger chortled. 'What kind of Russian moniker is that?'

But Bird ignored his little cockney's attempt at humour; he had no time for that now. Time was of the essence. 'As I was saying, between that Point and Krestorsky Island here, how far would I have to go to reach your Cheka HQ?'

Reilly pursed his thick lips. 'As the crow flies perhaps four miles, the first three across marshy difficult ground, before you reach the first road leading into Petrograd. But my dear young man,' he raised his voice in expostulation, 'surely you can't be thinking of making some absurd scheme of rescuing the girl?'

'That is exactly what I am doing,' Bird replied firmly without a moment's hesitation.

'Good on you, Dickie Bird!' the Colonial cried, obviously well aware now – perhaps from Ginger – who Anna was and what she meant to the young officer. 'Good on you!'

'But it's impossible, Bird. Well, first of all you don't speak a word of Russian—'

'Then I'll take you with me.'

Reilly shook his head firmly. 'No, it is not that I am afraid to go back, but I have other plans. Our lives are not important in the face of the future of the whole Western world. I must get to General Gough as soon as possible. Besides, what use would I be to you now? My photograph will be posted up throughout Petrograd. I am a wanted man. I should only be a burden to you.'

Bird considered for a moment. 'I have five hundred sovereigns with me,' he said. 'With that you should be able to find me someone who can speak Russian. Besides,' he made that gesture with his thumb and forefinger which he had first seen Anna use on the day they had landed in Finland, 'I've been given to understand you can buy everything in Russia, even in these days of proletarian power. Can't you also find me someone in the Cheka who is prepared to turn a blind eye?' He stopped and stared at the other man expectantly.

Reilly looked back at him with new respect. 'My dear Lieutenant I can see that you have learned a great deal very quickly since coming to our northern climes. Money does talk as you say.' He tugged his long hooked nose thoughtfully, his dark eyes gleaming with the new challenge. Finally, he spoke. 'If you ensure that I'm brought safely to Viborg railway station the first thing tomorrow morning—'

'I shall take you there personally.'

'Good. If that's a promise, this is what I suggest. The latest addition to my – er – network before I fled, was Countess Fleur de Courcy, a Russian woman of noble blood who married—'

'Oh get on with it, Reilly,' Bird snapped impatiently, 'time is running out.'

'Well, no one suspects her because no one knew about her association with the – er – network.'

'Would she help us?'

'Yes, but *not* for money. She has plenty of that in her late husband's Swiss bank account,' Reilly looked knowingly at Bird, his mind already making new plans – plans which would need the kind of financial backing that Fleur de Courcy could give him. 'Her price for helping you would be her freedom. *If* – and it is a big if – you did manage to rescue Anna and bring her out of that accursed country over there, you would have to take Fleur with you.'

'I promise,' Bird snapped hastily. 'So I would need details of where she lives etc and some sort of note of introduction.'

'You will have it, my dear Lieutenant,' Reilly said swiftly, realizing that the boy and his hare-brained scheme might be useful to him after all. 'You will also have a pass signed by me, identifying you an American reporter of social democrat persuasion. Ever since that fool Reed [1] was taken up by Lenin last year, American journalists have been able to go where they like and do what they like in Russia.'

'Good – and the other person in the Cheka?'

Reilly hesitated. 'That is exceedingly difficult. You must realize that the Cheka is the strong right arm of the Bolshevik movement. Its members are supposed to be one hundred percent dyed-in-the-wool Reds. However, in all organizations such as the Cheka with its unlimited power, there are always men who join because of some personal defect, some want, some desire that they could never attain under normal circumstances. Perverts, homosexuals, sadists and the like. You understand?'

'Yes. I understand. Get on with it Reilly.'

'Well, there is one such man in their ranks in Petrograd.' He tugged his chin thoughtfully. 'Krylenko, a Ukrainian, the chief interrogator, enormously fat, hairless, completely and disgustingly devoted to his belly and the pleasures of the table, in a country where one is lucky if one can obtain a piece of black

---

1. i.e. John Reed, the author of *Ten Days that Shook the World*, an account of the October Revolution, to which Lenin wrote the foreword. Reed died of typhus in Moscow and is buried in the walls of the Kremlin.

bread and a chunk of salt pork once a day. Of all my colleagues, he was the only one I was afraid of.'

'Why?'

'Because somehow or other I think he recognized in me a kindred soul. A person who was living two lives, and wasn't what he was supposed to be. I was a Cheka official, but in reality a British agent. He, too, is a Cheka official, but he is also something else.' He shrugged. 'What, I do not know. But of such men one has to be careful. Maybe he is your man?'

'And where can the Countess Fleur de Courcy find him, if she agrees to work for us?' Bird asked, clutching at this straw.

'Oh that is easy. Every evening you will find him in the Uncle Tom's Cabin, a *traktir*,[1] much frequented by black marketeers and the like, stuffing his face with as much food as he can shovel into it at black market prices.'

'Good, good,' Bird said eagerly. He swung round and faced the others. 'Listen chaps, you've heard there might still be a chance for Anna if we act quickly, and boldly. Didn't the Admiral tell us before we set off on the last show – "nothing is ever worth doing unless there's a risk attached to it. Always choose the boldest course." '

'Too right!' the Colonial said loudly. 'That little man in blue truly did!'

'Well, *I'm* going to choose the boldest course. I'm going to go in and get her out of that hellhole before the Admiral can ever find out. If I don't come back, well—' he left the sentence unfinished. 'Now, I can go it alone, but it'd be a helluva sight easier if you'd back me up.'

'All aboard for the *Skylark*,' Ginger cried. 'You can count me in, Skipper. Anything fer a larf!'

'And me too,' Shaw and the Colonial snapped as one. 'We might all get the big putty medal for this one, eh?' Behind them their mechanics raised their hands like schoolboys volunteering to answer some severe inspector's question, clicking their fingers in their eagerness to be taken along. 'We'll go, sir! *Us too!*'

Bird felt tears of gratitude well up into his eyes. Hastily he fought them back. 'Thank you, chaps, this is awfully ... awfully

1. Low class inn.

good of you. I don't know how to thank you!'

'No thanks called for, old lad,' the big Colonial said jovially, 'only another swig of that rotgut to keep up me courage, that's all.' Suiting his actions to his words, he picked up the stone jug and took a huge swallow of the fiery liquid, which set him off coughing and spluttering as if he would never stop.

Next to him, Shaw carried away with high spirits, thrust out his right arm in the old Roman salute and cried out in his best public school Latin: *'Ave Caesar, morituri te salutamus!'*

'Cor stuff a duck, what's that when it's at home, Mister Shaw?' Ginger Coates gasped.

'I'll tell you,' Reilly said, his dark face full of poorly concealed contempt at the foolish antics of these overgrown schoolboys in uniform, who would never see another spring. 'It means – "Hail Caesar, we who are about to die salute thee!"'

'Cripes, what a funny thing to say,' was Leading Rating Coates' sole reply . . .

2

Longingly Krylenko stared at the girl's unconscious body, the saliva of desire dribbling down his fat smooth hairless chin as she lay there on the table in the interrogation cellar. They had strapped her down in such a way that her fine breasts and the soft down of the Hill of Venus (as he liked to think of it in his romantic fashion) were thrust up in an unnatural, highly provocative manner, so that he could hardly concentrate on the report on her he was writing for his chief, Felix Dzerzhinski, the head of the Cheka.

In the end he dropped it onto the table in disgust, and absently took up his big blue-steel revolver, which he always kept at hand; somehow it gave him great comfort at such moments of despair. With his soft pudgy hand he stroked its hard powerful barrel, his little red eyes glued to her body. She was beautiful – very beautiful – in spite of the marks the torturers had left on her flesh. She had a true athlete's body: long muscular legs, trim small waist and small, yet tremendously desirable firm breasts, the nipples erect in the coolness of the Cheka cellar.

He licked his lips and recalled what had happened that morning when they had first brought her in from the Smolny Institute for interrogation. Systematically, almost clinically, they had raped her on that same table, the four of them, ripping down their pants and with them hanging around their ankles, thrusting themselves brutally into her writhing, struggling body. Then the last of his subordinates, that swine Alexei with his tough ex-docker's muscles and coarse vulgar tongue, had had the audacity to ask *him*, the chief interrogator, whether he would 'like to pump a little air into the murdering bitch?' When he had refused, the bastard had turned to the others and remarked as he pulled up his trousers with deliberate exhibitionist slowness, 'Boys, you know what they say about tall men, don't you? They're like tall houses – the bottom floor is the worst furnished!' And the rest of them had laughed knowingly in their vulgar manner.

Krylenko stroked the hard, long metal tumescence of his revolver and dismissed the matter. Alexei was always tormenting him, but one day he would force him to eat his words. Slowly he rose to his feet, still gripping his revolver firmly in his right hand, and stared at himself in the fly-blown dirty mirror which adorned one wall of the grimy, yellow-lit cellar.

Didn't he look immensely strong and tall, with miner's shoulders and thighs like those of a wrestler, the material of his cheap suit hardly able to contain them? He wiped the back of his pudgy hand across his thick, dark red lips and asked his image in the mirror when he, too, would experience the rapturous explosion of blood and body which was everyone's right? *When?*

He groaned out loud with the sheer misery of it all. Some had suggested fermented mare's milk in the Georgian fashion and he had drunk it by the litre; but to no avail. Others had recommended garlic and he had wolfed it down until his breath could have felled an ox at twenty paces. Still no use. Oysters, whores, stinging nettles, the knout – he had tried everything; yet he had still not been able to savour those tremendously exciting pleasures which were his birthright. Even these last months in the Cheka, which he had joined because he had known it would give him absolute power over the prisoners, male and female, had not yet given him that which he longed for so desperately.

Still holding the comforting, hard weight of the revolver in his hand, he walked slowly and thoughtfully to the girl, spread out in all her exciting nakedness – his for the taking. He swallowed hard and ran his little eyes over her body greedily, examining every inch of her – every delightful hollow, mound, secret orifice – feeling his heart beat more swiftly as he did so.

Gingerly he reached out his free hand and touched her firm woman's flesh. A shiver ran through his gross body, making the fat folds of his jowls quiver with passion. Gently he ran his fingers across her shallow breasts. How wonderful! He gripped the butt of the big revolver harder, and probed her unconscious body even further, running one carefully manicured forefinger into that dark, secret, damp orifice.

She groaned softly and squirmed. Her eye-lashes flickered momentarily, but she did not wake up; the beatings had been too severe. She remained unconscious.

His breath was coming in short, shallow gasps now, the saliva dripping from his slack open mouth onto her flat belly; his fist grasping the revolver ever tighter.

Suddenly he lost control of himself altogether. Moaning wildly, feeling the blood pound furiously at his temples, he ripped open his flies and prepared to mount her. But when he saw what was there – that terrible, hellishly disappointing nothing – he caught himself in time. Again it had not worked!

Sobbing almost hysterically, he staggered back across the cellar, his flies still open, his shame exhibited to anyone who might come in. He stared at his crimson, distorted, fat face in the mirror, the sweat-beads dribbling down its smooth hairless expanse. 'Krylenko,' he croaked, 'you bastard, you have failed again. *Failed!*' He flashed a bitterly accusing glance at his own features, his eyes filling with sudden tears of rage and self-pity, and half-raised the revolver to his right temple. He caught himself just in time. But one day – one day!

He pulled himself together. Slowly, savouring the comfort its long hardness gave him, he thrust the revolver into its leather holster and fastened up his flies. Now he would go to Uncle

Tom's and eat — eat, eat until his massive belly threatened to burst and he could fall into his bed, his body satiated with food and his mind blank, to fall into the blessed forgetfulness of sleep ...

*

The nightmare started to die away.

Framed against the whirling blood-red background of the cellar, the stark black, brutal features of the interrogator with his knout and harsh eyes began to fade away. Behind him those relentless, savagely-rapped out questions echoed and re-echoed, *'who put you up to this ... where did you get the Cheka uniform and pistol from ... what is the R-Network ... names, names, names ... where does he live ... what does she look like ... names, names, names?'* ... But slowly they, too, and her shameful answers disappeared into the distance.

The dark mist began to clear. With a sheer effort of will, Anna von Klaustein pulled her tortured body back to reality. At last the nightmare vanished to be replaced by the worse one of reality.

She opened her eyes and stared up at the naked bulb, burning above her head. For what seemed a long time she gazed at its opaque, fly-blown surface; then with infinite slowness she raised her head and stared round the empty, grey cellar. The full reality of her situation flooded back on her immediately. With a groan she let her dark head sink back on the wooden block once again.

In a flash, the happenings of the last twenty-four hours rushed by her mind's eye in all their terrifying detail: the failed assassination; the beating; the Cheka cellar and that hideous multiple rape, their greedy lips sucking at her mouth, her breasts, their hard paws biting deep into her soft flesh; and then the confessions. She groaned out loud. She had betrayed them all, every single one of them.

How could she? 'My God, how could I do such a thing?' she cried at the blank, unfeeling ceiling. 'I should have bitten through my veins ... seized one of their pistols and killed my-self ... *anything, but that shame*!'

For a while she wept softly, the tears streaming down her

poor battered cheeks without restraint, her body heaving, racked by her misery and shame like a small child. Then an almost fatalistic calm overcame her. Her breast heaved a couple of times more and the tears stopped for good.

Outside, the first tram was running down the Neva embankment, its bells muted by the prison's thick walls, but still audible. It was the first pre-dawn tram heading for the suburbs to pick up the workers, ringing its bell as usual as if to spite those who were still abed, although it was forbidden to ring a bell within the city.

Anna breathed out hard. It would not be much longer before the new day began. By nightfall they would have found the young ex-priest Serge, who had been one of Rosenblum's key agents. He would be the last. They would confront her with him, his face battered and terrified as had been the faces of the others on the day before. Then her usefulness to them would be at an end. They would execute her and toss her dead body into the sewers as they had done with those of the others – or so her grinning torturers had said.

As the city slowly began to come to life again, to face a new day, Anna von Klaustein realized she had thirty-six hours – at the most – to live. And she was glad . . .

3

The run in past the entrance forts on the northern channel, had been surprisingly easy, thanks to Shaw and the Colonial, and to Ginger's brilliant idea. As soon as he had returned from escorting the mysterious spymaster to Viborg on the first leg of his journey to the Finnish capital, Ginger Coates had approached Bird and said in his usual cockney manner, 'Skipper, I've been giving your plan some thought.'

'That's very kind of you,' Bird replied ironically. 'I hope it didn't keep you awake all night.'

Ginger, his brow creased in deep thought, had ignored the irony. 'Well, you see, it's like this here, sir. If we go in now, it'll be the third time and them Russkies'll know what we can and can't do. So they'll cotton on to us right sharpish this time. It stands to reason, don't it.'

'It certainly does,' Bird had been forced to admit, for the cheeky Londoner had given voice to his own unspoken doubts about the mission.

'Well, sir, it's them ruddy Thorneycrofts what attracts their attention to us, ain't it?'

Bird nodded.

'So, we go in *without* the engines!' he had grinned triumphantly at the officer.

Bird had looked at him, as if he had gone out of his head and asked sourly, 'Have you been at that Finnish firewater again, Ginger?'

'Ner, sir, I had a skinful of that rotgut last night! No, this is the way I see it. If we can rig up a rough-and-ready sail, we could use it to pass through and then when we're past the Russkie fortress, we can open up the Thorneycroft again. And perhaps we could get the other two gents to run their skimmers up and down the minefield so that the Russkies'll flash their searchlights out into the Gulf – and away from yours truly, Mrs Coates' darling boy.'

The idea had worked like a dream. With the Colonial and Shaw racing up and down at thirty knots beyond the Tolbukhin Lighthouse making a hideous racket, they had sailed past the guns by the way of the northern channel, without as much as a Russian even noticing them.

Now with the lights of Petrograd growing ever larger, they crawled in between the Elegin lighthouse and the township of Lakhta, the dark mass of the delta looming up as it came to meet them. 'Take her easy,' Bird whispered.

'Ay, ay, sir – easy it is,' Ginger replied, his voice equally low and tense.

'Cut the motor!'

Ginger obeyed instantly. The Thorneycroft died away in a flash and almost noiselessly they approached the dark hostile shore, which Bird surveyed anxiously, half-tensed for the angry shout and sudden crack of a rifle which would indicate they had been spotted by some Bolshy patrol.

Nothing happened.

Grasping his boat-hook, he began to take soundings, as the dense mass of reeds came closer and closer. Three foot . . . two foot . . . a foot. Suddenly they were in among them and the skimmer's progress was halted abruptly. 'All right, Ginger,' he hissed, 'leave the controls and get up on the stern with your boat-hook!'

Together, the two of them pushed and heaved with all their strength, forcing the light craft deeper and deeper into the steaming brown reeds. 'You want me to give yer a chorus of your old school Boating Song, sir?' Ginger quipped, gasping as a bunch of wet reeds slashed him across the face.

'Save your breath,' Bird replied, grateful for the little man's courage at that moment. 'Besides it wasn't my school.'

Finally Bird was satisfied that the skimmer was deeply enough hidden in the reeds. He whispered and the two of them commenced chopping reeds with which to hide the boat's deck. Five minutes passed. Ten. Somewhere far away Bird could hear a persistent rattling noise which he took to be the bell of a tram. It seemed an unearthly hour to run a tram – it was not yet dawn – but he hadn't the time to worry about it. They had to be across the two hundred yards of marshy land in front of them and on the shore proper before dawn broke.

'All right,' he gasped in the end, 'that'll have to do, Ginger. Come on, let's get the weapons and be on our way.'

Swiftly the two of them picked up the heavy German automatics and two Mills bombs and secreted them about their persons.

'Better ensure we're not given away by wet clothes, Ginger,' Bird decided and started tugging at his boots. 'Take your pants off.'

'Ay, ay, sir.' With the modesty of his class, Ginger started to do so, after first turning his back on the officer. Seconds later, with their boots and trousers wrapped round their necks, the two of them were wading carefully through the knee-deep icy water. They were on their way!

*

Dawn.

To the north the clouds were rolling away with dramatic

suddenness. As the first sickly light flooded the delta, the reed-covered marshy flat started to steam unpleasantly, while ahead of them the tall factory chimneys began to emit the first black smoke of another grey working day.

Cautiously, Bird peered out of the edge of the reeds. The dusty little country roads running to left and right were as yet empty. 'All right, Ginger – all clear, let's get on with it.' He rose hastily to his feet and Ginger followed. He took one last look at the lowering dark sky over Finland behind them then spat coarsely into the dust. 'Fer luck, sir,' he explained.

Bird grunted. They were going to need it that was certain, but he didn't tell Ginger that. Together they set off towards the first houses.

Bird's plan was bold, simple and extremely foolhardy. They would not attempt to use any form of public transport; that would involve them in conversation and could be dangerous. With the aid of the rough sketch-map and route Reilly had drawn for them, they would walk the five or six miles to the centre of the Russian city. If they were stopped by a civilian, he would shrug and use his half a dozen stock Russian phrases, in particular: '*Ya nie znayu* and *amerikani*.[1] If they were asked for their *Bumagi* by a Red Guard or anyone else in uniform, they would produce the rough-and-ready Cheka passes signed by Reilly and hope for the best, keeping their hands on the big automatics hidden in the pockets of their ragged overcoats. As they entered the great port city's suburbs, Bird told himself: 'if we're lucky – and then some, we might just pull it off. *Might!*'

Now the morning silence was being ripped apart everywhere by factory whistles summoning the workers to another day of back-breaking, unrelenting toil on starvation rations. But even if Bird found it a harsh sound, heavy with foreboding, the dun-coloured crowd which poured into the dripping, cobbled streets everywhere seemed unaware. Miserable, ragged, bent with undernourishment and worry, lack-lustre eyes fixed on the pavement, they shuffled to their factories like unseeing robots.

'Crikey,' Ginger whispered out of the side of his mouth, 'look at the poor beggars, sir. Faces only a muvver could love. Workers' paradise – my eye!'

1. I don't know.

158

'Shut up, Ginger,' Bird hissed. 'They might not all be so deaf or daft as they look. Let's speak as little as possible.'

In silence they trudged after the miserable hordes, penetrating deeper and deeper into the city. Everywhere the once magnificent streets and avenues were filled with drab human beings, scuttling hither and thither like ants. Red Army soldiers, burdened down with picks, spades, rolls of barbed wire, obviously work details being sent to the front. Pot-bellied, bespectacled men with shabby briefcases and even shabbier clothes – obviously the survivors of the city's once flourishing middle class – watching them pass in half-fearful, half-contemptuous contemplation. Slow-moving, homemade armoured cars, accompanied by policemen on horseback, their gleaming sabres crooked over their shoulders, as if they were ready to ride into the crowd, swinging their blades, at any moment. Fat peasant women, bundled up in shapeless rags, standing at street corners exchanging their vegetables and potatoes for whatever the starving city-dwellers had to offer them.

To Lieutenant Bird it seemed a city which was dying rapidly, whose citizens were only kept on their weary feet by a sheer effort of will; once they stopped and sat down, they would never get to their feet again. As Ginger put it in his own inimicable way, breaking their silence with a whisper, 'Gawd luv a duck, sir, if this is the workers' ruddy paradise, you can give me the hell o' Wapping any day o' the week.' Bird nodded sombrely. Ginger, as usual, had hit the nail on the head!

*

It was about ten when they finally reached the street which contained the Smolny Institute and the Countess's apartment. It, too, like the Cheka Headquarters lay not far from the wide sluggish snake of the River Neva. Suddenly pushing their way through the crowd which jammed the muddy, cobbled street, they turned a corner and were facing it: the graceful, smoke-blue cupolas of the Smolny Convent, and next to it the immense barracks-like facade of the Smolny Institute, which housed the Red leaders.

Bird nudged Ginger. 'Take out a cigarette and pretend to

light it,' he hissed, 'make it look as if the thing won't burn properly so that I can stop and recce the place.'

'Righto, sir,' Ginger whispered, 'One coffin nail coming up – smartish!'

Reaching inside his ragged coat, he took out one of his favourite Navy issue Woodbine and made a great play of lighting it, attempting unsuccessfully to strike the match on a nearby wall several times, while Bird's eyes darted up and down the crowded street, trying to find the number of the Countess's apartment.

Finally Ginger was forced to light his cigarette and they had to move on without Bird spotting the number Reilly had given him. They walked past the heavily-armed, leather-clad sentries at the door of the Institute, also sandbagged and protected by barbed wire hurdles, their heads bent, as if they were afraid to be seen looking into the centre of Red power. Finally they reached the end of the street. Still no sign of Countess Fleur de Courcy's apartment.

'Let's try the other side, Ginger,' Bird whispered.

'All right, sir. I'm shaking like a leaf but this gasper's helping.'

With Ginger puffing nervously on his 'gasper', they waited for a troop of mud-splattered ragged Red cavalry to canter past; then they crossed and began their search once more, pushing their way through the evil-smelling crowd of Russian civilians, who thronged the muddy pavement.

The minutes passed slowly. Bird began to grow anxious. If they couldn't find her, they didn't have a hope in hell of pulling off the rescue attempt. Where in the devil's name was the apartment?

Abruptly Bird forgot the Countess's flat. With a frightening sensation that sent the small hairs at the base of his skull standing on end, he realized that they were being followed. There was no doubt, although he had no knowledge of who was behind them. But he knew it for certain. Swiftly he nudged Ginger in the ribs. 'Keep moving and don't look back, Ginger,' he hissed urgently. 'I'm stopping here for a moment.'

Ginger reacted splendidly. As Bird dropped behind and pretended to be examining the nearly bare window of some pathetic clothing store, he walked on puffing his Woodbine, as casually as if he were strolling down Hull's Albion Street on a Saturday night out for 'a pick-up', of a factory girl.

The man who was following him was a big, bearded brute, his hand clapped on the leather holster which contained his automatic, and his nose, was raised to the air, as if he were trying to smell something. Then Bird tumbled to it. The Cheka man had been attracted to the odour of Ginger's 'coffin nail'; it was vastly different from the evil stench of the black untreated tobacco the Russians smoked!

His guess was confirmed a second later. Overlooking Bird entirely in his concentration on Ginger, the big Russian quickened his pace, pushing the crowd aside with a throaty '*pazhal'st tovarskchi*!' Catching up with the unsuspecting Rating, his dirty paw fell on Ginger's shoulder. '*Bumagi*?' he demanded.

Bird waited no longer. In a flash he was behind the big Russian. He rammed his knee hard into the back of the man's left leg. The man grunted and dropped his hand, caught off guard. '*Ginger!*' Bird rapped.

The cockney did not wait for any further invitation. He spun round, swung back his fist and crashed a left hook to the bearded Russian's face, with that lightning speed which had made him the old *Iron Duke's* middleweight champion.

The Russian yelled with pain. Staggering backwards, blood pouring from his split lips, he skidded full length into the muddy gutter.

'Come on, Ginger,' Bird yelled, 'let's hoof it – *quick*!'

Ginger needed no urging. 'Skedaddle it is, skipper!' he cried, breaking into a run.

Scattering surprised civilians to left and right, they pelted wildly up the street, while behind them the big Russian staggered to his feet, yelling '*Provocatori!*' through a mouthful of blood.

A revolver shot rang out. Women screamed and men flopped to the pavement. A slug struck the ground only feet away from them. They ran on. Behind them shrill whistles were beginning to blow and the women, their nerves on edge after the events of the last forty-eight hours, were screaming hysterically. Another revolver cracked. The slug struck a wall. Bird felt a burning hot splinter of stone strike his cheek. And then they were charging round a corner, pushing through alarmed civilians and running suddenly into a narrow, dark alley. Bird caught a glimpse of a once ornate door, pocked with bullet-fire, hanging crazily by one rusting hinge. 'In there, Ginger – *quick*,' he gasped, 'there might . . . be a back way out!'

Ginger staggered into the house, followed by Bird.

The filth was indescribable. Broken bottles, food cans and human faeces lay everywhere on the once priceless Aubusson carpets. On the walls, the oil paintings hung at crazy angles, their canvas slashed to strips with bayonets. The great fireplace was filled with still smouldering rags, as if whoever had looted the place had indulged in one great final orgy of burning.

But the two hunted men had no eye for the destruction around them in the looted house. Desperately they sought a place to hide from their pursuers. Then Bird spotted it. '*The table*,' he gasped, his chest heaving wildly. 'For God's sake, get behind the table, Ginger!' Ginger dived forward, crunching frantically over the broken glass. In a flash he had flung himself behind the great overturned oaken table with its charred legs. Bird followed the next moment. Outside the sound of running feet grew louder. Bird tensed, his hand clutched wetly around the butt of his automatic. Next to him, a pale-faced Ginger did the same.

Then they were swamped in the excited sounds of the chase. For an instant the running feet stopped. Someone yelled something in Russian, which Bird took to be an order. Hasty feet crunched over the glass. A matter of only feet away, the two hunted men could hear the sound of frantic breathing. Bird swallowed hard. His heart seemed to be thumping so loudly that he was sure that whoever was there on the other side of the table must hear it.

'*Nitchevo!*' a gruff voice reported.

'*Horosho,*' another commanded. '*Davai . . . davai . . !*'

Suddenly the feet commenced running once more and they were slumped there, drained, for a moment, of all energy, their mouths gaping stupidly, staring into nothing like a couple of village idiots.

'*Phew*,' Ginger broke the silence at last and mopped his damp brow. 'That was a proper turn up for the books. I thought they had us that time!'

Slowly Bird got to his feet, not trusting himself to speak for a moment. He eyed the sagging door, revolver still clenched in his wet hand and then a slow smile of triumph crossed his wet, tense face. Ginger stared at him wondering if he had suddenly gone off his head. Finally he could contain his curiosity no longer. 'What is it skipper?' he asked. 'Yer look as if you've just spotted a million nicker – without an owner.'

Bird forced himself to speak. 'I have, Ginger . . . I have. Just look at the number on that door. It's *hers*. We're where we wanted to be all the time.'

'Cor stone the crows, skipper, you're right. It's number clickety-click – sixty-six to you, sir.' Then his face fell. 'But skipper, this place don't exactly look as if it's lived in, does it?'

But Bird was not going to have his moment of triumph spoiled by Ginger's misgivings. 'Come on, my lad,' he said cheerfully. 'Get your skates on. The elusive Countess Fleur de Courcy must be around here somewhere, and we're going to find her if she is, Ginger.'

*

But in the end it was not the two Englishmen who found the mysterious Countess; it was she who found *them*. Prowling around in the dusty upper floor which looked as if it had been unoccupied for months, they halted, puzzled and frustrated, in front of a large carved Baroque cupboard. Suddenly, there was a metallic click behind them in the half darkness. Before they could grab their automatics, a soft voice commanded: '*Ruki verkh!*'

Even Bird could sense what that meant in Russian. His shoulders suddenly slumped in defeat, he began to do what the soft voice had commanded, and raise his hands. 'Ginger, we've been nabbed,' he told his surprised companion, 'put up your hands – or you'll get shot.'

'Did I hear you speak English?' the voice asked. '*English?*'

Bird's heart missed a beat. *Could it be?*

'Turn round,' the unknown commanded, 'and keep your hands up.'

Slowly they did as they were ordered and with a gasp of shock took in the woman facing them, a small ivory-handled pistol clasped in her slim white hand. There was no mistaking that elegant woman with her dark, sensuous, yet intelligent eyes, for anyone else than the person they had come to find.

'Countess Fleur de Courcy?' Bird asked.

The beautiful aristocrat's hand trembled visibly on the little pistol. 'Yes,' she answered, her voice suddenly wavering at the use of her name. 'But how do you know me?'

Hastily, his arms still raised above his head, Bird explained how Reilly-Rosenblum had sent him to her because she might be prepared to help them. 'You see, we have a proposition to make to you, Countess. If you would—'

With an imperious wave of her pistol, she indicated that he should be silent. 'You can tell me all about it in a moment,' she commanded. 'But now, please lower your hands.' She tucked the pistol in the pocket of her elegant gown. 'As we say in Russian – *S volkami zhitj po voltchi vitj*!'

'And what's that when it's at home?' Ginger asked his usual cheeky self, now that the danger had passed.

'When one lives with the wolves, then one must do as the wolves do.' She tapped her pocket. 'Luckily for you, I am not altogether wolf – *yet* – or I would have shot first and asked questions afterwards. But come, you can explain why you have come to visit me, in a much safer place than here on this landing.'

Turning, she opened the door of the great Baroque cupboard and raising one slim, black-stockinged leg stepped inside. A moment later they were in the snug little hiding place she had made for herself in the attic, its entrance concealed by the cupboard. Soon, they were sipping pepper vodka and putting their proposition to the Countess, while she smoked in attentive silence.

Finally Bird was finished with his explanation and in turn, waited in nervous expectation for her answer, on which the success of the whole crazy mission depended.

For what seemed a long time, the Countess considered, puffing at the long Russian cigarette in her elegant ivory holder, while the wind rattled the grimy window of the comfortable dark hideout she had made for herself under the eaves.

Finally she drew the holder from between her white teeth and said; '*Bon*, I will do it, if you promise to take me with you.' She shrugged in the Slavic fashion. 'Of course, we do not have the ghost of a chance. It is impossible. But even death is better than this, isn't it? . . .'

4

'Well?' Bird demanded, as she entered the hiding place, her normally pale face flushed and excited.

'She is still alive,' the Countess replied and reached for one of the cigarettes without which her long, elegant fingers seemed somehow naked.

'Thank God,' Bird breathed, 'thank God!'

'But will he do it, miss?' Ginger asked, as she thrust the glowing cigarette into her long ivory holder.

'Yes, for two hundred golden sovereigns.'

Bird pulled himself together, knowing that this was no time for any display of personal emotion. 'The money is no problem, Countess,' he tapped his money belt, 'I have it – and more. But what did he say?'

'Tonight after dusk at the Cheka headquarters. It is then that they carry out – the hangings.' She shuddered at the thought. 'The prison staff will be too busy with that task to worry about us, so he says. He will meet us at the gate to the courtyard, escort us inside and give us the key to the cell block. According to our gross friend Krylenko, there is no permanent guard on the block. The Cheka's prisoners are usually too far gone to have any thoughts of escaping. So he will give us the key and take his money – the rest is up to us. I have told him nothing about you save that you are Georgian friends of the girl. You can speak English. Like most Russians he'll probably take it for Georgian.'

'Do you mean, miss, there are Russkies who don't understand what other Russkies are saying?' Ginger asked curiously.

'Now then, Ginger,' Bird silenced him swiftly. 'We've got no time to go into that now.' He bit his bottom lip worriedly. 'But

Countess, don't you think it's all too easy? I mean, perhaps the man can be bought and he's greedy for the things money can buy and all that, but isn't he taking a devil of a risk? After all Anna has been accused of attempting to murder Lenin, himself. If she escapes, won't our friend himself be in serious danger?' He hesitated before expressing the fear which had plagued him ever since she had set off for 'Uncle Tom's Cabin' two hours before, to contact the Cheka Chief Interrogator. 'Could it be that he is going to pocket the sovereigns and then betray us, ending up with four prisoners instead of just one?'

The Countess exhaled a stream of blue smoke. She nodded her beautiful head sagely. 'Yes, who in his right mind would trust a Russian in this year of 1919, after the terrible things we have done to each other the last two terrible years? But somehow I have faith in him. He has the look of a man who is burned out, is sick of the world, sick of himself. A man who will seize the chance the money offers him – after all it is a small fortune in Russia today – to run and run, not from the world, but from himself. To eat and drink, and eat and drink,' she shrugged, 'until he is dead and grateful to be dead.'

Bird looked at her undecided, realizing that he would never understand the Russian mentality, with its terrible fatalism, even if he lived to be a hundred. Finally he made his decision. 'Very well, Countess, I see we have no alternative. But all the same it won't do any harm to be on our guard. What did this man say he was going to do, after he had handed us the key in return for the money?'

Her mouth made a pale imitation of a smile, but her dark eyes did not light up. 'Once he has given us the key, he wants nothing more to do with us. He was very determined about that. Apparently he intends to start spending his sudden wealth by celebrating. He has invited a woman of the street to his quarters.' The corners of her mouth drooped cynically, worldly wise, as if nothing would shock her any more – save virtue and honesty. 'That is the way of his type, I suppose. Besides the prostitute will provide him with a kind of alibi.' She rubbed her forefinger and thumb together in that gesture he remembered so well from Anna. 'It will be a case of instant love and for love, she will swear anything no doubt.'

'No doubt,' Bird replied coldly, repelled by the sordidness of the whole thing in spite of the way he had so rapidly dispensed with his middle-class British morality in the last few days. 'All the same, we shall take *some* precautions with friend Krylenko.'

'What precautions?'

'Once he has given us the key, he will return to his office and we shall go on to the cell block. Make sure you get full instructions from him on its location—'

'I know their location already, but no matter, continue.'

'Unknown to our friend, however, not all of us will go down to the cell block.' He poked his forefinger at himself. 'Only *I* will do so. You two—'

'Will be watching the Russkie's office to check that he doesn't decide to do the dirty on us.' Ginger was, as usual, quickest off the mark.

'Right in one, Ginger! You'll keep tabs on him Countess. After all, Ginger here is no Russian linguist and if he does decide to split on us, you give Ginger the wire.'

She nodded her understanding, the smoke from her holder curling up slowly in the still, little room. 'And if he does betray us? What then?' Ginger answered that question for her. He tapped the bulge of his automatic underneath his shabby jacket. 'The Russkie'll get a quick dose of lead poisoning, miss. *That's what then!*'

*

As they approached the grim grey façade of the 19th century villa which was now the Cheka HQ, a great yellow moon slid from behind the clouds and cast a sickly, eerie light across the still water of the Neva. Now, the embankment was nearly empty of pedestrians. Such civilians who were still about walked with a quick pace, their furtive eyes darting here and everywhere, as if they expected danger to spring from the shadows at any moment.

A convoy of police *troikas* clattered over the muddy cobbles, escorted by a squad of cavalry, bandoliers slung across their shoulders, rifles in their free hand. 'The witnesses for the hanging,' the Countess whispered as they disappeared into the courtyard of the Cheka HQ. 'Very proper our new Bolshevik masters,' she added cynically, 'they must have witnesses for their legal murders.'

Bird nodded, hardly trusting himself to speak. For the first time since they had set off on the impossible mission, he felt that they might pull it off. After all, they had got this far without too much difficulty and now Anna was only yards away from them. Yet, somehow, it was all proving too easy. There must be a snag somewhere!

'There he is,' the Countess hissed. 'At the gate. He's waiting for us.'

Bird caught a glimpse of an enormously tall, fat figure waiting in the shadows just outside the gate. Then he was shaking hands with a man who towered above them like a colossus, but whose grip was soft and flabby, and whose gross body gave off a revolting odour; a compound of cheap Cologne, stale sweat and – somehow – physical corruption. With a grunt, which indicated 'follow me', the Chief Interrogator swung round and passed inside. They followed quickly.

Across the dirty yard, littered with bits of paper, empty bottles and the faeces of those condemned who had not been able to contain themselves, they were preparing the prisoners for execution. A priest was on his knees, his hands clasped together, his great black beard bobbing up and down, as he pleaded for mercy. Next to him a slim boy sobbed silently, his shoulders heaving, as the line moved forward to the waiting gallows.

The Chief Interrogator stopped suddenly to let a cavalryman clatter by. On the scaffold they were arranging the noose around the neck of a big, rawboned woman clad only in a black petticoat. She stood there with animal-like peasant patience on the stepladder, accepting death as she had probably accepted everything in her short miserable, hard-working life.

Suddenly the hangman jumped the six foot to the littered cobbles. With one swift kick, he had knocked the ladder away from beneath her. Like a bird lifting its wings, she flew into the air. For one split second the movement was graceful, almost beautiful. Then, as the cruel noose bit into her neck, her hands flew upwards frantically. Only half way! They dropped, and the next moment she was whirling round back and forth in her death throes, her eyes suddenly bulging wildly, her tongue hanging out of her wide-gaping mouth, like a piece of raw steak.

'God almighty!' Ginger gasped, *'God bloody almighty!'*

Behind him, Bird fought back his nausea and told himself *that* would never happen to his Anna, come what may. As the soldiers began to cut down the dead woman, they hurried on in absolute silence.

A minute later, the big Russian stopped them in a little alcove off the main corridor, lit only by a couple of guttering yellow candles, which flung their shadows in giant distortion on to the dirty peeling walls. For a moment he dropped his eyes, almost as if (Bird thought with sudden fear) he did not want them to see the deviousness they contained. Wordlessly he held out a dirty, pudgy hand. Bird understood immediately.

Swiftly he grappled with the buckle beneath his jacket and released the heavy money belt. Krylenko took it, his gaze still on the ground, and weighed it in his hand. He nodded his heavy head as if satisfied, and reaching in his pocket brought out the key, which he handed to the Countess.

She attempted to say something to him, but he motioned her to be silent, as if he neither wanted nor cared to speak to them any further; as if the whole business repulsed him. It was a guess that Bird saw confirmed the next moment, as he turned to go to his office and the waiting prostitute. Krylenko's massive pale face was distorted by a look of absolute, complete self-disgust. A second later he was gone and they were left staring at the empty corridor.

'What now?' Bird broke the sudden silence. 'Which way for me, Countess?'

She responded immediately. 'Down there in the opposite direction. To your right you'll see a small flight of stairs. Take them – they lead to the cells. And be careful! Although Krylenko says there is no permanent guard on duty after dark, the cells are directly below the staff's offices.' She shrugged swiftly. 'It may be that someone might still be working up there.'

Bird nodded his understanding. 'All right, Ginger, you're on your own now. Take care of the Countess.'

'That I will, sir,' Ginger answered hastily. 'And I know what to do, if – well you know, sir.'

'Good chap! With luck I should have her out within the next five minutes. And that's all you need to give me. We rendezvous here then, understood?'

'Ay, ay, sir,' Ginger answered smartly, pulling out his automatic and snapping off the safety catch. 'And just one thing, sir.'

'Yes?'

'Just watch it, sir, won't you.' He attempted a pathetic grin. 'After all, sir, you've got a long career ahead of you in the Royal. With your promotion prospects you'll be an admiral of the fleet by nineteen hundred and forty-five, won't you?'

'Get on with you, you rogue,' Bird said, feeling a sense of warmth at the ginger-haired cockney's loyalty and steadfastness.

'Ay, ay, sir . . . come on, miss.'

A moment later they had parted and were hurrying on their separate ways. Now the great rescue operation had reached its most crucial stage.

*

'Here, whore,' Krylenko growled and flung the whore – the best Petrograd had to offer, and these days there were plenty of them around – a handful of the gleaming gold coins. 'Your wages!' She cried with delight and bending her knees began to gather them up, her fleshy naked thighs spread disgustingly to reveal a blurred vortex of dark thick hair, while he opened the Judas Hole and peered down at the woman prisoner's cell. The young Georgian – or whatever he was – had already opened the door to the cell and now they were kissing, their bodies pressed tightly together, her half-naked soft form cradled protectively in his strong arms.

'You like me?' the whore simpered.

He closed the Judas Hole, and swung round.

She had already hurriedly thrust the coins in her purse. Now she was leaning back against the wall, her dark eyes half-closed vamplike, holding up her heavy, dun-nippled breasts towards him, legs slightly spread to reveal those wet lips he desired so much, but yet feared. 'You like me?' she repeated the question in her husky, vodka-thickened whore's voice.

'Yes,' he answered, taking in her body, big and hefty in the fashion Russian lovers liked, with bruises and discolourations everywhere on her plump white flesh to testify to the passion of her many customers. Somehow the sight, which should have excited him, disgusted him. He felt ill and revolted.

'Come,' she whispered seductively and sank down on his untidy cot, 'come to me my little dove.' She arched her body in what she thought was a provocative manner and spread her legs slowly.

Krylenko hesitated. He picked up the glass and downed the fiery pepper vodka in one huge draught. Down below, still nothing stirred.

'What are you waiting for?' the whore asked.

'Please go away,' he cried out in sudden agony. 'I can't . . . can't help you.'

She laughed in her easy unashamed whore's way, as if he were trying somehow to tease her. Swiftly she sprang from the little cot, here eyes large and animal, her breasts swinging ponderously. 'Such a great bear of a man,' she cried. 'I bet you've broken many a girl's heart – and something else – with your strength.' She leered up at his fear-contorted, sweat-lathered face and reached out a greedy hand to seize him.

In a sudden panic, he avoided her grasp, knocking over a chair in his haste, backing against his desk, feeling instinctively for the heavy, hard comfort of his revolver, which as always lay there.

She came on, her teeth set in an animal grin, those greedy hands of hers reaching out to take hold of him.

'No please,' he stammered. '*Don't* . . . put your clothes on, you've got your money . . . go.'

Suddenly she grabbed his genitals and squeezed hard, grunting with real or false passion as she did so. 'Ah, my great bear, now I've got you where it—'

She broke off abruptly and stared up at his red, dripping face puzzled. 'What's the matter with you, Krylenko? I thought you – or perhaps you don't like girls?' She looked into his eyes with that all-knowing, mocking whore's gaze of hers.

Krylenko thought of the couple below, abruptly. His blood boiled suddenly at the thought of them pawing so obscenely at each other, his hands running wild with the prisoner's breasts and other things, while he was condemned to this – failure once again.

And now this whore was going to reveal his desperate inadequacy to all the world; he had no illusions about that. She would talk and grin; and they would sit and listen and laugh at his shame. 'Yes,' she would say, 'he can't get it up – a big bear of a man like that! Even one of the Czar's midgets could satisfy a woman ten times better than that giant!'

The fury welled up within him, a hatred that seemed to come from his very loins. With the big revolver he lashed at her face. 'Leave me alone,' he screamed, as she staggered back. He whipped the big revolver into her naked breast. She yelled with pain. He didn't care. He hit her again – and again.

'*Bitch . . . whore . . . !*' he cried, drowning even the sound of her screams, in a wild, exultant, all-consuming rage. Once more he lashed the heavy tumescence of the pistol across her contorted, tear-stained, terrified face and gasped with pleasure as she blood began to spurt suddenly from her smashed nose.

'*NO!*' she pleaded thickly, falling to her knees, her hands held up in front of her smashed face. '*NO, DON'T HIT ME AGAIN!*'

Far, far off, someone was shouting in alarm. There was the sound of heavy boots running. He didn't care. All he could see was that hated naked flesh, bounding and rebounding under his blows. Suddenly the door was flung open. He caught one brief glimpse of a flushed angry face under a mop of red hair. Then the automatic exploded deafeningly in the tight confines of the little room. Something exploded in the base of his stomach with an unbearable, burning pain. Abruptly his legs could no longer bear him. He crashed to the floor. The red-haired man towered above him, the automatic clenched in his hand. 'Please forgive me,' Krylenko wanted to say, but no words would come.

The man cursed in a language he could not understand. Helplessly he watched as the man's finger curled round the trigger again. *Crash!* The bullet exploded in his head all red and black. And he died as the sirens began to sound their stomach-churning wail of alarm and warning outside . . .

5

The four of them ran desperately down the long grey corridor, while the distant tumult grew ever louder. Whistles, cries, angry orders. Bird, in the lead, swung round a corner and skidded to a halt. A big man in his shirt sleeves, rifle in his hand, was standing there. Next instant a slug ripped into the wall only inches above his head. He ducked back around the corner. 'Quick – the window,' he yelled. 'The corridor is blocked!'

Ginger flung open the catches. In that same moment, Bird pulled the pin out of the Mills. Without exposing himself, he lobbed it under-hand round the corner. The running feet came to a sudden stop. A second later the bomb exploded with a dull thick muffled thud. A man screamed piteously, as the hot choking blast wave tore up the corridor.

'All right, sir,' Ginger cried. 'We're ready to go!'

'All right, you first,' Bird commanded. 'Give us cover when you're down. The women will follow!'

As agile as a monkey, Ginger swung himself through and down. Behind them, Bird could hear more running feet. He crouched automatically at the ready. 'You first Anna,' he cried. 'Then you Countess. Come, don't hesitate!'

A moment later they'd both disappeared from sight. The sound of the running feet was getting ever louder. Bird waited no longer. '*Davai!*' a hoarse voice cried. He caught a glimpse of a ruffianly bearded face and firing a wild burst in its direction, dropped cleanly through the window onto the cobbles below.

'*Ouch!*' he yelped with pain. His legs felt as if they had driven straight into the base of his stomach. But there was no time to worry about that now. Somewhere a machine gun was beginning to fire. At what target he didn't know and he was not going to wait to find out. Desperately he looked around for some means of escape. Then he spotted it. One of the police *troikas*, which had brought the witnesses to the hanging, had still not departed!

'There, Ginger,' he cried. '*That cart!*'

Ginger darted forward, while Bird grabbed the two shocked women and bundled them after him unceremoniously.

A vivid burst of flame exploded from the window. High velocity slugs struck the cobbles, sending up little vicious blue spurts of flame. Ahead of them the horses reared and plunged in fear. Desperately Ginger, the ex-drayman, hung onto the reins, crying 'Whoa Liza . . . *whoa!*' Just in time he managed to hold them before they bolted.

Swiftly Bird pushed the two women into the back. 'Get down – low,' he ordered. '*Quick!*' Without even aiming, he swung round and fired a burst at the window they had just left. Glass splintered. Someone yelped hysterically. Then the automatic stopped its frantic trembling in his tight fist. 'Blast,' he cursed. He had run out of ammo. 'Come on, sir,' Ginger yelled urgently. 'Don't muck about! They're trying to close the gate on us!'

Bird saw the danger immediately. Fifty yards away, a frantic guard was trying to swing the big door closed to block off their escape route. He jumped on the high seat beside Ginger. 'Right, off you go!' he gasped.

Ginger needed no urging. '*Gee up! . . . gee up, you buggers!*' he yelled and lashed the long black whip across the three horses' shining chestnut rumps. With a bound that nearly overturned the little carriage, they sprang forward, Ginger holding onto the reins with all his strength.

Bird reached across and felt into Ginger's jacket for his grenade. He found it. With feverish fingers, he ripped the pin out. The gate was looming up ever larger. In the light of the yellow lantern above it, he could see every detail of the guard's face as he pressed his shoulder desperately to the heavy door trying to close it in time. Balancing as best he could, Bird grunted and heaved the grenade at him.

The guard disappeared in an ugly, red burst of flame. The horses whinnied with fear and reared up alarmingly. Behind them the two women screamed. But Ginger was master of the situation. Cursing furiously, he lashed the trembling beasts' rumps and caught them just in time. Next minute they were swerving through the smoking gate, their wooden wheels lurching over the guard's outstretched gory body, and clattering wildly down the embankment and into the heaven-sent darkness.

*

Wildly their *troika* rattled down the embankment, Ginger whipping the steaming horses frantically, the reins cutting into his hand, half-blinded with sweat.

They careened round a corner on one wheel. Four militia men stood there, red lanterns in their hands. Ginger did not hesitate a second. Cruelly he lashed his horses. They shot forward. Their great sweat-lathered bodies crashed into the surprised militia men. Their lanterns smashed to the cobbles, as they dived for safety. One screamed shrilly, and went down beneath the flailing steel-shod hooves. The next moment the wheels had bounced over his prostrate body and they were rolling on at a tremendous speed down a narrow slum street.

But Bird knew that it would not be long before the pursuit would be taken up. 'Anna,' he called over his shoulder, 'can you guide us? We need the quickest route back to the spot where we landed you that time.'

The girl, her face swollen and bruised from the blows the interrogators had rained down upon her so mercilessly, pulled herself together, visibly shaking herself into reality. Dickie and Ginger had rescued her! She was still alive and free. Perhaps they had a chance after all?

Crouching behind Ginger, holding on desperately, she began to give instructions to the driver, as the horses' hooves hammered hollowly down the echoing, empty cobbled back streets and the cart swayed crazily from side to side, as the *Troika* turned corner after corner on one wheel.

The slum suburbs started to thin out. Ahead Bird could just make out the flat indistinct dark mass of the Neva Delta. Below, the cobbles gave way to dirt, and suddenly the clatter of their hooves on hard stone was replaced by a softer pad-pad. In that same moment they became aware for the first time, of the drumming behind them. Bird swung round and his heart sank.

'*Cavalry!*' he yelled. 'In heaven's name, Ginger step on it. There's a troop of cavalry at the back of us!'

Ginger cracked his whip desperately and the *troika* swayed and shuddered as they tore up the dirt road towards the reed marsh where the skimmer lay hidden. But now the sweat-lathered chestnuts were beginning to tire, and the cavalry was beginning to gain on them. More terrifyingly, they were fanning out from the road, extending to both sides like a pair of horns, so that the rear files did not have to ride in the lee of the leaders. Bird groaned and bawled at Ginger, '*Faster* . . . faster, or they'll have us!'

'It's no go, sir,' Ginger yelled back. He snapped his whip viciously over the horses' steaming rumps, 'they're about played out!' Angrily, Bird snatched Ginger's automatic and fired wildly at the leaders. One of them clasped his shoulder, as if he had been hit, but stayed in his saddle.

Now the Red Cavalry was gaining. The two horns were reaching forward ever more rapidly; their intention obvious. They were going to block the road in front of the *troika*. Bird, his brain racing furiously, trying to think of some way out, could hear the cavalrymen's cries, savage and exultant to each other. He threw a wild look behind him. The white blobs set against the dun-coloured uniforms were clearly visible now. It would be only a matter of minutes before they were overtaken, one way or other. He had to act.

'Damn you,' he roared in sudden rage, 'you won't have us!' The women, pale and frightened, stared up at him, as if he had suddenly gone crazy. But he paid no attention to them. 'Ginger,' he ordered, 'swing her round to the left and off the road – quick!'

'But the marsh!'

'I know . . . I know. But do as I say, Ginger. Trust me!'

Ginger hauled at the reins and then released them as the horses charged forward again. Bird heard a thin shout. He swung round. One of the horns had stopped abruptly and formed a little knot of excited, confused riders. But the horsemen on their immediate flank and some of those on the road had taken up the new direction at once. Still his little trick had cut down the number of their pursuers.

'Listen Ginger,' he cupped his hands over his mouth and yelled as the horses pounded over the still hard ground, nearing the reed marsh with every step, 'once we strike the reeds and slow down drastically, *jump*! You and the two girls. Then you're in charge, Ginger. Get to the skimmer!'

He repeated the message for the two women's benefit. 'And you, Dickie?' Anna gasped anxiously.

'Don't worry.' He tried to force a smile and failed lamentably. 'I'll try to hold them until Ginger gets into the skimmer and then I'll be after you like a—'

Suddenly the lead horse stumbled. They had struck the reed marsh! The horse beside it whinnied and desperately tried to save itself, to no avail. It slithered down, dragging the other two to their knees, whinnying in sudden terror. The *troika* slewed round horribly. A wheel cracked with a fearful splintering. The little cart sagged. Next instant they were hurled from the wrecked *troika*, the women screaming, Ginger cursing violently.

Bird felt his side smack against the hard heaving rump of the nearside horse. A fiery pain shot through his chest. He yelped with agony and flinging up his hands to protect his face slithered full length into the wet cold morass.

In a flash, he was up again, the mud dripping from his contorted face. 'Ginger – make a run for it. For God's sake!'

Ginger, his nose bleeding from the fall, grabbed Anna by the hand and hastily helped the Countess to her feet. A moment later they were blundering wildly through the reeds, up to their knees in muddy water.

Trying to control his madly heaving chest, Bird swung round to face the horsemen, dark shapes above the swaying reeds, slower now as their horses picked their way through the water-filled holes. Bird pulled out the last grenade. With fingers that trembled violently, he ripped out the pin, but kept a tight grip on the lever.

Now they were only a matter of yards away. Fifteen or twenty of them strung out in a slow, dark line, the only sound the jingle of the horses' harnesses and that of splashing water. Bird let go of the lever. It pinged off into the darkness. 'One – two,' he counted off the seconds under his breath, '*three* –

FOUR!' In that same instant, he flung the grenade into their midst and ducked.

The bomb exploded in a vicious burst of angry red and yellow. As the splinters hissed frighteningly through the air, he saw half a dozen of them silhouetted stark black against the scarlet glare, horses prancing wildly, whinnying piteously as they were struck, men cursing, shouting, falling everywhere.

Then he was round and had plunged into the reeds, half-running, half-wading through the knee-deep water, expecting a sabre to cleave open his skull at any moment.

*

It seemed an age before the Russians took up the chase again. Then a clear order snapped into the confused babble behind him. The screams, the cries, the curses died instantly. A moment later there was the sound of horses splashing through water in a hurry again. But now he had a hundred yards lead and was more difficult to locate in the marsh. His pursuers seemed to realize that, immediately. They began to spread out even more. Bird flung a rapid glance over his shoulder. In his immediate vicinity there was one solitary horseman floundering through the water, his horse's hooves throwing up a white froth as its rider urged it on. Suddenly he shouted. Bird did not understand the words, but their meaning was clear enough. The rider had spotted him! He turned and trying to keep his hand steady, fired. Scarlet flame stabbed the darkness.

Behind him the horse reared high in the air, its hooves flailing in an ecstasy of pain. Then the beast flopped to one side, and crashed into the water with a great splash. But its rider was an expert. Even as the horse fell, he had dropped out of the saddle with the ease of a circus rider and was plunging on after Bird.

Desperately Bird pressed the trigger. Nothing happened! Again he had run out of ammunition. With a curse of rage, he flung the useless pistol away and started running again. The man followed doggedly.

'Over here, skipper! *Here!*' It was Ginger. He had found the skimmer. Frantically Bird increased his speed, swerving to the right from which the cry had come. Now he could see them outlined against the sky, obviously standing higher than the marsh on the skimmer's deck. There was the first dry cough of a Thorneycroft starting. He had nearly done it!

Suddenly the Russian was on him, a massive figure stinking of garlic. Bird swung round and chopped his fist down on the man's outstretched hand almost instinctively. He yelped and his pistol splashed into the water. Bird didn't give him a chance to look for it. He smashed his fist into the man's face. The man staggered, but didn't go down. He flung himself on Bird, his hands grabbing for the officer's throat.

At the skimmer the Thorneycroft was giving a series of throaty coughs, which indicated that it might burst into roaring life at any moment.

Desperately, Bird tried to free the grip the soldier had on his throat, fear of being left behind lending strength to his weary muscles. He smashed blow after blow into the man's face. The soldier grunted with pain and the blood began to flow thickly from his broken nose. But he did not release his vice-like grip. Almost crying with rage and frustration, Bird's hands flew to the man's belt. As he'd hoped. *He had a bayonet there!*

Too late the Russian realized what the Englishman was going to do. He released his grip. In that instant, Bird had drawn the bayonet and rammed the shining steel into his stomach. As his scream rent the air, the skimmer's engine burst into triumphant, noisy life. For a moment, Bird could not move, held for what seemed an eternity by the man dying above him. He knew that as long as he lived, he would never forget that young unshaven face – eyes starting madly, mouth gaping wide in agony with blood trickling from the corner – dying only inches from his own. At last the Russian slumped dead on top of him, and he was wriggling his way from under him to stagger wildly to the roaring skimmer.

*

But they were not out of danger yet. As the women hauled him aboard, Ginger opened the throttle and the boat began to nose its way through the packed reeds into which they had poled it, the reeds effectively stopping him from opening up all out. Now the cavalry were on them again. Bullets zipped through the air. Lead whined off the metal and ripped open the wooden deck.

'Get down,' Bird sobbed and ran desperately for the Lewis gun. The women dropped. Wildly he swung it round and fired a crazy burst along the length of the deck at the hurrying figures. Men fell into the water everywhere, suddenly galvanized into frantic action, screaming with agony as they did so. But still they came on, firing as they ran. Bullet after bullet struck the light-skinned skimmer, making it reel like a live thing.

Bird fired again, keeping his finger on the trigger, slewing the gun from side to side, forming a wall of hot lead behind the skimmer, which was now beginning to gather speed, as it nosed its way through the last of the packed reeds. Just in time. To their right on the mainland, the searchlights flicked on, their cold white beams swinging across the dark water of the delta in search of the cause for this sudden alarm. But worse was to come.

Suddenly a star shell burst with frightening brilliance. It fell short, but as it bathed the sea in its icy glare, it illuminated two craft, sharp bows reared high in the air, the bone already in their teeth, as they sliced through the water a quarter of a mile away. The Reds had brought up their own torpedo boats to protect the Centre Fleet from any further skimmer attacks. Their way through the northern channel was blocked! As the great Thorneycroft roared to its full power and the skimmer's bow rose proudly in the air, Bird yelled desperately at Ginger – *'the Red Track Approach . . . for God's sake, Ginger – take the Red Track . . .'*

6

Now the skimmer was going all out, slicing the water at thirty-five knots an hour. Behind them the two Red torpedo boats, great bow-waves creaming from their long rakish hulls, were keeping up. But with five knots' difference in speed, they would not be able to overtake the skimmer. Bird knew that, but he also knew, that both Red craft would be armed, with a quick-firer at least to even things up. And once the skimmer was forced to reduce speed to enter the Red Track Approach – *if* they could find it – the skimmer might well be a sitting duck for the Red gunners. They must put more distance between themselves and their pursuers.

His face wet with spray, he swung round on Ginger, in full command of himself and the boat now. 'Can't you get anything more out of her, Ginger?' he demanded, his voice urgent but unafraid.

'We're going all out now, skipper,' Ginger roared, tensed over the controls. He inclined his head at the two women crouched fearfully on the wildly heaving wet deck. 'Extra weight, you see skipper.'

Bird did. Just as the closest torpedo-boat opened up with its six-pounder, he knew he had to make up for that extra weight.

Ducking instinctively as the first shell tore through the night, a trail of fiery sparks behind it, he ran across the deck. He winced as a tall, furious column of water rose just in front of the skimmer and the hull shuddered with the body-blow of detonation. The Reds were ranging in. He must lighten the skimmer, *now*! With fingers that felt like thick sausages, he released the number one torpedo lock. Behind him the first torpedo boat fired again. A flat heavy boom echoed across to him, as he bent, working in a sweating fury. Next instant the shell thudded over the water and exploded only fifty yards in front of them. The skimmer heeled violently. Seawater hissed over the upturned bows and drenched him. He gasped with shock then he pressed the torpedo button. There was a faint cloud of choking yellow smoke. Clumsily the fish struck the water and suddenly, lightened by two tons, the skimmer leapt forward.

Just in time! The third shell fell so close that the water from its explosion deluged him and nearly swept him overboard. Choking and coughing with salt water and the stink of cordite, he doubled over to the other torpedo. Now, they couldn't be more than five hundred yards away from the shallows. The angry, probing searchlight beams from Kronstadt were looming ever larger. Desperately he fumbled with the firing mechanism of number two torpedo, as the Red boats roused to a fury as their prey seemed to be escaping them, hissed through the sea, all-out, their quick-firers pounding the water all about the heeling quarry in frightening profusion. Finally he'd done it. He took a deep breath and pressed the button. Just as he did so, there was a sharp harsh whistle of a lower pitch than before. A deafening crack. Hot air slapped him in the face like a blow. Instinctively he opened his mouth to prevent his eardrums from being burst by the detonation. He dropped to his knees, his nostrils suddenly filled with the stink of escaping petrol, realizing with fear that tragedy had struck at last. The shell had somehow hit their feed-pipe. *They were losing petrol and speed rapidly!*

*

With almost fatalistic calm, ignoring the look of stark fear in the women's eyes, Bird gave his orders with convincing authority. 'Ginger, throttle back, try to save what fuel we've got!' 'Ay, ay, sir.' Ginger reacted instinctively, his face showing unafraid in the torpedo boats' searchlights. 'Twenty knots it is!'

Behind them the Red boats seemed to leap forward, every detail of their menacing bulk revealed, like live things, hissing forward to claim their just prey.

'Get on the Lewis, Ginger and—'

'Don't fire till you see the whites of their eyes.' Ginger beat him to it, as he raced to take over the gun.

Without looking down, Bird snapped at the girls : 'If we can manage to get within reach of the shallows before they overtake us, I want you both to go overboard. You can both swim, can't you?' They nodded, unable to speak now, with the air full of the roar of their pursuers' tremendous motors.

'It can't be more than three hundred yards to the shore and the water is only waist deep. You'll have a good chance. Once you're there—'

He broke off. The skimmer was slowing down rapidly with a series of alarming gulps, as if the Thorneycroft had suddenly developed a bad case of hiccups. He flashed a look at the green glowing speedometers. *Fifteen knots – ten!*

Behind him, Ginger pressed the trigger of the Lewis. It opened up with a frantic clatter, the tracer zooming off the torpedo boats' armoured sides like crazy golf balls. He had seen the whites of their eyes! The leading torpedo boat, confident of its prey now, belched fire. Angry red flames swept across the stricken skimmer's deck. Bird ducked instinctively, as they clawed about him and razor-sharp, white-hot steel splinters hissed through the air. The skimmer heeled alarmingly. Still she kept going, the splinters raining down on her ruined deck.

Five knots! Behind them – only two hundred yards away now – he could see every detail of the leading Red torpedo-boat, outlined in all its deadly menace by the white tracer of the Lewis. It could only be a matter of seconds now! When would he hear the bell of the sounding buoy, indicating the Red Track Approach, so that he could order the girls overboard. They must accept the only fate that the Bolshies could deal out to them now: killed honourably in battle at sea, or lined up as spies against some bullet-pocked prison wall and shot by a bunch of scruffy Red Guards. *When?*

The Thorneycroft had almost petered out now. The skimmer's bow had sunk back in the water. They were crawling along. Behind them, the great roar of the leading torpedo boat threatened to swamp them at any moment. At the gun, Ginger had stopped firing. It was useless! Fatalistically, he waited for the inevitable end. Bird tensed and stared at the hunter. She was plunging through every trough, throwing up great sheets of spray, while the seamen running to throw out lines, slithered and slipped on the heaving, soaked deck. Only the gun crew, strapped in in their leather harnesses, seemed unaffected by that tremendous, hectic, plunging motion, as they waited tensely to put an end to the relentless chase.

And then it happened! Suddenly at forty miles an hour, the Red torpedo boat stopped, as if it had run into a solid stone wall! The skipper went flying through the open front of the bridge. At the gun the leather straps burst, sending the crew flying to all sides. The sudden impact flung screaming, surprised seamen overboard and in an instant the torpedo boat, her keel ripped apart from end to end, her props revolving furiously in two inadequate feet of water, was sinking rapidly.

'Oh, *my holy Godfather, she's hit the Oranienbaum sandbanks!*' Bird yelled joyously, the tension snapping suddenly so that he felt like an elated child again. 'Don't you realize,' he cried, turning to the two frightened women lying on the deck, '*they've hit the damned sands!*'

But if they were too shocked to realize what had just happened, the skipper of the other Russian torpedo boat wasn't. In a great white heaving C, he flung his boat round desperately, just short of the newly brown water, her engines screaming in frantic protest, her huge bow-wave swamping her sinking running-mate and sending the men in the water bobbing up and down furiously like corks.

As the stricken torpedo-boat gave one final obscene belch of escaping air, before settling down on the bottom for good, and the damaged Thorneycroft came to a final stop, the jubilant young skimmer skipper heard the first faint tinkle of the sounding buoy. His heart leapt for joy as he realized what it meant. *The crippled skimmer had reached the Red Track approach – just in time!*

*

But they were not out of danger yet. Coasting slowly just off the sands, her screws just turning over as she picked up the survivors from her running mate, the other torpedo boat opened fire again. A shell tore flatly through the darkness with the sound of a gigantic piece of canvas being ripped apart violently.

Bird pulled himself together. They had had their moment of triumph, but they were still in enemy waters, and already the Kronstadt beams were swinging back and forth across the straits searching for them.

He threw a hasty glance to the north-west. The few, faint twinkling lights meant Finland and safety. But the Finnish coast was nearly fifteen miles away and there was only three to four hours of darkness left to cross that intervening space and reach safety.

The torpedo boat's gun spoke again, frighteningly. Another six-pound shell whizzed over their heads and crashed into the sandbank only yards away, sending the skimmer heeling from side to side crazily. Bird woke up to the immediate danger. 'Ginger, over here with those boat-hooks!'

The rating sprang forward with the poles.

'You,' he swung round on Anna, 'take over this wheel. You'll steer.'

'But—'

He gave her no time to object. Grabbing her hand, he thrust

184

it on the controls. 'It's simple,' he barked, 'just keep her away from that bell ringing to your right. We'll do the rest!'

'Countess!'

'Yes,' the other Russian woman answered at once.

'Get below and follow your nose until you find the place where the petrol's coming—' the roar of an exploding shell drowned the rest of his instructions. But she needed no further orders. Swiftly she pushed by him and disappeared into the skimmer's little hold.

Bird snatched the pole out of Ginger's hand. 'All right, Anna,' he yelled, 'watch your steering.' He flashed a look at Ginger, poised there, waiting for his order. '*Now*,' he barked, and took the strain, as yet another shell whizzed by them. '*Heave!*'

*

The next hour was one of the most terrible in all Bird's service career. While the Countess worked down below, trying to stem the flow of petrol with rags torn from her clothing, he and Ginger pushed desperately with the boat-hooks, pausing time and time again as yet another shell whizzed terrifyingly over their heads. Twice the little skimmer rocked violently as if it were going to heel over for good, and as they ducked in frightening haste, the all-engulfing roar swamped them, with shrapnel hissing viciously across the debris-littered deck. And all the time the searchlights continued to cast their frightening glare across the stricken craft, with almost mechanical regularity; yet without once settling on them for good.

But gradually, working frantically against time, with the firing starting to die away, as the sudden swell began to take them quicker through the Red Track Approach towards the open Gulf, their problem now became the sandbank. Without the Thorneycroft to aid them, steering was difficult. At a knot and a half speed, the only way they could avoid running aground was by pelting from one side of the craft to the other and pushing with all their strength whenever that danger seemed imminent.

Within a matter of minutes, both of them were lathered in sweat, their chests heaving like those of asthmatic old men, their hands holding the boat-hooks trembling violently with the tremendous exertion. But Bird knew they could not let up. At the wheel, Anna had got the hang of steering and was doing her best, but without the engine, there was little she could do once the drifting skimmer started to be carried towards the gap between the sounding buoys, except shout out urgent warnings which would send them staggering towards the threatened side.

And then Ginger slumped to his knees. 'Skipper,' he gasped, lungs labouring, 'I . . . I'm knackered . . . I can't . . . can't go on no more!' As if to emphasize the finality of his remark, the boat-hook slipped out of his hands onto the littered deck. A second later Ginger slumped on top of it, his shoulders heaving violently, as if he were sobbing.

Bird let his boat-hook clatter to the deck. He couldn't do it alone. At the two knots they were drifting now, his strength alone would not suffice to hold off the sand. What the hell was he to do? What the hell —

Suddenly he had it. A sea anchor! But what? Wildly he cast around for something he could use. Again his mind clicked. Down below! He pushed a surprised Anna aside and dropped into the little engine-room.

The Countess, her blouse soaked with petrol, her skirt and underclothing gone to reveal excellent legs in black silk stockings, complete with frilly garters, was patiently binding a white rag round yet another hole, her back to him. But he had no time for the Countess's undoubted physical charms. 'That can,' he gasped, 'give me that petrol can!'

She reacted immediately. With hands that were slippery with escaping petrol, she flung the tin. He caught it swiftly 'And the other two,' he commanded. They followed. He gasped his thanks and ran outside.

Ginger was staggering to his feet, swaying around, his knees too rubbery to hold him. 'Sorry, skipper, I didn't mean—'

'Get me that rope,' Bird cut him short. There was no time to waste now. Again the crippled skimmer was beginning to drift towards port, the ringing of the bell-buoy growing louder by the instant. Ginger flung him the rope. He caught it neatly and tied first one and then the other cans to it. The sound of the ringing was getting ever louder. Desperately, sweat standing out on his forehead, he raced against the sound. And then he had done it. With a quick gasp for breath, he heaved the improvised sea anchor overboard. For a moment nothing happened. Then the cans veered to stern. Their seemingly inevitable progress towards the sandbank stopped. The sea anchor was working. Bird breathed out hard and let his aching shoulders sink wearily. They had done it again.

*

One hour before dawn, they drifted silently beneath the guns of the fort on the extreme tip of Kronstadt Island, where the Red Track Approach ran out into the Gulf of Finland. Holding their breath, the four of them watched tensely as the squat, menacing mass of the fort loomed larger and larger. If they were spotted now, they were finished. Without the Thorneycroft's power to speed them out of danger, they hadn't a chance, if the guns opened up.

But those tremendous cannons did not fire. At a steady two and a half knots an hour, they drifted by the fort and out into the Gulf. At the controls, Ginger tensed. But Bird shook his head. It wasn't time yet. Besides he did not know how long the Countess's underclothing patch would hold up, once they started the Thorneycroft. He would wait a little longer.

Beside him the two women turned to watch the last of Russia fade into the gloom behind them. '*Dosvedanya*,' Anna whispered softly, tears in her eyes.

'*Dosvedanya*,' the Countess, next to her, joined in, and pressed her companion's hand tenderly; for as she knew, too, they would never see their beloved Russia again. This time they were leaving for good; there could be no hope of return. Now, for the rest of their lives they would be exiles.

Slowly Bird took a last look at the Red Track Approach, already falling behind them rapidly. A lot had happened in that narrow stretch of water in these last few weeks. He thought of de Vere and Bull and shook his head sadly. Weary, drained of emotion, he turned and nodded to Ginger. 'All right,' he commanded softly, 'you can start her up now, Ginger.'

Ginger needed no urging. He pressed the starter. The Thorneycroft responded at once, and burst into its tremendous, deck-shaking roar. Swiftly he throttled back and stared at his young skipper, his face aged and made gaunt by the events of these last terrible days. 'Your orders, skipper?'

Bird hesitated. Then he remembered how gaily de Vere had gone to his death, with that absurd phrase on his young lips. 'Take her home, Ginger,' he commanded, '*PDQ!*'

'*Pretty damned quick* it is, skipper,' the cockney chortled. He thrust the throttle wide open.

The skimmer responded at once. With a wild snarl, the lean craft leapt forward, its sharp bow tilting to the sky like a dolphin's head. Its speed rose instantly. At thirty knots an hour the battle-scarred little CMB hissed over the sudden waves, roaring away into the Gulf, heading for the twinkling lights of Finland. Within a second, she was just a wildly bucking speck on the face of the sea. One second later, she had disappeared for good.

Lieutenant Horatio (Dickie) Bird and Coastal Motor Boat Five had become part of the secret history of the British Empire . . .

EPILOGUE

'Egg and chips
Sausage and chips
Chicken and chips
Blinis and bortsch served to order.'

*Sign outside the 'Red Track
Approach' pub, Wapping, 1975*

Of the main plotters behind the Red Track Approach, as I have
cared to call those mysterious and exciting events off Petrograd
in the spring of 1919, 'C' – Captain (later Sir) Mansfield Cum-
ming was first to go, dying almost immediately after his retire-
ment in 1923, taking his many secrets with him to his grave.

But that master spy, the 'Irishman from Odessa', whom he
both admired and distrusted, Abraham Rosenblum alias Sidney
Reilly, still continued his one-man fight against Bolshevism in
spite of his old chief's death. Although he knew that the Secret
Service would no longer finance him, but believed he might
obtain funds from 'Marlborough',[1] Reilly contacted a mysterious organization within Russia calling itself the 'Trust'.

The Trust purported to be anti-Bolshevik with high ranking
agents at every level of the Soviet *apparat*, even within the
G.P.U., the successor to the Cheka. Reilly was tremendously
excited by the possibilities this mysterious organization opened
up for him, and – in spite of warnings about it from his old
colleagues in London, he smuggled himself into Russia over the
Finnish border, not far from the old skimmer base at Seehafen.
On September 27th, 1925 one of those old colleagues received
a card from him; the postmark was Moscow! And that was the
last anyone ever heard of the cunning-eyed plotter, who had
emerged so mysteriously from that long-forgotten expedition
to Brazil, to become Britain's master spy[2]

In that same year Horatio (Dickie) Bird returned from the
job he had taken on a Ceylon tea plantation, after leaving the

1. Reilly's code-name for Churchill.
2. Many still doubt his death that year. As late as 1956 an approach was made to Khrushchev and Bulganin on the occasion of
their visit to the U.K. for information on him. None was forthcoming.

Royal Navy because their Lordships had refused him permission to marry Anna von Klaustein. (In those days serving officers were not allowed to marry until they were twenty-five; and besides, their Lordships had not approved of the manner in which he had rescued her and the Countess from Petrograd). But now Anna Bird was dead – by her own hand. Two miscarriages and the oppressive heat had begun to play on her mind. In their conversations on those fly-filled, swelteringly hot evenings, she returned more and more to the terrible events of that spring, especially to what had happened to her person in the Cheka prison. One month before Reilly left for Russia for the last time and her husband was away three days 'up country', she took the big automatic he carried with him throughout the rescue operation, and blew her brains out.

In 1926, Bird applied successfully (his D.S.O. counted for a good deal) for re-entry to the Navy and began his rapid progress up the ladder of promotion. His firm – the *Daily Herald* called it 'ruthless' – handling of the near mutiny on his ship during the troubles of 1931, marked him out as a future admiral.

Ten years later that prediction by his contemporaries proved true, and he was made the youngest vice-admiral in the Navy. A harsh, arrogant man, with no apparent weaknesses, who lived solely for his job, driven by some inner force. In 1942 he was given command of the whole convoy system newly created to supply a hard-pressed Russia with supplies from the northeastern British ports. But to his anger, he found that although Stalin was continually screaming for more aid, the Red Fleet was doing virtually nothing to protect the hard-pressed British convoys, as they made the long and terrible haul from Hull to Murmansk. After the massacre of Convoy PQ 9 off Bear Island,[1] he lost his temper with the Russians altogether. Gaining no satisfaction from the British Liaison Mission in Russia, he decided he would tackle the matter personally.

In that typical, arrogant, high-handed manner of his, which was well in keeping with his first name 'Horatio', and reminiscent of the Great Admiral himself, he persuaded their Lord-

1. See the author's *TUG-OF-WAR* for further details.

ships to send him to the Red Fleet Naval HQ in Leningrad *by submarine*! And surprisingly enough, the daring mission through the German dominated Baltic into the Gulf of Finland, succeeded. On February 1st, 1943, the little sub, having evaded the German-Finnish forces still besieging the one-time Petrograd, surfaced in front of Kronstadt island and prepared to enter the southern channel, the one-time Red Track Approach, as soon as the Russians had opened the boom.

But Vice Admiral Horatio (Dickie) Bird, D.S.O., O.B.E., was not fated to re-enter the scene of his youthful exploits. In the same instant that sub's skipper threw open the conning tower to let his V.I.P. passenger get his first glimpse of Petrograd for nearly a quarter of a century, two lithe deadly shapes skimmed suddenly and alarmingly across the Gulf's smooth green water, in the same way his and de Vere's craft had done so many years before. '*E-boats!*' Bird had just time to cry out in alarm when the first torpedoes tore into their sitting target and he was lying in his own blood in the shattered conning tower, dying rapidly . . .

The fiery little Cowan survived him by another thirteen years. Although he had been forced to retire in 1929, ten years later at the age of 70, Cowan managed to wangle himself a job with – of all services – *the Commandos*! Captured on operations in the desert, he was repatriated because of 'his great age' only to volunteer for clandestine operations yet again. But in 1944 he was forced to retire for good, with a bar to his D.S.O., forty-six years after he got the first one in the Sudan. From then onwards, he lived alone in Warwickshire until at the age of 85, the man who had discovered the Red Track Approach, finally passed on.

Today only two of those youthful plotters of nearly sixty years ago are still alive, Ginger Coates and his common-law wife Fleur de Courcy, who was not fool enough to hand her Swiss francs over to Reilly for the sake of the counter-revolution. Instead 'Flo', as she is called by her regulars, put her money into a snug little pub in London's dockland, where she and Ginger, the landlord, serve *blinis* and *bortsch* on occasion as well as the usual egg and chips to the hungry dockers and merchant seamen who frequent the place.

The pub's name, you ask?

Can't you imagine? There is only one name that it could bear, isn't there? What else but the RED TRACK APPROACH...